The CAST AWAYS of HAREWOOD HALL

PHOTO: AMY LUCKETT

Karen Herbert spent her childhood in Geraldton on the midwest coast of Australia, attending local schools before moving to Perth to study at the University of Western Australia. She has worked in aged care, disability services, higher education, Indigenous land management, social housing and the public sector, and is a board member of The Intelife Group, Advocare Inc., and President of the Fellowship of Australian Writers WA. Karen lives in Perth, Western Australia with her husband, Ross. Her first novel, *The River Mouth*, was published with Fremantle Press in 2021.

The CASTAWAYS of HAREWOOD HALL

KAREN HERBERT

 FREMANTLE PRESS

For my parents, Wayne and Joan Schmidt.
Reading and writing were not optional.

Psalm 71:9
Do not cast me away when I am old; do not forsake me
when my strength is gone.

1 · MONDAY

HARLEY

Harley accepted the obvious. He lifted his head from Elizabeth's arm, left the bed, and climbed out of the window. It was time to move on.

2 · TUESDAY

JOSH

Rhubarb was out of season, but Pat wanted to stew some for dessert this week. Her grandmother used to make it when she was a little girl, she said. It was her favourite. It was also good for encouraging your bowels. She said that out loud and Josh turned red and looked around, hoping no-one else had heard. He didn't see her press her lips together in a secret smile, and trailed behind her with the shopping trolley as she searched the produce aisle. They had already found the whipping cream and sago, but rhubarb was the key and the other two were useless without it. Pat's circuit returned them to the asparagus and she made to go around again, her eyes scanning the shelves and her pen tapping the shopping list. Josh pushed the trolley up to her. She'd get tired if she stayed on her feet for too long.

'How about I ask someone?' he said. 'Maybe they have some out the back.'

Pat squinted up at him from her list. She blinked twice, considering. 'I'll ask. You can get me some flour.'

Josh passed her the trolley and walked back along the empty cash registers. The supermarket was quiet, with just a scattering of teenage boys in private school uniforms buying pastries and litre cartons of chocolate milk, their school bags dumped in a pile outside under the *No School Bags* sign. They kept their eyes lowered, hoping no-one would engage them in conversation. A few elderly shoppers wandered up and down, pushing shopping trolleys, taking their time. Josh knew that many of the oldies preferred to come in early, so they didn't have to negotiate traffic on the roads and in the aisles. He recognised a tall, grey-haired man in a navy blazer pushing a trolley loaded with toilet paper and cleaning products. He was here every Tuesday. They were eye-to-eye and, as Josh walked past him, the man nodded. Josh nodded back and stood a little straighter, then realised he had missed the aisle he needed. He turned around to walk back up the supermarket, eyes down like the schoolboys, hoping he wouldn't pass him again on the way.

In the baking aisle, Josh stood in front of the flour shelves. Why were there were so many different types? He picked up a blue-and-white one-kilogram packet and read the back. It was *plain* and the packet said it was for pastries and biscuits. Higher up on the shelves were *OO flour*, which was high protein and low gluten, and *semolina flour* which was high protein and high gluten. There was wholemeal flour and rice flour and gluten-free flour and self-raising flour. For each type, there were two different brands and up to three different packet sizes. Josh looked up and down the aisle. There were no shop assistants, just a cleaner with an oversized mop; one of the disadvantages of being an early morning shopper. He texted his mum.

> *What type of flours do I buy for Pat*

Flowers or flour?

> *Flour*

What does she want to use it for?

> *Baking*

Cakes, biscuits or pastry?

> *A cake I think*

White self-raising.

> *What brand*

Home brand. 1kg.

> *Thanks Mum*
> *xx*

Josh picked up a pink-and-white one-kilogram packet of white self-raising flour and took it back to Pat, who was now standing in front of the apples, talking with a shop assistant in a red apron. Josh stood at her shoulder, holding the flour, and waiting until they finished. The shop assistant said he didn't have any rhubarb, but Granny Smiths would be a good substitute if she wanted something tart and with plenty of fibre. Josh looked at his feet and ran his fingers through his hair, pulling the fringe lower on his face. The apples were five dollars per kilo loose or three fifty pre-packed. Pat pursed her lips, disappointed, then nodded. She would have the apples. The shop assistant bagged six apples and put them in her trolley. Pat thanked him and turned to Josh to inspect the flour. It was a different brand to what she usually bought. How much was it? Josh didn't know. Pat clucked her tongue and together they went back to check.

After Pat confirmed the flour choice and they paid at the cash register, Josh loaded the groceries into his car and helped Pat lower herself into the front passenger seat. He took care not to grip her arm too tightly as she lifted one leg and then the other into the footwell. Her skin was soft and thin, and tore easily. He had noticed that she walked slower than usual to get back to the car today, and now she closed her eyes as they turned out of the carpark and drove north through the suburb. It would only take ten minutes to get back to the retirement village.

Harewood Hall faced east from the top of a sandy hill overlooking school playing fields. Fig trees shaded the drive up the hill and the circular entrance and made purple stains on the tarmac. As he drove past the portico, Josh could see the office towers of the CBD and the flat-topped hills in the distance, hazy in the morning heat. More school students ambled past him in twos and threes, ducking down the stairs that ran down the hill to the school buildings, their school bags bobbing behind their heads. Some carried musical instrument cases; all wore blazers. Harewood Hall used to be a psychiatric hospital when such facilities were known by less politically correct terms. Loony bin, funny farm, sanatorium, mental hospital. He guessed the first two were never correct and filed them away to ask his girlfriend after work. She was a third-year psychology student and, on reflection, would probably deliver him a lecture on attitudes to mental health. Maybe he'd give it a miss.

These days, residents and staff referred to Harewood Hall's three-storey signature building as the *heritage building*. It avoided confusing conversations about Harewood-Hall-the-building versus Harewood-Hall-the-retirement-village and reinforced the village's status as a long-standing local landmark. Inside the portico, the entrance lobby and residents' lounge had soft armchairs, fresh flowers, and restrained chandeliers. Classical music piped through discreet overhead speakers in the mornings and was replaced with mid-century jazz in the late afternoons. It was, Josh supposed, more inviting than it had been in its former life. The building was warm in winter and cool in summer, and the smell of good coffee and sound of folding newspapers signalled a place where a person who had enjoyed a profitable career could spend an unhurried and thoughtful retirement. Josh could imagine his own grandparents living here someday.

Josh drove past the circular driveway and its rose garden, and around the heritage building to the villas on the western side. Here, he parked behind a white hatchback in Pat's carport. Summer grass was growing through the pavers behind the wheels and under the chassis. He'd move the car next week and pull them out, he thought, as he packed away Pat's groceries. She had refused his offer of a lift back to the heritage building for morning tea. She wanted to take Bobby for a walk, she said. He frowned, remembering her pace on leaving the supermarket but let it go. It wasn't his place to insist.

Josh drove around to the staff carpark. The warm morning easterly would keep the sea breeze and any clouds away until late afternoon so he parked the Golf under a bottlebrush, figuring that the benefit of shade would outweigh the cost of the litter on his roof at the end of the day. He unfolded himself from the car, banging his knee against the steering wheel, and walked to the staff entrance, where he turned down the stairs to the residents' garage rather than straight along the corridor to the staffroom. The door at the top of the stairs was chocked open with a triangle of wood, but the sunlight only penetrated so far. He reached over and flicked the light switch at the top of the stairs as he passed.

Josh was not due to see his next client, Martin, for another half hour. Martin was a stickler for punctuality, as Josh had been told by Fiona, the village manager, and he wouldn't appreciate Josh being early. Martin was a retired engineer and a stickler for a few things, Josh had discovered. He had a particular impatience with village management decisions that involved trade-offs between expenditure and risk. Management called these decisions pragmatic. Martin called them irresponsible. Josh had heard from Martin that the previous irresponsible management had traded off expenditure and risk in the construction of the retaining wall on the southern side of the village and the village was now at risk of sliding down the hill and killing them all.

At the bottom of the stairs, Josh turned towards the residents' storage units. Residents in the heritage building had access to underground car bays and secure storage units with numbers that corresponded to their apartments. This was a point of some contention in the village as the residents in the west-side villas only had open carports with attached storage. Worse, the west-side storage units were smaller than the heritage building storage units. The west-side residents believed this constituted an added unpaid benefit to the heritage building residents and had petitioned management to charge the heritage building residents for the extra cubic metres. This was denied. Josh had heard from the other support workers that the west-side residents were now considering an appeal to the State Administrative Tribunal.

Josh's third client for the day after Pat and Martin was Meira, and she had given Josh a key for her storage unit so he could help her move her belongings to and from her apartment. Meira avoided the basement. Josh thought that was fair enough for a ninety-year-old woman with a walking frame, but her aversion turned out to be convenient for Josh, as Meira's storage unit was at the back of the basement and for the most part unseen. Josh bent down to unlock the door to number five, ducked through, and walked along the narrow path he had made between the packing boxes, his hands splayed out to the sides to avoid knocking them over. The side of each box displayed a series of white sticky labels where Josh had listed the contents as he had searched and ferried them up and down between apartment and basement.

Against the back wall, Josh had built a waist-high shelf out of four of the same boxes (black-and-white dinner set, hats, black fur coat) next to an old bar stool. On top of the shelf sat a rounded, blanket-covered shape. Josh removed the blanket and sat on the stool, his knees hard up against the boxes. Two white mice looked up at him with expectant faces.

FIONA

Fiona heard Martin Havelock at the reception desk and looked up from the document she was explaining to Mrs Herbener. Mrs Herbener – Pam – had wanted to move into Harewood Hall for over three years. She and her husband Brian had attended each sales event Fiona had hosted but Mr Herbener was adamant. There was no need for him and Pam to downsize. They could still manage the family home perfectly well. Which was easy enough for you to say, thought Fiona, when your eighty-two-year-old wife does all the cooking, cleaning and gardening. Well, Brian passed away yesterday and here was Pam in her office asking if apartment six was still available. There is a God, thought Fiona, and she is good. But right now, Fiona needed to leave Pam with her tea and calm other waters.

'Please excuse me for a moment, Pam.'

'Of course, dear, I've got all the time in the world.' The round woman settled back in her chair and lifted a travel magazine out of her handbag.

Fiona left her office, closing the door behind her, and crossed the entrance lobby. Fiona's office had belonged to the last medical director of Harewood Hall when it was a psychiatric hospital and it held on to the solid wood and moulded cornice trappings of a time when offices were designed to elevate the incumbent and put visitors in their place. Jarrah floorboards, heavy bookcases, and sash windows were set off against pale walls, and the ceiling twenty-one feet above the floor supported a large plaster rose. A stern man in a suit looked out of a picture frame that had more surface area than was functionally necessary, and three deep armchairs circled a vintage occasional table in front of Fiona's desk. Pam Herbener sat in one of them. Fiona wasn't sure what universe had produced the interior designer who selected the chairs, but she was certain it wasn't one that contained eighty-two-year-olds who need help to get in and out of sitting positions. At least there was no oriental rug on the floor.

Fiona smiled an apology at Melissa, the village receptionist, as she worked to keep her composure with Martin. Fiona had seen Martin at the southern retaining wall with his spirit level when she arrived earlier and had hoped this moment would come later in the day.

'Good morning, Mr Havelock, how can I help you today?'

Martin was leaning on the reception desk and half turned his head, shaking it in frustration. 'Something needs to be done about that wall. It has shifted another half a degree. I've told you before. If you don't do something about it, the whole bloody place will collapse.'

Fiona gathered herself. The Harewood Hall retaining wall had been a subject of consternation since Martin had moved into the village. It had its own file on the shelf in Fiona's office.

'Perhaps Gerry can go with you to have a look later this morning. Or even now. How about we do that? Melissa, can you please call Gerry up from the maintenance shed and have him inspect the retaining wall with Mr Havelock?'

'I can't see what Gerry can do; he is only a bloody gardener. What would he know?' Martin protested. 'What you people need is to get a qualified engineer to do a proper risk assessment. I seem to have to do everything around here.'

'Thank you, Melissa. Mr Havelock, Gerry is on his way. Perhaps you could wait in the lounge? Melissa, can you fix Mr Havelock a cup of tea while he waits? Thank you.'

Fiona walked back across the lobby without looking to check if Melissa and Martin were making their way to the lounge.

'I'm sorry, Pam. You asked about our care services.'

JOYCE

When her husband was still working, Joyce lived all over the world. Beautiful places. She raised her children in a Cape Dutch house in Constantia in Cape Town and, after the children left home, she and Peter lived for a time in an apartment just below The Peak in Hong Kong. But now that Peter had retired, her favourite place in the world was her balcony in her apartment on the first floor of the Harewood Hall heritage building, back in the suburb where she'd grown up, in her hometown.

Joyce's husband was playing golf, so she had the apartment to herself this morning. She opened the bifold doors to the balcony to let in the easterly. At this time of the year, it was warm and gentle. I won't be able to do this in a few weeks time, she thought. The balcony was wide and tiled and furnished with two Adirondack chairs and a matching low table. Joyce bought those chairs in California and shipped them to South Africa and then Hong Kong and now here. When she sat in them, she could read for as long as she liked and look out across the school playing fields and the treetops to Kings Park. Nothing could bother her.

The best part of Joyce's balcony was the line of mature lemon-scented gums that shaded her reading chair and provided a home for the magpies that sang on cold mornings. Joyce had heard that magpies sing to keep themselves warm. She wondered if that were true. It would be nice if it was. There were three magpies in the trees now, probably twenty metres off the ground. Joyce laid out a line of birdseed on the balcony railing and went back inside to take out the chicken to defrost.

Joyce's kitchen was her second favourite thing after her balcony. Not that she cooked that much anymore. She and Peter didn't have the appetites they once had and Harewood Hall had employed an excellent chef, a local boy who had returned from London last year. Joyce and Peter ate in the residents' dining room three nights a week and at least one night each week they ate out. Usually locally but this winter they had ventured as far as Fremantle. The suburb had come a long way since Joyce left Perth forty years ago and its restaurants were just as good as Melbourne. But the clean lines and neutral colours in Joyce's kitchen were comforting and the appliances were German. It was a joy to cook in, she thought, even if she didn't cook much.

One magpie had come down from the gum trees and worked its way along the line of seed. It got to the end and peered into the kitchen, its head tilted to one side. Joyce went back out onto the balcony and tipped a little more into her hand. She couldn't see so well anymore but she thought this was the same bird that had brought her fledgling to the balcony last year. She was sure it had grey feathers on the back of its head – a female then – but couldn't make out any other distinguishing marks. She remembered how the little bird had hopped about under the trees and pestered its mother with begging calls and how the mother had obligingly supplied it with bugs she found in the leaf litter.

The mother magpie hopped towards Joyce's outstretched hand, pausing every couple of hops to study her.

'Come on, mum,' she whispered. 'I won't bite.'

The bird took a quick, hard peck into Joyce's hand, scattering most of the seed, and fled to the nearest gum. Joyce gasped and pressed her thumb into her palm. Not such a gentle mummy bird after all. Joyce inspected the bead of blood on her hand. That would be annoying if she was going to cook tonight. Maybe they would go out instead. Perhaps she would ask Bevan and Julie if they would like to join them. It was their wedding anniversary soon and she hadn't seen them in a while. The chicken would keep.

A grey car passed underneath Joyce's line of vision. She knew that Golf: it was Josh's car. Joshua was the support worker who visited Pat and Martin and who knew who else on Tuesdays and Fridays. He seemed nice enough – he had gone to one of the local private schools and his dad was in mining – but Joyce didn't approve of support workers in the village. Harewood Hall was supposed to be independent living but these days it seemed like everyone needed someone else to do their cleaning or take them shopping or give them their medication. And the number of scooters and walkers lined up outside the resident's lounge was too much. Joyce had to walk around them to get in the door.

She watched Josh park under the bottlebrush. At least management had planted natives so there would be food for the cockies. She had missed Australian native birds when she was overseas. As Josh passed under her balcony, Joyce could see that he had bottlebrush flowers in his hair where his head had knocked against the branches. Behind him, a small white dog trotted around the corner, trailing a red leash along the ground. Joyce frowned. After a moment, the dog was followed by a woman wearing a lemon-coloured cardigan and a white dress.

'Oh, for goodness sake,' Joyce muttered. She watched the slow progress of dog and woman along the path towards the residents' cafe. If Joyce went down there now, she would be stuck for an hour. But perhaps if she was quick, she could go and warn the others. If Pat joined them, they would never have a decent conversation and would have to listen to the story about that damn dog three times. That was another thing that shouldn't be allowed, Joyce thought. Once people had dementia, they shouldn't be permitted to stay in the village. How can you live independently if you couldn't remember to turn off your stove? In any event, if Pat set fire to her villa, Joyce herself would be fine. Pat lived in the new section, on the western side, in a semi-detached villa with a pocket garden and no balcony. Those could all burn down, as far as Joyce was concerned. She was confident that emergency services would arrive before the heritage building was threatened. She and Peter would be safe. Soothed by this reflection, she went inside to change and go down for coffee with the girls.

PAUL

There was some crusted glue on the surface of the pine table. Paul could feel scratches in the wood around the edges of the small lumps where someone had tried to scrape it off. He rubbed the tips of his fingers over the uneven surface and wondered whose grandchildren or which craft group had been here, gluing and sticking. Probably whoever had made the Christmas decorations stored in the cupboards at the end of the room. The decorations were in shoeboxes and sorted by type. Angels (clay, paper, and toilet roll, with and without wings, some with more legs than others), reindeer (all with red noses), baby Jesuses (male and female, infant and toddler) and an array of dinosaurs representing each of the Triassic, Jurassic, and Cretaceous periods. Paul himself preferred store-bought Christmas decorations in a single colour scheme. He was shamefully pleased that the entrance hall Christmas decorations were traditional red and white, and the shoebox decorations used solely for decorating the more functional spaces in Harewood Hall.

Paul looked at his watch. Roy had been speaking for ten minutes now and was repeating himself. He'd taken longer to circle back to the beginning than most people Paul knew these days. Perhaps he should let him go on while he was still coherent. But he could see that the other committee members had had enough and were giving Paul meaningful looks. He knew what meaningful looks meant and the consequences for ignoring them. He looked up. Meaningfully.

'OK, Roy, thank you for explaining that. Does anyone have any questions about Roy's proposal?'

'I do, Paul,' said Jean.

Jean always had questions. Jean used to run to Harewood Hall Residents' Committee before Paul became president and Jean's husband, Geoff, was active on the state retirement villages residents' association. Jean took a set of papers out of a green plastic folder. Looking across the table (Jean always sat directly opposite Paul, where she could catch his eye), Paul could see that the papers included Jean's Harewood Hall residential lease and a copy of the *Fair Trading (Retirement Villages Code) Regulations 2015*. Jean had tagged sections of both documents with red and yellow sticky tabs. Paul settled back in his chair. His fingers found the remains of the glue.

'I don't have a question as such,' said Jean, 'but would like to point out a few crucial matters that are important to our discussion.' The other committee members also settled back.

I know, thought Paul in sympathy, no morning tea for us today.

'The Village Rules that Roy proposed that we change are appended to all of our leases.' Jean turned the pages to one of the red tabs. 'Section 2(f) of the Village Rules state, and I quote: *We are responsible for the common property gardens and grounds. You'* – here, Jean looked meaningfully at each of the committee members – '*are responsible for your courtyard/ patio/balcony only. You may not locate potted plants, shrubs or trees in your courtyard/patio/balcony which have an adverse visual impact to the exterior of your residence, or which are inconsistent with the general landscaping and planting theme for the Village.'*

Jean paused and took a sip of water. Committee members shuffled their feet and recrossed their legs. Paul found a loose edge under one of the lumps of glue.

'However, clause four point two of your lease states: *The residents may by special resolution and with our agreement (such agreement not to be unreasonably withheld) change or revoke the Village Rules.* A special resolution is defined in the lease, which of course you all know.'

Another pause and another sip. Paul thought that, with another ten to fifteen minutes, he might unpick one of the glue lumps.

'This means that Roy is correct. We can change the Village Rules if we successfully put a special resolution to a meeting of the residents.'

'Thank you, Jean,' said Paul, unsure of Jean's point but keen to close the discussion. He sat forward and picked up his pen.

'However,' Jean gave Paul a look and he settled back again. 'Roy's proposed change to the Village Rules will not allow him to achieve what he wants to achieve. I refer you to clause six point one of the lease. Clause six point one states that a resident *must not plant or remove or prune any plants, shrubs or trees in the Village (other than those in the rear courtyard of your residence) unless you are authorised to do so by us.* Roy's motion won't change clause six point one.'

'So I'm afraid, Roy,' said Jean (not looking apologetic at all), 'you can change the Village Rules all you like but you still won't be able to plant a liquid amber in your front garden. Clause six point one of your lease won't let you. It is quite clear.'

Everyone looked at Roy. Roy looked at Paul.

'Well,' said Paul, 'this is clearly a complex matter, but I think we are out of time. Perhaps we can come back to it at the next meeting. Thank you, Jean, for again raising these important clauses in our leases. Do we have any items of other business? No? Good then.'

He read out the actions arising from the meeting and looked around the table for confirmation.

'Joyce won't like our decision about the trees, you know,' said Roy. One last dig.

'Yes, I know, but our decision was unanimous and reflects the views of the residents. The trees are a hazard and must be pruned. I expect that all committee members will communicate that position when they discuss the matter outside of this room.' Paul's tone was becoming curt. It was time to wrap it up.

The committee members gathered up their papers and headed out of the room, avoiding eye contact with Roy. Paul looked at the crucifix on the opposite wall and gave a silent thank you for a meeting that was less fractious than usual. He tidied his agenda papers, put a clip around the bundle, pushed in the chairs, and wiped down the surface of the table.

Roy was waiting for him in the corridor.

'There is another thing, Paul. Have you seen your statement this month? Did you see the increase in water charges? They are up by more than ten percent over the last month. We are only at the end of spring, and it has been a mild season at that.'

'No, I haven't seen them yet, Roy, but I will be sure to have a look.'

'Well I can tell you; I have been monitoring the water bills over the past four months and they have been increasing since April. Over winter. During water restrictions. I've made up this spreadsheet ...'

'Is that right, Roy? You must have gone to a lot of trouble. Tell you what, bring the spreadsheet to the next committee meeting and we'll put it on the agenda. If you will excuse me now.'

Paul didn't wait for an answer, and headed out into the residents' lounge, where he hoped to find the last of the morning tea sausage rolls.

As he passed the village manager's office he paused, then thought better of it. He could brief Fiona later.

MARTIN

Martin knew it would be a waste of time showing Gerry the retaining wall. The retaining wall problem was a failure of the structural engineer to observe the Australian Standards for Steel Reinforcing in Retaining Wall Systems AS4100. Gerry was a gardener, or perhaps the maintenance man, Martin couldn't remember, and couldn't be expected to know about Australian Standards and retaining walls. In Martin's view, it was another example of management irresponsibility. Anyway, gardener or maintenance man, Gerry was no use. They needed a qualified engineer to assess the wall. And besides, Josh was due at 10.30am and Martin needed to be upstairs.

But Melissa had already made Martin a cup of tea. Quite efficiently, he thought. Martin understood from his wife, Maureen, that when a person fixes you a cup of tea, it was impolite not to drink it even if you were not strictly thirsty. It would cause offence and hurt feelings. Martin thought that it was irrational to drink a cup of tea when hydration or thermal comfort were not required, and a person whose feelings were hurt over a not-drunk cup of tea lacked emotional resilience. But Maureen had got angry when he said that, so now Martin drank cups of tea when they were offered. To give credit to his wife, he had noticed that this seemed to please the tea-makers and make future interactions with them more amenable. He sat by a window in the residents' lounge, scalding his tongue as he drank his tea as quickly and politely as possible.

As he sat, he ran his hand over the surface of the occasional table next to him. It was well finished, he thought. Someone had taken the time to sand the wood back and apply at least three coats of varnish. Remarkable, given that the tables were imported cheap from Indonesia and cost half the price of local products. He turned his hand over and ran his fingers around the lip. He felt a sudden sharp pain, swore and a small amount of hot tea escaped his own lips and ran down the side of his chin. The edge of his fingers had caught on something rough that had not been sanded back and coated with three coats of varnish. He was bleeding.

Someone had neglected to finish the underside of the table, not thinking of the end user and creating a risk of injury. Careless. Martin took out his handkerchief and wrapped his injured finger. He carried his half full cup and saucer over to the bar and returned to the table, which he cleared of its lamp, and up-ended on the floor. As he thought, the underside was ragged all the way around. And there were four unnecessary staples fixed to what looked like pieces of a torn plastic bag. It also smelled like – Martin put his nose down to the wood – cat pee. Disgusting. What if one of the ladies caught their dresses, or their hands on this mess? Old ladies' hands take a long time to heal and are susceptible to infection. Martin huffed in frustration at the lack of attention to detail in the world. Did he still have to do everything himself? But it was 10.25am already. He righted the table and, not waiting for Gerry, went to the stairs to fetch Joshua.

Martin liked Joshua. He was punctual, polite, kept his hair short and seemed to maintain his car. He was still built like a foal, all awkward arms and legs, but he was young, and Martin could see that he would fill out in time. He did a thorough job of cleaning Martin's apartment, paying attention to tricky corners and following Martin's instruction list. This surprised Martin and he had needed to write a note to himself not to assume domestic competence based on gender in the future. Martin suspected that Josh also took instructions from Martin's daughter Elise to check that Martin took his medication. He didn't mind this. He thought that he would do the same in Elise's position.

Martin understood that Joshua studied environmental science at university. Joshua had been unspecific about what environmental scientists do and who employed them, but Martin had googled *what do environmental scientists do?* and discovered that Joshua would most likely become an academic, a government regulator, a consultant, or work for a mining company rehabilitating mine sites. He also found an especially useful website that benchmarked salaries for environmental scientists working in various positions. He had printed out job descriptions for each one and handwritten the salary ranges in the top right-hand corner. He would give them to Joshua today to help him get some career direction.

Martin stopped at the top of the stairs to catch his breath. There was Joshua, at the front door of Martin's apartment, pleasingly on time.

'Look, I know you are not terribly good at men's things, but you have to come down to the basement to get some tools. Never mind the cleaning.'

HARLEY

In storage unit number eight, Harley had found a soft woollen rug folded on top of a box. The box was wedged between an old refrigerator and a bookcase, creating a safe and comfortable nook for the type of animal that needs eighteen hours sleep each day. Harley's ears twitched when Martin and Josh walked past and unlocked the door to number seven, but he kept his eyes closed and his head down. Martin's presence in the basement was unremarkable to Harley. Martin was often carrying tools and sandpaper and bits of wood and metal back and forth, and Harley's stomach was still sufficiently full of Elizabeth's chicken from the night before not to have to worry about bothering humans for another day.

3 · WEDNESDAY

JOSH

Josh woke at six, pulled on his running gear and headed north at a slow jog along the street. The easterly was cooler than yesterday but foreshadowed a warm morning. The traffic to the south along the highway was still quiet ahead of the daily march towards the city. Water vapour hung in the air over every third verge from sprinklers that obedient residents had timed to observe watering restrictions. The footpath had been sprayed for weeds by the council earlier in the week and Josh ran along the road to avoid the chemical smell. At the end of the street, he turned right and then left to track along the eastern edge of the cemetery towards the train line.

As he ran, Josh rubbed his thumbs over the edges of his fingers, feeling the rough skin and ragged nails from his efforts yesterday with Martin. Josh's usual routine on a Tuesday was to clean Martin's apartment, check for expired food in the kitchen and write a grocery list for the next week. On instructions from Martin's daughter, he also surreptitiously checked Martin's Webster pack and the expiry dates on his medication. Yesterday, however, he spent the whole visit sanding back the undersides of the five small tables in the residents' dining room. Martin wasn't a bad old sort, Josh thought as he ran. An odd bod, certainly, but well intentioned. He was a stickler for detail though, and Josh thought he wouldn't like to have worked for him back in the day. Martin had checked every table – apparently Josh could not be relied on to do this – and instructed him to remove the staples fixed to the underside of the tabletops and sand back the lips where Martin deemed them to be too rough. After sanding, each table was checked a second and third time, and there were two that Martin had found necessary to finish off himself. Josh was told they would be varnishing when he visited Martin again on Thursday.

When he reached the road that ran beside the train tracks, Josh turned left to continue along the cemetery boundary. He preferred to run inside the cemetery but during magpie nesting season it was safer to stick to the roads. Even then, he had to remember to keep his eyes to the ground. He checked his watch. Twelve minutes to the corner made it two six-minute k's. He should be home by quarter to seven. He had a two-hour lab at nine and then he needed to finish an assignment by four. He'd been putting it off. It was about population modelling and, unlike Emily, Josh couldn't get enthusiastic about statistics. His favourite subject so far was Zoology. He had also enjoyed Animal Behaviour and Animal–Plant Interactions and Principles of Wildlife Management. He liked vertebrates.

Environmental science had not been Josh's first choice of career. He had wanted to be a vet. At high school, for his work experience placement, he had worked at a small animal clinic on the highway. He loved it, looking after the cats and dogs as they waited for their surgery and doing the jobs that the veterinary assistants obligingly relinquished to him – scooping out litter trays, hosing down cages and cleaning consulting rooms in between patients. By the second week, they let him sit in during surgery, provided he didn't touch anything. It was all going great until he worked out what the pleasant room at the far end of the corridor was used for. After that, every animal that came through the front door filled Josh with dread, as he wondered which Molly or Pepe or Rusty would be walked down the corridor for the last time. He was relieved when the placement ended and, when the time came to nominate his preferences for university, he put Environmental Science first, second and third at three different universities.

Josh rounded the corner of his street and gave himself one last push, sprinting the last two hundred metres and ducking under the hanging branches of the street trees. He pulled up onto the front lawn, gasping, and walked slow laps of the lawn, his fingers interlaced on top of his head. He must remember, he thought, to stop at the pet shop on the way home this afternoon and pick up some mouse food. He hadn't known what to feed the mice at first, but he googled *mouse food* and had bought some ordinary looking pellets from the local pet shop. To these he had added sticks of celery and apple that he cut up in the morning and carried in a plastic ziplock bag. He figured he must be doing it right because one of the mice looked pretty fat. He sat down on the grass and stretched, then went inside to shower.

MARTIN

Martin was on his morning walk. Every day at seven, he left through the main entrance doors, walked around the circular ornamental garden bed and climbed down the limestone steps to the private school at the bottom of the hill. He turned left and walked along the bitumen service road behind the science classrooms, turned right before he came to the tennis courts and then did a loop of the school playing fields. On most mornings, he passed a golden retriever with his middle-aged male owner and a striding woman wearing white sneakers and shalwar kameez. The football season had wound up by this time of year and the grounds were quiet. There was just a trickle of students carrying musical instrument cases into the auditorium for early morning concert band practice.

As Martin completed his circuit of the ovals and came back to the playground near the school buildings, he took two plastic shopping bags out of his pocket and collected the rubbish left behind from yesterday's lunchtime. He placed the plastic wrap and food scraps in one bag and the cardboard, tins and plastic recyclables in the other. He put the first bag in the green landfill bin and tipped the recyclables into the yellow recycling bin. He then used the empty second bag to collect the remaining lunch boxes, drink bottles, freezer bricks and utensils, and hung the filled bag on the nearest classroom door for the teachers to find later in the morning.

Coming back up the stairs to the top of the hill and the looming front façade of Harewood Hall, Martin turned right to begin his circumnavigation and daily inspection of the village and its grounds. The northern boundary was lined with five mature lemon-scented gums that had been planted when Harewood Hall was built. There had been a beehive in a cavity in the first tree until management blocked it with an ugly yellow substance that looked like concrete. This was both irrational and irresponsible in Martin's opinion. He couldn't see how any substance could block all the holes that a bee could crawl through. It was a waste of money and doomed to failure. He was mollified two months later when he saw the bees, who had at first seemed to disappear, swarming around the tree again. Also, concrete – if it was in fact concrete; Martin could not tell from ground level – was not manufactured to bend and flex and would in time damage the tree as it moved in the wind. He shook his head. He didn't understand why people didn't do their research. Especially when it was so easy these days with all the world's knowledge accessible from a home computer. Surely the village manager had access to the internet from her office computer. Martin thought he would check when he returned. She could use his if she didn't.

A public pedestrian path ran between the gum trees and the southern fences of the private houses to the north of the village. Neighbourhood residents walked their dogs along the path and Martin had observed that although not all of them kept their dogs on a leash, they all carried yellow dog poop bags and were diligent in cleaning up after their pets. Today, the path was poop- and dog-free. The garden bed under the trees was damp from the morning's watering. It was planted out with clivias and snake vine. The clivias were finished now, their orange flowers gone until next spring, leaving just their dark, fleshy leaves. Martin begrudgingly approved of the clivias. They weren't endemic to the area, so were not ideal, but as natives of southern Africa, they were hardy and waterwise and could withstand both the hot summer and the three months of sprinkler bans in winter. The snake vine was a more recent planting and although it would eventually cover the entire garden bed, there were still some bare patches of soil. One of these caught Martin's attention as he reached the western end. Here, he could see water collecting on the ground. He poked at it with a stick. It had clearly received much more water than the rest of the garden bed. Perhaps the sprinklers were watering unevenly. Martin knew that would cause reduced pressure in the other sprinkler heads, shortening their spray radius and ultimately causing dead patches in the garden bed. He made a mental note to tell Melissa at the end of his walk. Someone should fix it.

Martin continued around the western and southern boundaries of the village, checking the verge-side lawns for dead patches as he walked. It was not uncommon to find that vehicles had been parked or driven over the verges and had squashed the reticulation. This resulted in broken risers spraying jets of water straight up into the air and sending rivers of precious, potable water down the road and into the stormwater drains. Martin had estimated that a broken riser spraying water for ten minutes three days per week (the watering time allowed by the Water Corporation) delivering ten millimetres per spray with a radius of two metres, would waste 377 millilitres of water per week and almost fifteen litres per year.

Martin had brought the matter to the attention of the management and the Residents' Committee, but they had declined to follow his recommendation to install *No Parking on the Verge* signs. They said that the village wanted to be a good citizen and preserve its reputation in the neighbourhood as a place that welcomed local families to share its facilities. The local council had also declined, citing a shortage of parking for residents and visitors.

In the end, Martin had taken it on himself to check and replace broken sprinklers each day. In doing so, he had discovered that he could lower each sprinkler by three centimetres and still achieve the same spray radius. Further, if he also installed a twenty-centimetre concrete sprinkler guard instead of the ten-centimetre plastic ones that management had installed, the combination of lowering the sprinkler and providing a guard meant that the problem was fixed. Martin had himself witnessed a car drive over one of his lowered-and-guarded sprinklers without harm. There were no broken sprinklers today.

Martin turned left before he returned to the front façade of Harewood Hall and walked down the sloping vehicle entrance to the basement carpark. From here, he could see his own balcony, looking out from the south-facing wing of the first floor of the heritage building. It was a good position, if a person was inclined, to monitor the comings and goings from the basement. Martin knew that Peter Wise left at dawn three days per week to play golf, returning at midday, and that two of the residents on his floor never drove their cars at all. Once, he had watched Joyce Wise drive out of the carpark, around the perimeter of the village and return, seemingly content with her short trip.

Using the swipe card tucked into his mobile phone case, Martin let himself into the carpark by the pedestrian gate and walked past storage units one to six to his own storage unit against the southern wall. There, he collected his spirit level from the tool board mounted on the wall, leaving an oblong shape picked out in black marker, and an A5 yellow-backed notebook from the shelf. A red-and-black striped pencil (B2) was attached to the spiral coils of the notebook with a piece of string and secured in place with a bulldog clip. As he reached over his workbench, he sniffed. He could smell vermin. He bent down to check under the bench for droppings but in the low light of the basement couldn't see anything. He straightened up and took his torch from its place on the shelf and had another look. There was no sign of rodents under the bench and nothing on the shelves. Still, he knew what he could smell and resolved to buy some mouse traps this week. There was no point leaving it to management, it would never get done. Locking the storage unit behind him, he headed back out the vehicle entrance to check the lean on the retaining wall.

PAUL

The closing notes of the *Resurrection Symphony* sounded, and Paul leaned back in his chair with a heavy sigh. He had been sitting forward for the fifth movement, elbows on knees, anticipating the declamatory final statements. *Sterben werd' ich, um zu leben!* He sighed and ran his hands over his face. Die in order to live, indeed, he thought. Perhaps Lord, you could let me do that before it gets hot again this summer. Paul reached for the remote control, switched off the sound system and made his way to the kitchen with the remnants of his now-cold breakfast tea and toast. But I need to write these minutes and have another cup of tea before I start eternal life, thanks, or I will never hear the end of it.

While the kettle was boiling, Paul opened his laptop on the kitchen bench and checked his email. He opened a Word version of the October committee meeting minutes, copied it and renamed it 'Residents' Committee Meeting Minutes November 2019'. Still standing at the bench, he updated the attendee list and apologies and entered in the meeting start time. Years of writing parish council minutes had given him a reliable template for meeting records, and he saw no reason to abandon what he had already perfected. In half an hour he had finished the minutes, checked them over, and printed off three copies: one for his own records, one for the committee file, and one to post on the residents' noticeboard.

As he washed his teacup, Paul remembered Roy's comments about the water bills. Residents didn't receive their water bills directly from the state-run Water Corporation because there was a single metered supply line into the village. Management paid the Water Corporation bill and then recovered the amount from the residents on their monthly invoices. It was a good system that meant residents didn't need to worry about remembering multiple household bills. (Although once every two years, a new resident would write a heated letter demanding an acquittal of the Water Corporation bills against the residents' invoices in the belief that management took a cut from the supply.)

Paul knew his invoice for the last month was in a pile of unopened letters at the front door. Might as well take a look, he thought, and retrieved the pile. He opened all the personally addressed letters and put them to one side with the local community newspaper. The discarded envelopes and advertising material he gathered up and carried outside to the recycling bin. Back inside, he sorted through the addressed letters and pulled out the invoice. It listed the monthly management fee, his restaurant and café charges, telephone, water, and the monthly charge for the emergency call system. A line at the bottom of the page reminded him that the amount would be paid by direct debit from his nominated bank account on the second Tuesday of the month. Paul used his hole punch to make two neat holes in the left-hand side of the invoice and took it across to his invoices file on the desk in his sitting room. There he compared the water charges with the previous month.

Roy was right, there was a ten percent increase from the previous month and another from the month before that. Going backwards through the file, the increases tailed off until Paul reached the end of last summer where they stopped completely. The increases didn't amount to much, but there was a clear pattern. Paul took out his notepad and copied down the amounts for the previous six months and marked it 'For discussion with Fiona'. He tidied up and headed out the front door to post the minutes on the residents' noticeboard.

The morning easterly brought the scent of gum trees through Joyce's balcony doors as she tidied up after breakfast. Writing a note, she left instructions to the cleaner to sweep and mop the balcony floor and wipe down the handrail. She gathered up her keys and purse, folded a tissue into her pocket, and wrapped a blue-and-grey patterned scarf around her neck. It was a present from her children on Mother's Day from her favourite boutique and she had worn it all through winter. She didn't need it this morning, but it gave a bit of interest to her outfit (white-and-grey sequinned Golden Goose sneakers, white Jac + Jack cotton trousers, dark blue linen Country Road long-sleeved tee). She ignored her lanyard with its emergency call fob and left it in the fruit bowl.

Joyce checked her face and hair in the mirror next to the front door, applied more lipstick, locked the door behind her and walked down the wide corridor past the elevator to the central staircase. She made note of the cleanliness of the carpet and the orderly line of portraits along the wall. They were all former medical directors from Harewood Hall's former life as a hospital and in Joyce's mind spoke to a reassuring connection with knowledge and tradition. She frowned at the skirting board and the heavy dark line it made between the cream carpet and the Antique White walls. She knew the contrast was intentional, designed so that cognitively impaired residents could navigate the corridor without walking into the walls, but she didn't appreciate the reminder of the company she now kept and thought it insensitive to the more able residents. Other retirement villages that she visited had also installed grab rails along the corridors and even put seats in the elevators. Joyce couldn't stand them. They made her feel depressed and angry. At least at Harewood Hall, for the most part, she could feel comforted that the limitations of aging were not yet part of her world.

Joyce and Peter's apartment was on the first floor of the heritage building. This meant they could choose the elevator or the central staircase to access the residents' lounge and dining room. Joyce preferred to use the staircase. Retained from the original building, it was broad, with a heavy jarrah balustrade worn smooth from years of ascending and descending hands. Few residents used the staircase now. In fact, Joyce believed she only ever saw herself, Peter and Martin Havelock on the stairs. Meira Jacobs in apartment five, who used a walking frame, relied on the elevator, and it was two months since she had seen the Johnsons from apartment sixteen. Poor Mr Leeuwenburg in apartment six had been a stair user until he had a stroke three months ago and then passed away in the Mount Hospital. Joyce hoped management would find a younger person for apartment six. Someone with a bit of life about them, and preferably a couple or a single man. There were too many single old ladies here already.

The stairs ended at the parquetry floor of the reception area, where a resident could turn right to the residents' lounge and dining room, or left into a café that was open to the northern sun. Joyce turned left, towards the sun and the smell of fresh apple cakes. Three of the morning-tea girls had already arrived and sat at a table in a sunny part of the room. As usual, Jean held court. Joyce couldn't hear the conversation but from the open newspaper on the table, figured it was a continuance of yesterday's discussion about the proposed master plan for the local shopping precinct. Joyce called a good morning to Melissa at the reception desk, who waved back, and then smiled as Fiona walked out of her office.

'How are you this morning, Joyce? How was dinner last night?' she asked.

'Dinner was nice thank you, Fiona. We went to Manuka and shared the fish.'

'Lovely. I haven't been there yet. Were the desserts nice?'

'You will need to book if you haven't already, it is terribly popular. We went with Mayor Worth and his wife, Julie. Bevan and Peter have known each other since their days at Scotch, you know. Peter was best man at Bevan and Julie's wedding; we flew all the way back from Cape Town especially. They got married in the College chapel and the reception was in Peppermint Grove at Julie's parents' house overlooking the river.'

'How wonderful that you have remained friends all this time. Perhaps we will go there this weekend for Jack's birthday if we can get a booking.'

'Has Jack come back from Bali already?'

Fiona's younger son had stepped up into the league team at the local football club and joined the squad for their end-of-season trip to Bali. Fiona had been worried that the accompanying parent-chaperones might be too intent on their own socialising and the boys would get up to mischief. Joyce recalled that a student from Jack's school was injured after riding a motorcycle under the influence on the island the previous year.

'You have a good memory, Joyce. Yes, he has, thank you. The boys had a wonderful time – they all drank too much of course, but no-one ended up in hospital or jail – and they have a good break now before pre-season starts. I might put him to work in the gardens.'

Joyce blanched at the implication that her memory was a thing to be commented on. 'Well that should keep him out of trouble for a while,' she said, and turned back to the café. Jean looked up and waved her over.

'Good morning, Joyce, you look very put together as usual. Such a yummy mummy!'

'More a yummy grand-mummy,' said Elaine, giggling.

'What's yummy?' asked Molly.

'Joyce, sweetheart,' said Elaine. 'Isn't she gorgeous?'

'Oh yes,' said Molly, blinking upwards at Joyce as she approached. 'Joyce, you are gorgeous. Your scarf is so pretty. Was that a present from your children?'

Joyce unwound her scarf and passed it to Molly. Molly had commented on Joyce's scarf all winter. She and Elaine lived in villa twenty-seven on the western side. Molly was ninety-seven and one of the oldest residents in the village. She was less than five feet tall and looked like a possum, all soft and plump with enormous, round fringed eyes and a little pointed nose. Elaine was her live-in carer. From their conversations at morning tea in the café, it seemed to Joyce that Elaine had been caring for Molly for an extraordinarily long time. They could talk about a shared history of travels to Europe, South America and across Australia; births, deaths and marriages of various relatives; and even early career anecdotes. It wasn't apparent why Molly had needed a live-in carer for all of those years, and no-one had been forthcoming when Joyce had mused about this out loud. All she got was Molly's sweet smile and a fond look at Elaine. 'Yes, she has been a saint to me, hasn't she?'

Ignoring the yummy-mummy comments, Joyce lowered herself onto one of chairs around the café table. Melissa came over with her coffee and an apple cake. The staff took the time to remember residents' coffee orders, another small touch that Joyce appreciated at Harewood Hall.

Sipping her coffee, Joyce looked down at the paper. In between 'Dog Thief Strikes Again' and 'Local University Professor Defeats Deadly

Parasite' was a quarter page schematic drawing of the proposed master plan for the local town centre. She noted with approval the many green circles lining the streets, and the pedestrian paths linking the shopping areas with the adjacent parks and residential precincts. To the north of the main shopping area, an orange rectangle showed where disused railway sheds were to be converted to a collective art space and community garden. To the north again, and across the road, the existing tennis courts, swimming pool and public golf course were proposed to be retained and upgraded to improve access to the lake from the shopping area and train station.

Putting her cup back down on the table, she looked up at Jean, Elaine and Molly, who watched her read with bright looks on their faces.

'What do you think, Joyce?'

'Well on the face of it, it seems quite sensible for once. But the devil is in the detail, as you know.' She looked down again at the paper. 'What is this?'

A large blue square was drawn over the four blocks to the north of the swimming pool, its western side with a quarter circle bite cut out to exclude the lake. Joyce couldn't read the writing against the blue shading and the editor had removed the legend.

'The article says the residential areas on the north of the railway line will be zoned R-60,' said Jean, glancing in anticipation at Molly and Elaine.

Joyce looked up at her. Jean looked rather happy about imparting this news. No doubt Jean expected her to be incensed at the creep of urban infill northwards through the suburb. The streets to the north of the shopping area were lined with turn-of-the-century weatherboard worker's cottages with iron lacework, picket fences and jacaranda verge trees. Joyce and her neighbours drove through them each time they went to the shops. It would be a shame to lose them. But what Jean didn't know, thought Joyce, was that she and Peter owned three of those cute houses, all in a row, and if the council approved the master plan in its current form, the development potential could give them quite a windfall.

'Hmm,' she said. 'Well I suppose people have to live somewhere and at least is it walking distance to the train station. Transit-oriented development is so important for creating sustainable cities, you know.' She lifted her plate and took a delicate bite out of the cake. Take that, Jean.

The four women turned as the external glass doors opened. Pat Warburton's dog, Bobby, trotted through, red leash trailing behind him.

Anticipating his morning treat, he made straight for Molly, who now had Joyce's scarf folded over her knees, and sat at her feet with his head on the scarf, drooling through his overbite. Molly placed her left hand on his head and rubbed the back of his neck with the tips of her fingers.

'Good morning, Bobby,' she said. 'Have you been good today? Are you a good dog? Have you had a treat?' She blinked up at Pat as she followed in through the door. 'Bobby says he hasn't had any treats today, Pat.'

'What's that, Molly?'

Joyce rolled her eyes. Molly and Pat had this exchange every morning and still Pat had to ask Molly to repeat herself.

'Bobby says he hasn't had any treats today, Pat.' Fractionally louder.

'Oh! No, he was saving himself for you, Molly.'

'Well, he'll be waiting a while. Wrong team,' said Elaine. 'Anyway, she's shut up shop.'

Molly leaned forward in her chair and crumbled the remains of her cake onto the plate. Pinching some between her fingers, she sprinkled them into her left hand, which she lowered down to the dog, tucking in her thumb as though she was feeding a horse. Bobby gathered up the crumbs with care, licked Molly's hand clean, and looked up again for seconds. Molly reached over to the table and started the process again.

While Molly continued feeding the dog, Pat sat down at the last vacant chair and received her cup of tea and plate of cake from Melissa.

'Is that our very own Vincent Tredwell?' she asked, nodding at the newspaper.

Joyce looked down at the paper again. Yes, it was. She had missed it. The owner of their village and seven others, all located across the city's more gentrified suburbs, was standing next to the Local University Professor. A major sponsor of the renowned research centre, the article said, without whom it would have been impossible to obtain the research mice that were vital to the successful program. Of course, he was, thought Joyce. Mr Tredwell was well known for picking winners. As well as his retirement villages, he had a furniture import business with a shopfront on the highway, and Joyce believed he also owned property back in Sydney. Joyce had heard that his children were already climbing corporate ladders after completing internships abroad. She wondered if she should invite him to the concert on Sunday afternoon and then dismissed the idea. Vincent could be unpredictable in a social setting and it was best to restrict him to his official capacity at resident meetings and Christmas dinner.

'I was sad to hear about Elizabeth yesterday,' said Molly.

'Didn't she live next door to you, Pat?' asked Jean.

'Yes, in between me and Molly and Elaine.'

'What was she, ninety-two?'

'She passed away in her sleep, lucky girl.'

'I heard she was found by her cleaner on Monday.'

'I thought she had a cat. What will happen to the poor animal now she's gone?'

'No, it was just a stray that she fed from time to time.'

'I heard she's been here twelve years.'

'That's a long time for a cat.'

'I hope they get someone nice for her villa. We need some younger ones around here.'

Joyce ignored the chatter and continued reading the article about the university research. She hadn't known Elizabeth, just seen her in the dining room from time to time and at village functions. Joyce had been told that Elizabeth moved to the village with her husband from Albany where he had managed the local hospital. So not from around here. The husband – Joyce forgot his name – was diagnosed with liver cancer weeks after they had moved and had died within two months.

Jean turned to Joyce. 'The Residents' Committee minutes have been posted. Have you seen them yet?'

FIONA

The Harewood Hall budget contained forty-one items, ten for income and thirty-one for expenditure, all of them laid out in a neat table in front of her. This year, Fiona had budgeted for income to exceed expenditure by a modest three percent. If she managed the budget well for the rest of the financial year, this would give her a fourteen-thousand-dollar surplus that she hoped she could convince the Residents' Committee to put towards grab rails and contrast tiles around the indoor pool. It would be a contested proposal. Some of the Harewood Hall residents resented any age-related safety modifications and Fiona had been reminded several times during her three-year tenure that Harewood Hall was promoted as independent, not supported, living. It was a firmly held view, if only voiced by a few, that residents unable to live independently should be required to relocate elsewhere. Sitting at her desk, she looked pointedly at the visitors' armchairs. Yesterday, she had needed to lift Pam Herbener to a standing position from one of them, and she was determined to allocate future surpluses to the chairs' relocation elsewhere.

The budget results for the year to date showed that Fiona was on track to generate her surplus. Income, which came from residents' monthly management fees, was exactly to budget, although she had more vacant residences than she would have liked. Head office was required by law to pay the management fees on behalf of vacant residences and Fiona was under pressure to fill them. *Head office can't subsidise you forever* was a sentence that regularly appeared in emails from her boss at the end of each month. On the expenses side, wages were higher following the government's decision to increase minimum pay rates in July, but the mild winter had resulted in lower power costs. Sliding her ruler down the spreadsheet, she noted that water consumption was higher than she had budgeted, although that too could be put down to the lack of rain and residents hand-watering their gardens during the winter months.

Fiona marked the budget papers as read and put them to the top left-hand corner of her desk. She pulled across the statement for the Reserve Fund. The Reserve Fund was a point of great interest for her residents and generated most of the questions at committee meetings and resident AGMs. The fund was made up of payments that became due when a resident's lease ended. This generally meant that the resident had moved into a nursing home or had passed away. Fiona's residents took an unsettling delight in scrutinising the monthly Reserve Fund statements to see how much their departed neighbours had paid. Nothing for this month, everyone, thought Fiona, although you will all be pleased with Elizabeth's contribution when it comes through.

The thought of Elizabeth Collins made her pause. Fiona had been alerted to Mrs Collins' absence from morning tea yesterday and had called in to her villa just before lunchtime. Letting herself in with the master key and feeling the still air, she had known what she would find and went straight through to the master bedroom where Elizabeth's body lay, tucked up under the patterned quilt, her little silver head just visible. Fiona had sat with her for a few minutes, letting her hand rest on Elizabeth's shoulder. It was the way everyone wants to go, she thought, asleep in your own home in your own bed. Few are so lucky. Sitting there, she had taken in the open window in Elizabeth's bedroom and smiled. It didn't matter how many visits Harewood Hall had from the local police, some residents refused to lock up their homes at night. They were of a generation that believed in the restorative powers of fresh air and the inability of criminals to cross the threshold of their law-abiding suburb. She looked about the neat room with its 1950s furniture. The glass on the dressing table might have been speckled from age but it was perfectly dust-free. On the left-hand side, Elizabeth and her late husband William stood by a red-and-white caravan in front of white sand and a whipped ocean. Esperance, Fiona guessed. On the right, a group of children had been arranged in a line, shortest to tallest, grinning at the camera. They wore bathers and shorts and were barefoot and tanned. A postcard of whitewashed boxy houses and steep streets against a deep blue sea was propped against a crystal ring holder.

Later that day, Fiona had spoken with the eldest of the children, Bill junior. It had been a shock. The family had not expected their mother to pass away. Mrs Collins had been withdrawn for some time after their father's death but had been back in the Harewood Hall café over the past few weeks and even attended Friday fish and chips twice last month. She had looked forward to attending her eldest grandson's twenty-first birthday in December.

Fiona sighed and turned her attention back to the village accounts. The Reserve Fund balance stood at $851,000. Fiona expected to withdraw fifty thousand in the next month as the first progress payment for a new rooftop photovoltaic array. The project would generate eighty kilowatts of solar energy and reduce residents' electricity bills to almost nothing, not to mention the reductions in heating the indoor pool and common areas in winter. Although it would drive a sizable dent in the Reserve Fund balance, solar power would be a significant selling point for the village and Fiona had fought hard with head office to make it happen. She checked the payments into and out of the fund for the past month and, satisfied that they were correct, turned to her computer to forward the accounts to the president of the Residents' Committee for tabling at the next committee meeting.

As she hit the return key, there were three taps on the open door, and she looked up. Joyce Wise asked if she might see her for a moment.

'Of course, Joyce, come in.' Fiona came around her desk and sat in one of the tub chairs. Joyce took a seat across from her. Joyce and Peter Wise were two of her younger residents and, although Peter was more interested in his golf outside of the village, Joyce had become an active user of the village facilities. She was a regular swimmer in the village pool and had organised some of their most successful social events. She still took care over her appearance and Fiona complimented her on her outfit, observing that she was fussing with her scarf, her hands busy and tense.

'What's troubling you?'

'Well.' Joyce set her shoulders. 'I have just seen the minutes of yesterday's committee meeting and I have to say, Fiona, I am quite distressed about the tree decision.'

Of course. Joyce would have seen the draft minutes posted on the residents' noticeboard. Paul's email with Fiona's copy was still unread in her inbox, but he had given her the heads-up before the meeting yesterday that the tree pruning would be approved. Joyce had protested about the plan to prune the lemon-scented gums and had threatened to take the matter to council if it proceeded.

'Yes, I'm sorry it didn't go your way, Joyce. I knew you would be disappointed.'

'It is completely unnecessary, Fiona. It will destroy the magpie nests and expose the northern façade of the heritage building to the full sun. Including my balcony. It makes no sense at all. You must refuse it. If you don't, I will take it to the council and call our member of parliament.'

Fiona was used to threats to call in higher authorities. The local council, members of parliament, the State Administrative Tribunal, the High Court of Australia, the Human Rights Commission, the Hague. If there was one thing her residents knew about in their retirement years, it was their rights and channels of appeal. In Fiona's experience however, higher authorities, if they were contacted as threatened, tended to write polite letters of inquiry. These were often satisfied with equally polite responses setting out whatever policy and legislative framework applied to the appealed decision and how it had been followed to the letter. They all went away quietly if you knew how to handle them.

'Joyce, you know we had the council's environmental officers assess the impact to the local birdlife and they gave us the all clear. You read the report yourself. If we don't prune those branches, they might break off and damage the building. They weigh a tonne, you know, and could even kill a person walking past if they fell at the wrong time.'

'That report was full of errors, Fiona, as I said in my submission to the Residents' Committee. I fail to see how anyone could reach an informed conclusion after a half hour stroll around the gardens. They spent most of their time drinking tea in the café. It's ridiculous. The officers were clearly incompetent and didn't know what they were doing.'

Fiona had no reply. She had already been around the block on the competence of the council's environment team with Joyce, and nothing Fiona could say would persuade her otherwise.

'I will have to take this up with the council myself, Fiona. I know people on council and the mayor is a good friend of ours. It is not personal to you; I am just doing it for our native birdlife. Do you know how many native species we lose to clearing each year?'

Fiona didn't know and chose to treat the question as rhetorical.

'Well, you should do that then, Joyce. I think it is admirable that you care so much about the environment. And, of course, I don't take it personally. I know you are acting for the right reasons.'

Both women rose up out of their seats and said their thank yous and goodbyes. As she left, Joyce turned from the office door.

'Oh Fiona, has Jack come back from Bali yet?'

Fiona looked back over at Joyce and paused for a moment. 'Yes, he has, thank you. Last month. The boys had a wonderful time.'

'I'm so pleased to hear that. I know you were worried.'

HARLEY

The temperature in storage unit number eight was lower than in Elizabeth's bedroom overnight and by midday Harley needed to warm up in the sun. He stood and stretched, and then jumped up to the top of the refrigerator where he stepped between the unit's dividing bars onto the tool shelves in number seven. Walking along the top of the shelves, he could smell the two mice in number five. He had sniffed them over when they arrived two weeks ago, but it was apparent they were unreachable underneath the blanket and behind their own bars. And he didn't need to concern himself with live prey when there were plenty of full pantries upstairs.

At the end of the shelves, Harley made the small jump to the top of the brick basement wall and flattened onto his belly to crawl through a hole in the limestone footings. He was a small, neat cat and, despite his age and regular diet of raw chicken, had not yet developed the rounded underbelly of other well-fed domestic pets. He drifted along the shadow of the southern wall of the Harewood Hall heritage building and settled on his haunches at the western corner. Lifting his head, he could smell the sea, the clean scent signalling the breeze that would reach the village later in the afternoon. Heat came off the path that ran along the western side of the building where the sun now touched the red bricks. On the other side of the path, between the heritage building and the west-side villas, the native shrubs were still and quiet. The resident blue-tongue lizard would be dozing under the bark and leaf litter. Behind him, Harley heard the lunchtime siren at the secondary school at the bottom of the hill. If all else failed in his search for today's dinner, there would be discarded sandwiches and yoghurt pots on the school grounds in an hour.

A small white dog trotted out past the northern end of the building, also heading west. Following its nose and off its leash, it tracked the brick path until it came to a banksia, where it lifted its leg. Harley flattened onto his belly, legs tucked under, watchful. The dog sniffed its own pee and inspected the garden bed, wandering nose down through the grevilleas and pigface. On the street, another dog, this one a half-grown brown labrador, came into Harley's view. It was intent on moving forward, huffing and ignorant of the smaller dog in the bushes, and followed by a short, blonde woman who leaned backwards to counter the dog's pull on the leash. Harley dropped his head lower and eyed their progress east up the hill.

As they passed, Pat Warburton also turned the northern corner of Harewood Hall. She kept her eyes down and on the brick pavers as she tracked the motion of each foot. Harley softened. This lady was Elizabeth's neighbour and sometimes dropped shortbread pieces on the floor when she stopped by for afternoon tea. No-one scolded Harley for cleaning up the sugary crumbs, and if he got close enough so she could reach without bending down, Pat would scratch his head. Pat's hands smelled of sugar and flour and milk and the dog. She walked with the shuffly, shushing sound that foretold the approach of many older people at Harewood Hall. He also knew that, after morning tea in the café, she would forgo lunch and spend the rest of the afternoon asleep on a brown leather recliner by a sunny window in her villa and the dog would sleep on the carpet at her feet.

When Harley was satisfied that both dogs and women were gone, he stepped out of the shadow of the building and onto the path, where he stretched himself out along the warm pavers. Lifting his head up and to the side and with his belly facing the sun, he pulled his tongue along his right shoulder, working his way across his upper back and then down to his elbow. Raising his right front leg, he continued down his shin and across the top of his paw. He lifted his leg higher and tucked his chin so he could clean across his chest and to his left shoulder. He stretched his right elbow backwards to reach his lower chest, where he made long downwards tongue-strokes, moving from right to left. An unexpected shadow passed over him mid-stroke and he paused and looked up, the tip of his tongue caught outside his grey muzzle. Nothing marked the sky except the edge of the Harewood Hall roof and the branches of a bottlebrush. Interrupted from his flow, he stretched out again, rolled over and half closed his eyes.

4 · THURSDAY

PAUL

Paul liked to have morning tea every Tuesday and Thursday morning in the Harewood Hall café. Tuesdays and Thursdays were savoury morning teas and, after being served five decades worth of cake, Paul was ready to embrace a late-life conversion to mini pies and sausage rolls. An added benefit these days, was that two sausage rolls midmorning could see him through to dinner time. This was as much a benefit to Paul's wallet as it was to his waistline. Unlike many Harewood Hall residents, Paul was not a privately funded retiree and relied on the government pension. His accommodation at Harewood Hall was by virtue of a commercially inclined parish council, who had negotiated lifetime residency for retired ministers as part of their sale of the old church-run hospital. This meant that Paul was able to live in a luxury that he could never manage on his pre-retirement income. Nevertheless, Paul's government pension was only just enough to cover his monthly management fees and living costs and didn't stretch to daily morning teas or other luxuries.

Morning tea today was quiche. A good-sized individual pie with bacon, asparagus, and pumpkin, with onion jam on the side. Paul ordered a latte to have with it and settled at a table in the café to wait. The current edition of *The Post* newspaper was open on the table from the previous reader and Paul bent over it to read the latest news of the plans for the local shopping strip.

Fiona crossed the entrance lobby floor to the reception desk, and he raised his hand in greeting. She smiled back.

'Good morning, Paul, are we still on for ten o'clock today?'

He nodded, his mouth full of coffee. She gave him a thumbs up and turned to Melissa with a sheaf of papers. Paul swallowed and watched her, competent and in charge, and had a twinge of tenderness and nostalgia for the little girl she was thirty years ago. Paul had been the minister at Fiona's family parish and had baptised Fiona and her sisters. They were intermittent churchgoers. Certainly not Christmas and Easter Anglicans, but not week in, week out regulars either. The girls had been well behaved and well dressed, attending kids' church and once or twice taking part in the Christmas play. The parents were small businesspeople and ran a successful chain of bicycle shops. There was one on the highway near the church. They had come to services less and less often after the girls had left home and the girls themselves not at all, but Fiona had returned with her own husband and children after she married, and Paul had baptised both boys before he retired. And now here he was, being served by a woman whose family he had served when she was a child. He felt the pleasure and completeness of it, of responsibility passed on, and of his own good fortune to be comfortable and cared for in his retirement.

Paul blinked himself out of his musings. He folded the newspaper and took out his papers for his weekly meeting with Fiona. As president, his job was to ensure that residents had a say in how Harewood Hall was run. This meant holding monthly committee meetings, listening to resident complaints and meeting with the village manager. At Harewood Hall, these things were proving relatively simple and the job was miles removed from the drama of running a church parish. The Harewood Hall residents were a contented lot. Successful professionals and businesspeople, they had made their money and raised their kids, and were free to kick back, relax and enjoy life. Many were still active in their own parish councils and on boards and committees, and some continued to lever an influence in state politics. Several of the ladies, and also Martin Havelock, volunteered at the school at the bottom of the hill. Most residents used the gym and pool daily and ate in the residents' lounge two or three times per week. If they could afford it, thought Paul, everyone should move into a retirement village while they were young enough to enjoy the lifestyle.

It was not without its dramas though. Most residents were unused to living in a close community. While some people thrived in the new environment, with its ready companionship and freedom from household chores, others found the rules of community living hard to bear. Some, like Roy, actively railed against them. For Roy, if it wasn't the water bills, it was the rule about the front gardens. The year before, Roy had fought a battle over staff driving their cars through the western end to get to and from the carpark. The year before that, he had campaigned for all residents to be allowed to install solar panels on their roofs (paid for by the village of course). This last one had resulted in a working party which then turned into a project control group which would soon become a $250,000 investment in an embedded energy network powered by photovoltaic arrays on the roof of the heritage building (discreetly hidden from view as required by the local community and the state's Heritage Council). Unfortunately, from Roy's perspective, this necessitated mandatory participation by all residents, resulting in Roy being the sole dissenter to a project that he himself had initiated. Such is life, thought Paul.

Paul's meeting with Fiona was, as he expected, uneventful. He briefed her on the actions arising from the committee meeting and they discussed Joyce's disappointment with the tree-pruning decision and the most likely options for the residents' Christmas party. The Social Club Committee was leaning towards a formal, plated dinner in the residents' dining room. Last year they had held a cocktail-style event with finger food in the café, however this had been too much for the older residents who were unable to stand and juggle drinks and food. Many of the residents had requested individual plates and cutlery from the kitchen and taken their satay sticks and beef sliders to the dining room. Paul and Fiona both agreed that the sit-down meal option was the better choice for this year.

'And what are they thinking in terms of a theme this year, Paul?' Fiona asked with a smile.

Paul grimaced. 'This year I hope it will be the birth of Jesus Christ.'

Fiona laughed out loud. For a reason that Paul couldn't fathom, the Social Club Committee found it necessary to have a theme for the annual Christmas party. Last year it was Hollywood, which wasn't so bad as it simply meant that everyone dressed up a little better than usual. But the year before, it was Mexican. They had a piñata and a wandering mariachi band. Gerry the gardener had worn a fake moustache, red pants and a bandolier, and all the women had bought white embroidered off-the-shoulder blouses and worn red flowers behind their ears. The tables were laid with red, green and white striped cloths and they had eaten a lot of beans and corn chips. Paul had gas for days afterwards.

'Hawaiian perhaps?' she suggested. 'Oh, my goodness no, think of the hula skirts!'

'I'd rather not.' The men would be able to get away with a coloured shirt and boardshorts, but the ladies would indeed be a sight. Paul got up to leave and Fiona walked out with him through the café. Together they looked up at the lemon-scented gums.

'Just imagine if one of those branches came down on a passing dog walker,' mused Paul.

'It doesn't bear thinking about. How much do you think they weigh?'

'No idea. Oh, I forgot to mention, Roy said something about the water bills going up. Do you know anything about that?'

Fiona thought back to her accounts. 'The usage has been a little higher than usual, but the rate has stayed the same. What is he worried about?'

'Exactly that. He thinks usage is up this winter for no good reason. We don't have a leak somewhere do we?'

'I'd be surprised, but it is always possible, I guess,' Fiona said. 'I assumed it was because the winter has been dry, and residents were hand-watering their gardens. I'll have Gerry investigate anyway.'

'Thanks, I appreciate that. It will keep Roy off my back for a few days.'

'All part of the service, Mr President.'

Josh drove past and they both waved as they watched him park his car in the staff carpark. They looked at each other with a smile as he knocked his head against the underlying branches of the bottlebrush.

'Nice lad, that one,' commented Paul.

'Yes, he is,' replied Fiona. 'Martin and Meira are quite happy with him.'

They stood in the sun while Josh made his way towards the building and turned down the stairs to the basement carpark.

'What's he been doing in the basement?' asked Paul. 'Martin says he's been down there a lot in the last few weeks.'

Fiona paused for a moment. 'I don't know. Probably moving things for Meira.'

Fair enough, thought Paul. 'Well, I'd better let you go. See you tomorrow.'

'Yes, see you tomorrow. And I'll let you know what Gerry finds out.'

Back in her office, Fiona completed the paperwork authorising the first payment for the solar project and took it out to reception.

'Happy days, Melissa,' she said with a smile, handing her the paper. 'The committee has endorsed the solar project. This is the approval. Can you scan it in and send it to finance? Maybe follow up with a phone call and ask that it be paid by the end of the week.'

Melissa beamed. 'With pleasure!'

Fiona knew Melissa would be delighted. All the young people are little greenies at heart, she thought. 'Maybe also give Solar Solutions a call with the good news and let them know they can expect payment by Friday.'

'I'm onto it.'

Telling Melissa that she would be out of her office for half an hour, Fiona walked through the café, greeting the morning-tea ladies, and headed back out into the sunshine. She looked up at the lemon-scented gums again. She must follow up with the tree-pruning contractor. His office had said they wouldn't be able to start until Monday week but would check their schedule and fit her in if any jobs were cancelled. Fiona was anxious to get the work done before they had any summer storms.

She turned left and walked along the staff-access road, taking in the gardens and resolving to congratulate Gerry on how tidy they were looking. As she approached the staff entrance, Bobby rounded the far corner of the building, trailing his leash on his way to morning tea. Fiona waited for him to come to her and bent down to pick up the end of the leash. After a moment, Pat also appeared from around the corner and Fiona waved. She walked slower and slower every day. But at least she was out and about. So many Harewood Hall residents found it too hard to get themselves out of their villas and apartments and use the common areas. Every month, Fiona seemed to add another person to the list of residents who wanted meals taken to their homes instead of eating in the residents' dining room. It broke her heart to contemplate the loneliness. Meira Jacobs would be the next one. Fiona barely saw her anymore and wondered if Josh was now the only person Meira spoke with on a weekly basis. Perhaps she should revisit Meira's care plan and see if she would agree to having Josh visit for an extra day each week.

'Here he is, Pat,' she said as the little woman reached her. She passed her the leash.

'What's that?'

'I stopped Bobby for you.'

'Oh yes. He knows where he is going,' Pat replied. 'He never gets lost on the way to morning tea.'

'I'm sure he doesn't, but you know you must keep him on the leash when he is out.'

'Yes, yes. But he doesn't bother anyone. He's such a good dog. Aren't you, Bobby?' Bobby glanced up at his name and then refocussed on the direction of the café. Pat bent down to pat his head, wincing at the effort. 'You're a good dog.'

'I know he's a good dog, Pat,' Fiona said, helping her to stand up straight again, 'but it would be awful if he tripped someone over and they got hurt, wouldn't it? It is important to keep hold of his leash.'

'I know, I know. You are quite right. Come on, Bobby, let's stay on the leash now.'

Pat and Bobby continued on their way to the café. Fiona knew that the next time she saw Bobby he would be off the leash again and it wouldn't be too long before she got another complaint from the Residents' Committee. But she wouldn't press it. If Pat didn't have Bobby, she would become one more resident who never left their home.

Fiona continued up the access road and waved as Bill Collins Jnr drove towards her in a large blue four-wheel drive and towing a trailer. He pulled to a stop and wound down the window.

'Goodness, Bill, that was quick.'

'The benefits of running your own business, I guess,' he replied. 'I can come and go as I please. I've got almost everything out of the villa. There's still a bit left, but I'll have it all by tonight.'

'Are you sure? You don't have to rush you know. Take your time if you need it.'

'No, I'm good. I spoke to your tradies yesterday – thanks for that contact by the way, makes it easier than calling around to get quotes – and I've got a painter coming in tomorrow.'

Fiona smiled. The fleet of retirement villages owned by her boss generated enough work to support a home renovation business and was, of course, on the top of the list of contractors that Fiona gave residents' families when the time came to refurbish their loved ones' homes. Tredwell Trades had also arranged the supply of Harewood Hall's new dining room chairs, imported from Indonesia at a quarter of the price local suppliers had quoted.

'You are very efficient, getting it done so fast.'

'I had a good teacher.' Bill gave her a forlorn smile.

'They were lovely people, your mum and dad. They lived good lives.'

'Not bad for a couple of kids from Albany.' He looked up at the sandstone walls of the heritage building, blinking in the sunlight. 'They loved it here. They thought they were in paradise. And you were so kind to all of us after Dad passed.'

'We loved having them here. I will miss your mum.'

'Do you know who will move into Mum's villa?'

'Not yet, but it won't be vacant for long.'

'Waiting list?'

'Always.'

'I hope it's someone nice. Anyway, better get going.' He put the car into gear and pulled away, waving through the open window.

Fiona turned into the staff entrance and stepped through the chocked-open door to the residents' basement. She flicked on the light switch and walked down the stairs, taking care in her heels. What was Josh doing down here? The basement was well ventilated but cold. The floor was clean and the walls and ceiling free of cobwebs. The cleaners were doing their job, she thought, pleased. Fiona did a circuit of the car bays, noting who was in and who was out. Peter Wise's car was out – Thursday golf – and his wife's bay was also empty. The apartments had one car bay each. Residents could use the excess bays in the staff carpark for free if they had more than one car, but Peter and Joyce paid extra for a second bay in the basement, preferring to keep their vehicles out of the sun. The Johnsons were in. Two more residents who you never see, thought Fiona, but at least they have each other for company. Martin's car was in, but Fiona knew that Martin was out, volunteering at the school at the bottom of the hill. Good for him.

There was nothing unusual around the car bays and Fiona walked over to the storage units. Simple wire cages with lockable doors, they were used by the residents to store belongings that they couldn't fit in their apartments and had been reluctant to discard when they downsized.

Some contained furniture, some had stacks of packing boxes, some had metal shelves packed with books and DVDs and electrical equipment. Fiona had the basement sprayed every year and was confident that her residents' belongings were undamaged by moths and silverfish and mice. The storage unit closest to the entrance was used by Tredwell Trades to store equipment and was unnumbered. It gave off a faint smell of ammonia.

Starting at the back wall and moving along the front of each unit, Fiona peered into number five, Meira's unit, taking in the furniture and packing boxes. The light was poor at this end of the basement and she had not brought her master key. She could only just make out a blue shape against the back wall. Moving on, she saw that number six, Mr Leeuwenburg's old unit, had not yet been emptied and she made a note to call the family and remind them. It would need to be cleaned out before Pam moved in. Number seven was set up as a workshop. True to character, Martin had discarded anything that could not be stored in his apartment and was putting the storage unit to practical use. Fiona smiled at the pegboard with its black outlines for each of Martin's tools. The light was better at number eight and along one side she could see a folded blanket on a box between a fridge and a bookcase. The blanket had a round indent in the middle. Fiona had heard a rumour about a stray cat that the residents were feeding. So, this is where you live, she thought, and guessed that the cat was Josh's interest in visiting the basement. She would let him have his little secret. Satisfied, she went back upstairs. She made another mental note, this time to call Tredwell Trades and have an extra light installed in the storage-unit end of the basement.

JOSH

Josh sat on a milk crate and pushed a piece of carrot through the bars of the cage. It was the end of the day, and although he had already visited at the start of his shift, the fatter mouse had its pink nose against the frame, asking for more food. In the past two weeks, one mouse had become larger than the other. At first, Josh hadn't been able to tell them apart. Both mice were white, the same size, and had pink noses. They had no distinguishing marks or, as far as Josh could tell, different personalities. But now one was a little bit bigger and the other was, well, a lot bigger.

The reason why the fat one was so fat did not take much guesswork. He pushed his nose through the cage bars as soon as Josh lifted off the blanket and sniffed the air for treats. The other mouse sniffed about a bit as well, but with less enthusiasm, and after a nibble or two was happy to snuffle around the shredded paper in the cage. Josh had changed the paper once. It had become stinky after a week, so he took some of the paper from the shredder in the staffroom upstairs and used it to re-line the cage at the end of his shift. The problem was, he didn't have anything to put the mice in while he cleaned out the cage, so he used his empty lunchbox. The mice hadn't minded being picked up and put in the little green plastic box, and the lid had one of those plastic vents for reheating food in the microwave so at least they had air to breathe while he did their housekeeping. He was careful with them, holding their small, warm bodies against his chest so they felt safe as he transferred them back and forth. They also hadn't seemed disturbed about the change in their cage lining when they went back in. He wondered if mice noticed these sorts of things.

Josh reached into his ziplock bag of vegetable sticks and pushed another piece of carrot through the bars of the cage. The same mouse gobbled it down. It was nice to come in here after work, he thought. There was something about sitting and feeding the little animals that slowed him down, made his mind go still. Josh had never looked after a real live creature before. His family had a dog, which had been around since Josh was ten. A miniature schnauzer named Stan; he was a happy, friendly dog who loved everyone. Josh loved Stan back, but Stan was Mum's dog and looked to her for walks and food. The mice were different. They relied on him alone for food and shelter now, and he felt a tenderness and sense of responsibility towards them. He was their saviour. Josh snorted to himself. Imagine if Emily knew he thought that.

Josh's dad had wanted Josh to become a vet and hadn't been wild about his switch to environmental science. Josh's dad was an engineer.

'There's only good money in environmental consulting if you're not one of those ideological tree-huggers,' he'd said. 'You've got to take a practical approach; understand the commercial realities of the industry. Ideology just gets in the way and that doesn't help anyone.'

By *the industry*, Josh's dad meant mining. It employed the most people, earned the most export income and made the most millionaires in the state. Josh knew that the mining industry had paid his private school fees, funded the family's skiing holidays and would, in time, give him a deposit to buy his first house. He had reassured his dad that his course was taking a very practical approach, that one of his lecturers was an engineer, and that a mining company sponsored their graduation event last year. He didn't tell his dad that he preferred marine over land-based environments and was unlikely to ever consult in his dad's industry.

Josh had kept the mice for two weeks now and it was fair to say that three weeks ago he hadn't planned on having pet mice in his future. A friend from school was doing his honours project at the university's medical research centre and on a Friday afternoon at the university tavern had been telling him about knockout mice and the centre's research program. According to Mike, the centre used mice that had their genes deactivated – *knocked out* – so the researchers could test their impact on diseases like cancer. Mike reckoned the mice were pretty cute and said that, even though it was discouraged by the ethics committee, the staff gave them names according to the gene that had been knocked out. One was named Serena because she was genetically modified for studying anxiety disorders. Josh's friend Tim had needed that one explained.

Later that night, after the Tav closed and a few too many beers consumed, Josh, Mike and Tim thought it might be cool to visit Serena and her mouse pals. Mike had his security pass on him and the centre was ten minutes away, so the three of them walked across campus and let themselves in. The labs were warm. Mike said this was because the mice needed to be kept between twenty-three and twenty-eight degrees Celsius and they became sluggish and dopey if they got too cold. Josh had to admit that Mike was right: the mice were cute and seemed happy to have someone to chat to, even if he couldn't stroke them on the other side of their locked glass cages.

'What are they testing them for?' he asked.

'Don't know,' said Mike.

'Hey, maybe they've been infected with anthrax,' said Tim, his nose against a cage of six white mice.

'Yeah, right. They wouldn't be sitting around on benches in the open then would they.'

'Or some sort of mutation that turns them into tiny little tracking devices. Like real-life search drones.'

'How come they are all white?'

'Or maybe the zombie virus.'

'Nah, the main dude is all about parasites in cat poo.'

'That's gross.'

'To you maybe, dumb arse, but these things kill people. Cats eat the infected mice, make infected poo, and then humans touch the cat poo and die.'

'I'd die too if I touched cat poo. That stuff is evil. Have you ever cleaned out a litter tray?'

After they had said hello to each mouse in its glass cage, they spent some time crouching under a bench because someone thought they saw Security. Then Tim had to piss, and Mike said they should go anyway and make sure they didn't leave anything behind. Josh had gone back to get his beer from the other side of the lab and seen the carry cage underneath and, well, he swiped it.

He didn't make it far. As it turned out, Security had been patrolling outside and as he crossed the carpark, he saw the officer talking with Mike and Tim. He ducked over to the verge and placed the cage under the bushes out of sight.

Josh put the ziplock bag of carrots back into his backpack and reached between the bars of the cage to coax the not-as-fat mouse into a head scratch. He was catching up with Emily after his shift today. They were going out for ice-cream before coming back to his parent's house for dinner. Josh and Emily had been dating for eighteen months. For their twelve-month anniversary, Josh had taken her on a surprise picnic at the beach. They had eaten cheese and hummus, tomatoes and bread on a picnic blanket, and watched the waves. Josh got sand in the hummus tub and they couldn't eat the rest, but then Emily pulled her own surprise out of her backpack. She'd booked them both an introductory session at a rock-climbing wall in the city. Josh had been apprehensive, but after his first attempt he'd revelled in stretching his long arms and legs across the rock face and dragging his lean body upwards. For once, he appreciated being thin for his height. And it hadn't hurt to watch Em stretch her own limbs. They'd had so much fun that they'd now been back four more times.

Josh gave his mice a final scratch and put the blanket back over their cage. He knew he couldn't keep them here forever. He would have to make a plan. But right now, he needed to pick up Emily.

MARTIN

Martin liked to eat at 6.30pm. This evening, he was cooking teriyaki chicken and, according to the recipe at healthyfitnessmeals.com.au, he needed to start at 5.30pm. He opened his iPad, rechecked the instructions, and stood it up on the kitchen bench for reference. He set out the ingredients – chicken breast, vegetable oil, sesame seeds, broccoli, asparagus, capsicum, mushroom, soy sauce, water, garlic, ginger, honey, sesame oil and corn flour – on the kitchen bench next to the iPad and chopping board, and took out a small saucepan, a frying pan, his chef's knife, and measuring spoons and cups. Following the recipe, he measured out the soy sauce, water, garlic, ginger, honey and sesame oil into the saucepan, cooked it for two minutes and turned it up to boil. He dissolved the corn flour into the mixture, boiled the sauce for another two minutes then turned off the gas and left it to cool.

Martin opened the top cutlery drawer under the kitchen bench and took out his sharpening steel. He drew the chef's knife across the steel three times on each side, checked the blade, and placed the steel back in the drawer. He sliced the vegetables into even pieces to the sizes recommended in the recipe and wiped down the knife. Moving the sliced vegetables to one side of the chopping board, he laid the chicken breast flat on the surface and sliced the meat into one-centimetre-wide strips. He turned to the stove, measured out a teaspoon of oil into the frying pan and lit the gas. When the oil started to shimmer, he added the vegetables, tossing them with a slotted spoon so they were coated, and added a pinch of salt and pepper. After three minutes (he liked the vegetables to be firm), he added two tablespoons of water and continued cooking until the water evaporated. He turned the vegetables out onto a dinner plate, wiped down the pan, and returned it to the stove. He measured and added two more teaspoons of oil and when it was hot, laid the chicken strips evenly around the pan. After three minutes, he turned the pieces over using tongs and cooked them for another three minutes. Poking the meat with the back of the tongs to check that it was cooked (he liked to be sure), he added the vegetables, sauce and sesame seeds, and turned off the gas.

Martin closed the iPad and wiped down the chopping board. He turned half of the teriyaki chicken onto the dinner plate, collected two chopsticks out of the top drawer, and took his meal to the dining table. It was 6.29pm.

Martin had the same six-seater table and chairs set that his family had sat at to eat evening meals since he was married. A wedding present from his parents, it had a grey pearl laminex top and polished chrome legs with rubber stoppers on the feet. The chair backs and seats were covered with butter-yellow vinyl and foam cushions with white piping. A focus of embarrassment for his children during the faux-Victorian 1990s, the table and chairs were now fashionable again and Martin had established that they were worth $1,500 from antiques traders. Not that he would be selling them, but it was good to know the value of one's assets.

From Martin's seat at the table, he could look across his sitting room to his balcony and the valley to the south. The sun had just set. The tall gum trees in the primary school on the other side of the main road through the suburb were darkening and a flock of black cockatoos were heading north to roost for the night, their voices announcing their progress across the valley. The lake made a large dark shape in the middle distance. This was Martin's place. The suburb where he had attended school and where he had raised his own children. The base from where he had made dozens of trips to and from north-western mining camps and had driven his daily commute in and out of the central business district. He knew its seasons and its daily routines. He had walked the banks of the lake when it was still designated a swamp and knew its smell when it dried out in summer. He knew the heat of the footpaths before the sea breeze came in and the barking that sounded across from the east when it was mealtime at the dog refuge. He knew that the lights he could see on the other side of the lake were from the boys boarding school and the boarders would now be sitting down to their own dinner in the dining hall before returning to their rooms and their homework. The year twelves would start final year exams soon, he thought, and frowned as he remembered his own children's fraught final two years of high school.

He looked down and was surprised to see that he had finished his meal. Well then. Time for a cup of tea and dessert. When Martin's wife was alive, she used to stew leftover fruit at the end of each week and the family would have it for dessert with ice-cream and a sprinkling of Rice Bubbles. Martin liked the stewed apricots best, but the children had preferred the apples. Fortunately, enough fruit was stewed each week so that all preferences could be accommodated in one meal. It was two years since Martin had taken the last container from the freezer (it was apples). Six months later, and after several burnt saucepans, he was making his own. In fact, he thought his was better than Maureen's (she had used too much sugar). He put the kettle on and spooned some stewed apricots out of the Tupperware container that he kept in the fridge. He would forego the ice-cream tonight.

Martin poured the tea and took his stewed apricots to the living room where he placed the bowl on the coffee table. He walked over and pulled the balcony door closed and slid the lock into place. Something caught his eye and he leaned forward to look through the reflections in the glass. There was a cat on the balcony. Martin stood for a moment. He didn't know much about cats. They had never been part of his life. He did know they had no place in Australia and were responsible for destroying numerous small native animals, but aside from that, nothing. How do you approach a cat? Or do you leave it alone until it goes away? He couldn't see it well through the glass door, which he was inclined to keep shut, but it seemed small and was grey with black markings. It was watching him.

Martin decided that leaving it alone was the better choice with an animal he didn't know and returned to his dessert. After a moment, he got up again and drew the curtains. Later that evening, after showering and brushing and flossing his teeth, he collected his iPad from the kitchen bench and typed *domestic and feral cats* into his browser.

The dinner dishes were in the dishwasher and the kitchen benches wiped down. Joyce took her coffee to her desk (antique bureau plat parquetry, French c.1860, purchased at Brans, Mosman Park) and opened her silver MacBook Air. The recipe for tonight's dinner (swordfish con sarde by Alberto's Lounge; gourmettraveller.com.au) was still on the screen and she closed it and opened a Word document.

> *Dear Matthew,*
>
> *RE: PRUNING OF TREES – URGENT ATTENTION REQUIRED*
>
> *Thank you for your time on the phone this afternoon. As you suggested, I am writing to ask the Council to prevent the planned pruning of the five Lemon Scented Eucalyptus trees on the northern boundary of the Harewood Hall property on St James Avenue. The trees are an important part of the greenway that supports the movement of birds across the regional lakes system. Magpies roost in the trees and forage underneath. They are a constant source of delight for the residents of Harewood Hall, many of whom have served this community for decades, including as elected …*

Joyce paused in her typing. Elected what? She couldn't think of the word. What was it? Peter looked up from his newspaper.

'Writer's block, darling?'

Joyce could feel herself flushing. She knew what she wanted to say but the word wouldn't come. She looked down at her hands, willed them to find it for her, and saw that they had a small tremor.

'Are you OK, love?' Peter leaned forward to catch her eye.

'I can't think of the word I want.'

'Uh oh, you know what that means,' Peter teased. 'I'd better think about booking you into a nursing home.' He chuckled and returned to his paper.

'And how is that funny exactly?' Joyce snapped. Mortified both by the memory lapse and the tears she could feel coming, she left a space for the missing word and finished her letter.

elected [...] and we are deeply concerned for their welfare should the trees no longer provide adequate shelter. In addition, nesting season is well underway, as I am sure you are aware, and pruning at this time of the year will have a devastating impact on this year's nestlings.

The Western Suburbs are prized for their leafy streets and the many mature trees that have been protected by residents and the Council, withstanding constant development pressure from the State Government. It is this amenity that makes our suburbs the most desirable place to live in the state and this is reflected in property values and council rates. It would be short-sighted to continue with this poorly thought through decision.

I urge you to put an immediate halt to the pruning while Council reconsiders its approval in the interests of our green corridors and our native wildlife.

Yours faithfully,
(Mrs) Joyce Wise.

Joyce read back over her letter. She wasn't sure if it was the welfare of the magpies or the elected *things* that she had said she was deeply concerned about, but she felt she had got her point across. She saved the document, closed the laptop and went to bed. She was sure she would remember the word in the morning. Peter could fix his own cup of tea.

HARLEY

After leaving Martin's balcony, Harley made his way to Meira's apartment. He hadn't eaten since Wednesday afternoon, when he found some sharp cheese and licked out a half full tuna tin and the remains of a tub of vanilla yoghurt at the school playground. Meira was generous with dinner, but her door was often closed, and she didn't always come when he called from the balcony. Tonight, the door was open, and he walked straight in, announcing his arrival. She greeted him with raised eyebrows.

'So, you are back. And I suppose you expect chicken?'

Harley trotted to the place by the fridge where Meira always fed him. She set down a paper towel and then a side plate with a large mound of minced chicken. She stood back to watch him eat, arms folded.

'Have you read any good books lately? I finished our book without you, you know. You were right. They weren't nice people. I didn't like them either.'

Harley paused and looked up at her. She didn't move, so he finished the chicken then took himself to the carpet between the couch and the television. He was thorough in his toilette. Meira followed him and sat on the couch next to a round wooden table where she had arranged the television remote control, a plate with half a quiche, and a gin and tonic. She had a rug over her crossed knees and held a large book on her lap. She took off her glasses, picked up the quiche and a fork, and continued to speak.

'The main character in my new book is an interesting man. Not at all like those silly Irish girls. He is damaged, traumatised by what happened to him when he was a little boy. Now he separates himself from the present in the same way he separated himself from the abuse while it was happening.'

She took a sip of her drink. Harley paused mid-toilette to watch her, left leg in the air.

'He sleepwalks through his life. He doesn't hear what other people say to him and they get angry when he doesn't reply. He eats his supper but doesn't taste the food. His boyfriend, he feels that he does not see him anymore.' She looked at Harley with a solemn face and he mewed and trotted over to her. She uncrossed her legs and reached down to stroke his back as he wound backwards and forwards across her shins.

Meira finished her quiche and put down her plate. She stood, closed the curtains against the cold seeping through the glass, and walked around the bench that separated the kitchen from the living room. As she switched on the kettle for tea, she turned her head to Harley, who jumped onto the back of the couch to watch.

'But he can't turn off his brain at will now,' she said, the tone of her voice changing, and twisting her hand next to her ear. 'He needs some help. So, he takes a knife and he cuts himself. Here, and here, and here.' She cut across one arm with her other hand. 'Sometimes he cuts so much that he loses consciousness. His friends find him in pools of blood on the floor. It is so sad, this poor man.'

Meira sighed as she brought her tea back to the couch, a heavy exhalation that made her chest sink inwards. Harley jumped onto the couch and curled into a circle beside her.

'There is so much pain in this life, and yet here we are, you and me. Two old souls. We have come through it to live quietly in this beautiful place.'

5 · FRIDAY

JOSH

Josh laced up his running shoes and headed down the street. He needed to be at uni at 9am for a lecture and then a two-hour lab. Then his classes would be finished for the week and he could work on his last assignments before meeting Emily and their friends at the Tav at five.

In many ways, Emily was just like any other girl that he had gone to school with. They all had shiny hair and big eyes and cute little noses, and after they turned fifteen, they had become softer and rounder and good to look at. They never stopped talking, which suited Josh because he could just sit and listen to them, and make reassuring, confirmatory noises when they paused for breath. That seemed to work for girls and Josh had never been short of female friends who would happily chat at him, uninterrupted. The old people at Harewood Hall were the same. If he asked a couple of stock questions and then kept quiet, his clients could talk through an entire visit, content to chatter away while he worked. They surprised Josh with what they would tell him sometimes. Once, an old lady told him that her brothers and sisters were not her brothers and sisters at all but her cousins. Her real mum had secretly given her to her mum's sister when she was a baby. No-one knew that the woman she called Mum was her auntie, and the woman that she called Auntie was her mum. Not her brothers and sisters or even her own husband. Josh had thought she'd got it wrong, but she had shown him photos of herself as a little kid with her family and it was obvious to Josh that she was different to the rest of them.

Emily was a talker too. Like the oldies, she had no filters and blurted out everything that was on her mind. Josh sometimes wondered if there was anything he didn't know about Emily. Unlike the girls from school, Emily let Josh talk back, and to Josh's surprise, he did. He told her about mine rehabilitation and how open-cut pits can be reshaped and seeded with native tree species. He told her how Sachin Tendulkar was the greatest batsman in the history of cricket, making his test debut at sixteen years old and becoming the highest run scorer of all time in international cricket and the only player to score one hundred international centuries. He explained how Virat Kohli was on track to surpass the Little Master with his ability to stay at the crease under pressure. He even told her about the time he found a dead possum on the side of the road when he was out running and had been so upset he came home and cried in the shower.

Emily had listened to Josh. To be fair, the schoolgirls had listened too, with delighted eyes and pats on his arm and plenty of advice. Josh half suspected that his *sharing*, as they called it, might have been re-shared, especially the time he told Sarah Teo about breaking up with his previous girlfriend. But Emily didn't pat his arm or give advice. She just sat there. She asked questions, sure, when she didn't understand what he said, like when he explained Kohli's flick shots, but mostly she just sat and listened. Not in an ignoring-you kind of way, but in an I'm-listening kind of way. Josh liked that. It felt good. He was pretty sure she didn't re-share.

Josh hadn't told Emily about the mice and he felt bad about that. She would have told him if it was her, he was sure. There was no way she could keep a secret like this to herself.

Josh sprinted the last hundred metres to the house and pulled up on the lawn, breathing hard. His brother's car was in the driveway. Josh watched as he unfolded himself from the front seat, wondering how he did it without knocking his knees on the steering wheel. Unconsciously, he twisted his knees to the right, in imitation of his brother's movements.

'Hi Josh,' said Matt, 'been out for a run?'

Josh walked over and shook his brother's hand, processing the question. It was a strange thing to ask. What else would he have been doing? He wondered if it was a trick. Matthew had always been smarter that he was.

'Yes,' he said, then added, because he knew it was the answer to the next question, 'five k's; twenty-seven minutes'.

Matt raised his eyebrows and nodded. 'Good one.'

In the kitchen, over breakfast, they discussed weekend plans and the test series that was starting in two weeks. They both wanted Australia to win but agreed that New Zealand was shaping up well ahead of the tour. It would be close. One of Matt's clients had offered him four tickets in a corporate box for the local game. Did Josh and Emily want to come? Of course they did.

'How's Greg?' Josh asked. Greg was the dachshund puppy that Matt had bought his fiancée, Alice, after they purchased their first apartment. Last Sunday, Greg had chewed through a set of noise-cancelling headphones – Matt's twenty-sixth birthday present from Alice – and one of Matt's audit files. Josh looked down at his lap where Stan was resting his head and tracking the progress of Josh's hand between his plate and mouth. Stan didn't chew anything that wasn't food. Josh tore off a piece of toast and fed it to him.

'Living a life of luxury,' Matt replied. 'He gets three meals a day on weekends and has his own toy basket.'

Josh grinned as his dad walked into the kitchen, ruffling the back of Matt's head as he passed.

'Doesn't the world of tax auditing pay you enough to afford breakfast at home?'

'I was just telling Josh that all the money goes on the dog.'

'I told you, didn't I?' said his dad, starting the coffee machine. 'Next thing you know, he'll be sleeping on the bed.'

Josh looked across the table at Matt, eyebrows raised. Greg already slept on the bed. Matt flicked milk out of his bowl into Josh's face.

'Are you still working for that dodgy boss of yours?'

'Who, Fiona?' Josh looked at his brother, perplexed.

'No, doofus, the big boss. Big, blond guy. Looks like he spends half his time in the gym and the other half on a tanning bed. Mr Vertical Integration.'

Josh could sense a lecture on accounting-something coming on and pushed his chair back.

'Yeah, still there. I've got to get to uni. See you next week.' He put his dishes in the dishwasher and jogged up the stairs, Stan trailing after him.

The printer hummed and Joyce's letter spooled out onto the paper tray. The word was *representatives*, of course. She remembered as soon as she'd woken up, and she had gone straight to her desk to finish the letter and print it out. Now she stood over the desk in her grey marl Country Road pyjamas, satisfied. This morning, she thought, she might cook a nice paleo breakfast for herself and Peter and they could eat on the balcony. Later, after the rush-hour traffic, she would drive to the council offices and deliver her letter in person. She would miss morning tea with the girls but perhaps she could have coffee in town and then treat herself. She had received an email from her second-favourite shop announcing a new delivery of Isabel Marant and she quite liked the look of the blazers. Was a boyfriend style too casual for someone her age? She didn't think so. She signed and reread the letter, then folded it into an envelope and put it into her handbag.

Later that morning, she sat in a glass meeting room with the council's senior environmental officer, Michael D'Souza. Michael was rather young, it seemed to Joyce. Younger than he sounded on the phone on Wednesday. He was explaining the process for appealing council decisions. Joyce had heard this all before, but if she knew anything it was that local government officials needed airtime before they did something for you, and this is what she would give him.

'Under the *Local Government Act*, council can delegate decisions regarding certain matters to council officers. This is necessary because so many matters come before council that they couldn't possibly deal with everything within a reasonable timeframe.'

Joyce smiled in sympathy.

'Before they delegate a decision, council must establish a delegation schedule specifying what matters can be delegated and to which officers. This also applies to decisions regarding appeals against previous decisions.'

'Very sensible,' she murmured. 'Very orderly.'

'Yes, it is,' responded Michael, pleased that she appreciated the framework of his working life. 'Fortunately, in your case, the senior environmental officer is the council delegated authority for considering appeals against tree maintenance decisions.'

'And you, Michael, are the senior environmental officer.'

'Yes, I am.'

'A responsible position.'

'Yes, it is.' He glowed.

'What happens now, Michael?'

Michael passed her a trifold brochure and opened it to a flowchart. 'I am required to advise you in writing of my decision within three working days. Can you see this step here?' He pointed to an orange rectangle a third of the way down the page. Joyce couldn't read it but muttered something confirmatory. 'That means you will receive a letter from me by Wednesday.'

'So efficient. I am most impressed.' She lifted her handbag to her shoulder, leaving the letter on the desk, and stood up. 'Thank you for your time, Michael. I look forward to your decision.'

Pleased with the meeting and confident in a favourable decision, Joyce went shopping. She liked the blazer, which the shop assistant had paired with a white logo t-shirt, so she bought that too. Further down the street, she found a pair of low-heeled black ankle boots with an interesting zip detail and, crossing the road, she bought another bottle of her signature perfume. The new Italian café had a table free outside under the trees, so she deposited her bags on one of the chairs to claim it and went inside to order.

Back at the table, Joyce took her laptop and phone out of her bag and began her plans for the Harewood Hall Christmas Party. Joyce loved Christmas, and the Harewood Hall Christmas Party had become her favourite event to organise. Everyone in the village came to the Christmas party, even the ones who no-one saw during the rest of the year. It needed to be special.

She opened a new Word document and began to type.

Christmas 2019	
Date and Time:	*noon, Friday 20th December*
Venue:	*Residents' Dining Room*
No. people:	*approx. 90 (TBC no later than 6th December)*
Theme:	*White Christmas or Desert Island Castaways*
Entertainment:	*jazz pianist, City Professional Entertainment*

	Services (White Christmas); Beach Boys
	cover band (Desert Island Castaways)
Menu:	*three course plated lunch with two options*
	for mains and two options for dessert
	(Options TBA depending on caterer)
Catering:	*Ultimo or Elegant Touch*

Run sheet:

Thursday 2pm	*Hang decorations (Peter and Roy)*
	Receive wine delivery (Joyce)
Friday 9am	*Caterer arrives*
	Dress tables (Social Club Committee ladies)
11:30am	*Social Club Committee members to be*
	present in dining room
noon	*Guests arrive*
	Pre-lunch drinks
12.15pm	*Mayor arrives*
12.30pm	*All guests to be seated*
	Welcome speech
12.45pm	*Entree service commences*
1.15pm	*Village Manager speech*
1.25pm	*Main course service commences*
2pm	*Mayor speech*
2.30pm	*Dessert service commences*
3pm	*Mayor departs*
	Coffee and tea served

Joyce's phone buzzed on the table.

'Darling, good morning.' She waited with a small frown while the caller spoke.

'Of course, yes, we are all ready for this Sunday

'Yes, the numbers are confirmed. Eighty-six.

'That's right, six canapés per head.'

Joyce looked up and spotted a dark-haired woman in a business suit across the road. She waved to her as she listened to her caller.

'You have full access to the kitchen as per our usual arrangements.

Guests arrive at three and you can come in anytime after noon. We plan to wrap up by five.'

'Lovely, darling. See you then. Ciao. Ciao.'

Joyce blew kisses into the phone and looked up at the suited woman who had now crossed the road and stood next to her table.

'Darling, how lovely to see you. How is your beautiful Allegra?'

The woman rolled her eyes and adjusted her black handbag, her red nails bright against the leather. 'Busy, busy. She has three engagements this weekend.'

'I know, darling, and one of them is for me. I hope her voice has recovered from that nasty virus.'

'Yes, yes, she will be fine for your little concert on Sunday. Are you working?' She tilted her chin at the laptop on the café table.

'A woman's work never ends. You know that, darling.' The two women laughed and kissed, Joyce stung by *little concert*. She'd like to see Allegra's mummy organise a function for eighty people. The woman sashayed back across the street and Joyce gathered up her bags, thanked the wait staff, and walked back down the road towards the council offices where she had left her car. On the way, she waved to the shop assistant who had sold her the blazer and t-shirt and stopped to chat with a young man who she thought was the son of one of Peter's cousins.

Returning to her car, she turned left at the traffic lights to drive west down the highway. She passed the row of riverside private schools, noting the light traffic at this time of day, and was thankful she had never needed to negotiate the school rush that clogged this part of the western suburbs every weekday during term time. Raising her children abroad had gifted her with nannies and private drivers who had done all the school gate chores for her. That reminded her, she must call both children this evening and arrange their own family Christmas dinner.

When she reached the T-junction at Marine Parade, Joyce stopped, puzzled. Why was she at the beach? She looked right, then left, then checked in her rear-view mirror as though there might be some clue on the road. Had she arranged to meet someone for lunch? It was almost noon after all. She picked up her phone from the passenger seat and checked her calendar. No lunch appointments. A car honked behind her, reminding her that she was in the middle of the road, waiting at an intersection. Shrugging, she indicated right and turned onto the beachside road heading north and back to Harewood Hall. It was a lovely day to drive along the beach front; perhaps that was what she had intended to do all along.

HARLEY

The vehicle access gate to the basement trundled open and the Tredwell Trades van pulled in and parked outside the unnumbered storage unit. Curled on the warm bonnet of a recently returned resident's car, Harley watched as one of the painters from Elizabeth's villa unlocked the storage unit door and took a trolley around to the back of the vehicle. Earlier that day, Harley had left Meira's apartment looking for a sunny spot out of the wind. Cloud cover meant that his favourite places were chilly, so he sat on Pat's fence for a while watching Bobby. Bobby had been in the garden, sniffing at an ant trail. He had half-barked when Martin walked past and then, noticing Harley, furiously complained at the intrusion on his privacy. He didn't stop, so Harley followed Martin around the village instead, waiting while he talked with the painters and ducking through the door when Martin returned to the basement to collect his spirit level and notebook. In the gloomy light after Martin left, Harley had inspected the covered mice and then waited until Peter Wise returned from early morning practice at the driving range before taking advantage of his warm Jaguar. Harley had then spent a contented and uninterrupted twenty minutes, dozing in a circle listening to the ticking of the cooling engine, only opening one eye when Paul came into the basement and scratched his head.

The van was a surprising interruption. In Harley's experience, the painters usually parked outside the vacant villas for the duration. He watched as the driver took drop sheets and paint tins out of the van's back doors and put them on the floor. Then he lowered the trolley ramp, unloaded two packing boxes onto the trolley and rolled them into the storage unit. He did this four more times, then lifted the ramp back into the van, reloaded the tins and drop sheets and swung the van around and out of the basement again.

Curious, Harley jumped down from the car bonnet and slid between the bars of the storage unit door. The boxes were stacked towards the back, wedged behind ladders and white paint buckets. Several were dented and thick plastic wrapping poked through their broken corners. There was a sharp smell of paint and something more astringent. Two short tables were upended on the floor. Absorbed in his mission to find the source of the smell, Harley startled when the garage door trundled open again and Joyce's car pulled in and drove around to its allocated bay. Harley crouched behind a table as she walked past and up to the stairs. When she was out of sight, he pushed back through the bars of the storage unit door, trotted over the car, and curled himself into a circle on the warm bonnet.

FIONA

Fiona and Gerry sat across from each other at Fiona's desk and bent over the plans of the village. Gerry traced his finger over a line, showing the location of the ring main for the village's water supply. He explained that potable water entered the property at the south-eastern corner and was reticulated via the ring main, a series of one-hundred-millimetre PVC pipes that circumnavigated the heritage building approximately five-hundred millimetres below ground level. The PVC pipes were connected by flexible polymer couplings held in place with hose clamps. The heritage building, the garden reticulation system, and each villa was connected to the ring main through a system of taps and smaller pipes. Gerry explained that each tap was located below ground inside a covered pit box for ease of access and that it was possible to isolate each section of the water supply by turning off those taps.

In fact, that was exactly what Gerry has done last night, at midnight, when he returned to the village to determine the location of the suspected water leak. Gerry discovered that the water meter in the south-eastern corner had continued to turn over even after he closed off the supply to all the different sections of the village. This meant that either the taps he had used to switch off each section were still letting water through, or there was a leak somewhere in the ring main. Gerry proposed that today at 2pm, when most residents were either napping or out of the village, he would switch off each tap in turn and check whether water still flowed into the isolated section. When he found the faulty tap, he would go to the hardware store near the railway line, buy a new one and replace it today.

'It's that simple?' asked Fiona, anxious for a quick resolution.

'It's that simple.' Gerry grinned, pleased with himself.

Fiona sighed, relieved. 'This is great, thanks Gerry. And thank you for coming in last night. I appreciate it.'

'Happy to help out, Mrs Boston.'

Fiona smiled. Like Josh, Gerry was a local boy who she had known since he was in primary school and he couldn't bring himself to call her Fiona. Gerry wanted to be an engineer but didn't get the marks in his final exams. Now he worked for her while he completed a bridging course at TAFE. She was torn between wanting to keep him forever and hoping he would be accepted into university and on the road to his dream career.

When Gerry left, she sent out a notice on the village intranet that the water supply would be interrupted for forty-five minutes from 2pm today. Apologies for the inconvenience and late notice. She printed out the notice on an A4 sheet of paper and walked out to reception to pin it on the resident noticeboard.

PAUL

Friday night fish and chips had become Harewood Hall's primary gathering for residents, and the principal distribution point for village information, both official and unofficial, accurate and surmised. It was at Friday fish and chips that residents learned about the birth of grandchildren, the career trials and triumphs of adult children, and which residents were absent on holidays and where. They compared notes on the performance of share portfolios, tax minimisation strategies, and discussed the federal opposition's proposal to cap franking credits, the last ending in resolutions to write to their local members of parliament that were usually forgotten by the next morning. They gossiped with happy abandon about the staff, passing judgement on weight gains and losses, speculating on the sexual orientation of those who were single and arguing about the course selection of those who were studying at university. Invariably, conversations turned to expressions of amazement at the various illnesses, injuries and decline they themselves had encountered in their older years.

'I had a new glasses prescription only this time last year and I need stronger lens again already.'

'This is the third skin cancer I've had cut off and apparently there are two more. There'll be nothing left of me when they have finished.'

'His doctor said his blood pressure won't change until he loses weight.'

'They replaced the top of her femur with titanium.'

'All she did was trip in the shower and now she'll be in hospital for six weeks.'

Although the conversations were predictable and he had no tax to minimise, Paul enjoyed these evenings with his neighbours. Just like at church, everyone had a story to tell and the less he spoke, the more he learned. Tonight, standing at the bar with Roy, they had been joined by no other than the elusive Martin Havelock, who was attending fish and chips for the second time in a row after never being seen at resident functions outside of Christmas, even when his lovely wife was alive. Martin was a funny fish, thought Paul, as he watched him enter the room and block the doorway as he decided which way to go. Tall and ungainly like a teenager who hasn't worked out how to coordinate his adult self, Martin at eighty-plus had a somewhat alarming physical presence, compounded by his habit of standing too close. Paul was a shorter and rounder man and found looking up at Martin's face and those long dangling arms and big hands both disconcerting and comical, like talking with Lurch come to life. Martin swung himself over to the bar, ordered a beer and raised his glass at Paul and Roy.

'Good evening, Paul, Roy.'

'Good evening, Martin.'

'Nice weather we've been having.'

'Yes, it is.'

'No sign of rain for another week.'

'Good for the harvest.'

'Indeed.'

They all sipped their beer and looked down into their glasses. Martin tried again.

'Did you hear if Smith has been declared fit for the game?'

'Against Pakistan? Doubt it.'

'They'll be in trouble if he isn't.'

'Warner's back in form.'

'And Labuschagne and Paine can bat.'

'Hmm.'

They all took another sip.

'I hear you fixed a problem with the chairs in the dining room, Martin.'

Martin brightened at the conversation opening. 'I did, I did.'

He explained the problem at length, describing the failure of the workmanship and the risk to residents of cutting themselves and the consequent potential for infection. He told them about the foul smell of ammonia – *that's cat urine, you know* – against the wood, how someone had thoughtlessly left staples embedded in the underside of the tabletops and how he had needed to remove them with a pair of pliers. He explained his calculations of the amount and grade of sandpaper and varnish required, the drying time that had to be allowed between successive coats, and how he managed this so he and Josh could attend to other chores without delaying the overall project or his scheduled housework. Overall, he had completed the project over two and a half days with no downtime.

'It sounds like we have you to thank for saving us from some grazed knees and cut fingers,' said Paul. 'You weren't out of pocket at all were you? The Residents' Committee should reimburse you for any money you spent.'

'No, not at all. Happy to be useful.' Martin looked embarrassed and waved his suggestion away with his plate-sized hand, almost knocking Paul's head. 'I see you had a committee meeting this week,' he said, changing the subject. 'I read the minutes. I didn't understand the problem with the gardens.'

At this, Roy straightened up. It was his turn. 'I can tell you all about that. It's a disgrace what's been happening.'

Paul took the opportunity to excuse himself and find a seat. There was an empty chair at a table next to Peter Wise, who sat next to his wife as well as Molly, Elaine and Meira. Peter looked up and smiled as Paul sat down. He could feel the other man's gratitude. Elaine had just finished describing the refurbishment of Elizabeth's villa and was now telling the table about the doctor who might be moving in.

'His name is Doctor George Godden. He was a GP around here for years until he retired. Molly and I googled him, didn't we, Molly?'

Molly blinked at her.

'Godden is an old English name,' said Meira. 'It means good friend. Very auspicious.' She nodded her approval. 'It is also in the *Domesday Book* of ten eighty-six I believe.'

'Goodness, Meira, the things that are in that head of yours,' exclaimed Elaine. 'Anyway, he will cause a lot of excitement. He is quite handsome, isn't he, love? In a tall and rugged kind of way.' She patted Molly on the arm. Paul considered the word rugged and doubted whether it could be said of any man over the age of seventy and still be a compliment.

'I suppose so. Conventionally handsome,' replied Molly. She sipped her wine and made a face. 'Not my type. A bit too, well, masculine, although I guess the single ladies might like the look of him.'

Meira rolled her eyes and Elaine laughed. 'Bless you darling, you are so funny.'

Joyce looked back and forth between the three women and then changed the subject.

'Paul, I have to say I am disappointed in the committee's decision to endorse the tree pruning.'

'I expected you would be, Joyce,' Paul replied, serious and conciliatory. 'But the committee felt that the risk of damage to life and property outweighed the other arguments.'

'I think it is only right to tell you that I have appealed to the council.'

'It's your right to do that, Joyce, but I do appreciate you letting me know.' He attempted what he hoped was a reassuring smile.

Joyce huffed and took another mouthful of wine. 'I see the committee hasn't considered the dementia matter yet.'

'No, we haven't, Joyce. I'm afraid I don't expect that we will either.'

'Why not? The residents have a right to say who comes into the village and who doesn't. Clearly, people with dementia are not capable of contributing to village life and will eventually need full-time care. Peter and I didn't come here to live in a nursing home and neither, I expect, did any of you.'

Peter, Molly and Elaine looked down at their glasses. Meira pursed her lips and reached for a piece of cheese.

'I don't mind a confused brain here and there,' she declared. 'We will all go that way, some just sooner than others.'

'You will mind when Martin Havelock starts wandering the halls in the middle of the night and comes knocking on your door stark naked,' Joyce retorted.

Paul snorted into his beer. He knew he would never unsee the mental image of a naked Martin raging through the Harewood Hall under the gaze of the past medical directors.

Meira laughed, throwing back her head. 'Trust me, Joyce, he wouldn't know what to do with me.'

Paul intervened to prevent any further invocations of unseemly resident behaviour.

'But we don't have anything like that here, and if we did, I'm sure Fiona would handle it.'

'But that's not the point. The point is that they shouldn't be here in the first place.'

'I think the point is that we don't have a right to say who comes into the village and who doesn't,' Meira stated mildly. 'And neither should we; it is against the law to discriminate.'

'Well, I think we should have the right. This is our home and we shouldn't have to share it with just anyone who wants to come here.'

Elaine and Molly looked at each other, eyebrows raised. Saved by the dinner service, they shuffled their glasses to make way for their plates. Molly looked up from her fish and chips and raised her wine.

'*Bon appétit!*'

MARTIN

Friday fish and chips night was something that Martin attended as a means to an end. Martin's doctor had recommended that Martin be more proactive in maintaining his mental health as he aged. Martin took this to mean he was at risk of becoming depressed, so he googled *depression in older men*. The top results after advertisements were a selection of government-sponsored mental health services. They all agreed that being socially active is important for maintaining one's mental health in older age. Apparently, *regular social routines* contribute to a sense of connectedness, meaningfulness and overall contentment with life. University research, he was pleased to learn, had demonstrated that connection with family, friends and the wider community can be a protective factor against anxiety, depression and may even delay the progress of dementia. People who have strong relationships also need less support and continue to live independently for longer.

All of these sounded to Martin like reasonable things to achieve, so he had worked through an online self-reflective questionnaire and asked himself *am I as connected as I'd like to be.* After completing the questions, Martin felt that he was, in fact, as connected as he'd like to be, but suspected that he was not as connected as mental health practitioners would like him to be. Following the academics researchers' advice, he had made an Action Plan for improving his social connection.

Goals	Actions	Achievements
I would like to meet some like-minded people in my local community.	*1. Call the local council and find out what activities are on.* *2. Trial some activities that I am interested in.*	*I tried a tai chi class, book club and walking group. I liked the people in the book club and will go once a week.*
I want to improve my social connections as a protective factor against anxiety and depression.	*I will attend the weekly fish and chips night.*	*I don't have anxiety and depression yet.*
I want to find a sense of purpose to avoid dementia.	*I will volunteer in the workshop at the local school.*	*I don't have dementia yet.*

Martin had attended fish and chips night for the first time last Friday. He had made a good start on his Action Plan, he thought, talking with Peter and Joyce Wise for thirty minutes. They lived on his floor in the heritage building and he already knew them on a wave and say hello basis. He recalled that Maureen and Joyce had served on the Social Club Committee together and this gave him an opportunity to take an interest, as Maureen had once advised him to do in social settings.

'Take an interest in what a person does, and they'll tell you all about themselves,' she had said. 'Then you don't need to worry about coming up with conversation ideas yourself.'

Martin had been sceptical at first. What if the other person had nothing to say that interested him? Or worse, what if they said things that were poorly informed or lacked coherent reasoning? Martin knew from experience that both situations could end a conversation sooner than he had intended. But Maureen had been right, and with the support of a few practised phrases – *That's interesting; tell me more about it* and *That must have been hard for you* and *Then what happened?* – he had conducted several successful conversations in a social setting and was well on his way, he thought, to his Action Plan Achievements.

Last week, he had asked Joyce about the current committee's plans and had been rewarded with a beaming smile and twenty minutes of conversation about the Christmas party. She had even asked his advice about the theme. He had been confused about the concept of a theme for a Christmas party until he recalled the Mexican Christmas two years ago. He liked the White Christmas theme she proposed. He had always been a fan of Bing Crosby and had seen the movie with Maureen. He wasn't so sure about the Castaways idea and suggested to Joyce that the double meaning of the phrase might not sit well with some residents, even if it might be fun to have tropical cocktails and decorate the dining room with seashells and fishing nets. He then spent ten minutes listening to the details of Peter's golf game that morning (he had remembered seeing Peter leaving the carpark and had initiated this conversation himself). Martin didn't play golf, but he also remembered reading that physical activity was a factor in maintaining good mental health in older age and thought that he might ask Peter about it again.

So far tonight, he had exceeded his achievements of the previous week. He had already spent fifteen minutes telling the president of the Residents' Committee about the dining room chairs, and twenty minutes listening to Roy tell him how the village gardening policy needed to be fixed. Apparently, according to Roy, management were arbitrary in their administration of the policy and let some residents plant bushes that would grow to more than 1.5 metres and denied the same privilege to other residents. Roy wouldn't go so far as to accuse anyone of deliberate misconduct of course, but he felt that there might be a case for arguing that management discriminated against some residents on the basis of gender when it came to gardening decisions. He wanted residents to support him in removing the gardening policy altogether and intended to put a motion at the next residents' general meeting.

Mindful of his own recent gender assumptions, Martin had suggested that Roy obtain a record of all of the gardening policy decisions for the past five years to determine on the basis of facts whether management was indeed discriminating against residents of a certain gender in administering the gardening policy. Roy agreed that he would do this first thing Monday morning. Satisfied that he had achieved a meaningful social interaction with the extra benefit of making a contribution to his village community, Martin excused himself and went to find a seat at one of the dining tables.

HARLEY

At sundown, Harley made his way up to Martin's balcony. The balcony, which the last time he visited was empty except for a wooden chair, now had a shallow dish of water in the corner and there was a musty, human smell that wasn't there before. The apartment itself was dark and the balcony door closed. Apart from the fridge and the high-pitched buzz of the television on stand-by, there were no sounds. Harley drank the water and began to sniff out the source of the smell. On the chair he found a blanket, folded so the edges lined up exactly with the edges of the seat. It was not as soft as Elizabeth's blankets and had a more pungent smell that reminded Harley of the basement and the dust and pollen that blows in on the easterly wind, but it was better than a bare wooden seat. There was no food though, and Harley jumped up onto the blanket and thought through his options. He had already tried Meira's apartment and found the door closed and unresponsive. It seemed to Harley that Martin was not home either. He curled up for a short doze.

After a time, the balcony door slid open and another shallow dish appeared a hand's breadth outside on the floor. Harley kept still until he was sure Martin's footsteps had taken him well back inside the apartment. He sniffed for the scent of the dish, slipped off the chair, and ate the small pieces of raw chicken before the bowl could be taken away again.

6 · SATURDAY

MARTIN

When Maureen was alive, she looked after everything to do with food. She shopped, cooked, packed lunches for the children, cleaned out the expired food each week and replaced it with fresh. Martin followed her example and prepared weekly meal plans and shopped to a list. This week, he planned to cook:

> Saturday: roast chicken with potato, pumpkin and broccoli
> Sunday: chicken and vegetable soup (use the leftover roast chicken)
> Monday: stir fried beef with oyster sauce, mushrooms and bok choy
> Tuesday: lamb chops with steamed broccoli, cauliflower and baked potatoes
> Wednesday: spaghetti bolognaise (use the second half of the bolognaise sauce from last week)
> Thursday: potato and tuna bake (freeze half for the following week).

On Friday night he would attend fish and chips night again in the residents' dining room.

Martin preferred not to shop on a Saturday. Mondays were best. Saturday grocery shopping was for people who worked during the week. While he was still working, Martin went with Maureen to the shops on a Saturday once, to buy work shirts. It was awful. There were multitudes of parents, hurrying through the aisles, trying to fit a week's worth of shopping into the time they had between cleaning the house, doing the laundry, and ferrying children to basketball games and ballet lessons. Often, they were pushing children in prams or pulling them along on foot. There were announcements over the supermarket public address system directing shoppers to half price gourmet pizzas in the frozen foods section. Children from a local school played violin, discordant against the piped shopping centre music, and lights flashed in shop windows. Frazzled infants cried and parents called for toddlers who had wandered out of sight. Otherwise pleasant smells from the bakery competed with the rotisserie, which competed with the fruit and vegetables, which were overtaken by the cleaning products in aisles twelve and thirteen. Mud tracked in from sports grounds mixed with orange juice knocked from shelves, and yellow and black signs cautioned shoppers against wet floors.

Martin couldn't see how a person could shop in such an environment. The parents didn't stand a chance of comparing products and obtaining the best prices, let alone checking the sugar, salt and fat contents of the food they planned to feed their children. Martin himself appreciated the new system of displaying prices that included the cost per unit of weight, although he still calculated it himself – sometimes they were not correct. Shoppers could not assume that larger, bulk packages were always cheaper by weight than smaller packages of the same product. Sometimes, especially when the shops were discounting, which they always seemed to be doing these days, multiple small packages were cheaper than a single large package, with the added convenience of staying fresh for longer, and this could only be determined by calculating the unit cost by weight yourself. Martin couldn't fathom why some shoppers chose to grab items of the shelf without checking, denying themselves potential savings. He had vowed he would never go back.

Weekday shopping, Martin had learned since retiring, was completely different to Saturday shopping. Almost enjoyable. The traffic in the shopping precinct flowed as the road system engineers intended, he always got a parking bay in his preferred aisle of the covered carpark, the atmosphere in the shopping centre was unhurried, and he could compare prices at leisure and in relative silence. There were no violins. The first time he shopped on a weekday was a revelation to Martin, although he was taken aback by the femininity of the place. There were, quite literally, no men shopping. Only women. Middle-aged women, some escorting much older women on slow rounds of the aisles; tired-looking women with prams; and young women, some wearing the uniform of the nearby hospital, browsing through the dress shops. None of them looked rushed and all of them appraised shop windows and carefully discussed their purchases with smiling salespeople. The café exuded a gentle murmur of female voices conversing while silent toddlers ate muffins and drew on thoughtfully provided sheets of paper. And the smell, he realised, was sweet and floral, from the feminine deodorants and body lotions and perfumes these women had used in their homes before they brought themselves to the shops. It was a different world.

But Martin wouldn't go to that calm and pleasant world today. The cat needed cat food, according to the internet, so Martin would brave the weekend madness and do his shopping on a Saturday morning. He finished his shopping list and made a note at the bottom to visit the pet shop and ask about balanced diets for domestic cats.

JOSH

Saturday mornings were chore mornings for Josh. This morning, he had to prune the hedges at the front of the house for his mum and sweep out the garage for his dad. He also needed to fill a prescription at the pharmacy and buy more flea treatments for Stan. While he was at the pet store, he would also buy some mouse food.

After his morning run and breakfast, Josh opened the garage door and took the hedge trimmer down from its shelf. He had put the battery on charge last night after Emily left and now he took it off the charging station and slotted it into the trimmer handle. He removed the plastic cutting guard and gave the motor a quick test. Good to go. His mum and dad had planted box hedges down each side of the driveway, and these were to be cut back to keep their shape. There were also larger hedges on the fence lines at both sides of the garden that needed tidying and Josh was the only one tall enough to reach them. Josh didn't mind doing chores for his parents. His mum and dad made his life pretty easy, letting him live at home while he finished his degree. Lots of Josh's friends had moved out of home and into share houses. Whenever vacant rooms came up, they tried to cajole him into moving in. So far, he had resisted. It looked like fun, sure, but right now he could go to their parties and then come home to a quiet bedroom and not have to pick his way through the after-party slop the next morning. He thought it might be nice to move out with Emily, but – he knew this was pretty clichéd and that his friends laughed at him – right now his mum cooked him dinner every night and there was always food in the fridge and paracetamol in the pantry.

Josh worked his way through the hedges. When he finished, he raked up the leaves and swept out the garage. At his dad's workbench, he cleaned and oiled the cutting blades, slid the plastic guard back on, took out the battery, and put the trimmer back on its shelf. Upstairs in his room, he changed into jeans and a t-shirt, picked up his wallet and keys off the floor, then headed out for the shops.

After he had hidden the mouse cage under the bushes two weeks ago, Josh joined Mike and Tim and talked with the security guy for a while. It turned out he surfed the same break as Josh, and he said a late storm forecast for next week was going to push the swell to over two metres. Josh should get down there, he said; decent waves were rare at this time of year. Josh thought he'd probably be working that day.

Then they walked home up the highway. The buses had stopped running by that hour and they couldn't get an Uber because everyone's phone was flat. Tim lived at the colleges anyway, so he didn't have far to go. On the walk home, Mike reminded Josh that he still had a vacant room available. Emily could come too if she wanted. Josh laughed it off but felt queasy at the thought of Emily living in the semi-squalor that was Mike's share house. No, if he and Emily ever moved in together, it would be their own place or at least with someone who practised the principles of basic hygiene. Maybe a girl. From what Josh could see, girls were less likely to put up with sticky floors and soap scum.

Early the next morning, Josh had taken an old blue dog blanket out of the linen cupboard, told his mum he was going running along the river, and drove back to uni. At that time of day, there were plenty of parking bays near the research centre. He parked next to the lab entrance, found the cage easily enough (the mice were still there, looking up at him with startled eyes), strapped it into the back seat and covered it with the blanket. He reversed out of the carpark, drove around to Matilda Bay, locked the car, and headed west on the running track towards the city.

During the drive home after his run, Josh had congratulated himself on the mouse retrieval but was perplexed about what to do next. There was no way Mum would have mice in the house and he couldn't see Emily being too thrilled about them becoming a birthday present. They couldn't stay in the car all day – they were probably like dogs that overheat and die horrible deaths in locked cars – so he had to come up with something soon. Tim couldn't hide them in his college room. Mike would lose it if he told him. But he could stash them in the basement at Harewood Hall for a couple of days while he worked it out.

So that's what he did. The only person who saw him that Saturday was Bobby, wandering around the gardens on his own. Josh had taken the mice to Meira's storage unit, set them on the floor, and rearranged the storage boxes to create a shelf against the back wall. He'd sat with them for a while, stroking their little mousy backs, until it occurred to him that there was no obvious food in the cage, and they would need feeding sometime. Probably that day. He had no idea what mice eat so he'd taken out his phone – by then fully charged and to his surprise with four bars down there in the basement – and googled mouse food.

That was two weeks ago now and, as usual on a Saturday, the shops were busy again. Josh had to queue to get into the carpark and then spend ten minutes searching for a bay. As he trawled the rows of BMWs and Volvos, Josh reflected on how a couple of days had become a couple of weeks and today he would need to buy his third bag of mouse food. He had tried two different types, one that provided a 'healthy and nutritious meal' in the first week and one that gave 'your rodent friend a vibrant life' in the second week. The mice hadn't seemed to notice the difference and had gobbled down everything put in front of them. Today he thought he might get them 'healthy skin and coat'. In front of him, the reversing lights blinked on at the rear of a large four-wheel drive, and Josh flicked on his indicator to claim the bay.

Upstairs it seemed like all the people in the western suburbs were in town. He was stopped three times on his way to the pharmacy by friends or mothers of friends from school. He learned that Tim's parents were visiting from the country and taking him to the game this weekend; that Sarah's brother had switched from law to medicine; and he was invited to a party. When he eventually made it to the pharmacy and handed over his prescription, his phone pinged. It was Emily.

R u @ shops? Sarah saw u @ Coles

                                             Yeah. At pharmacy now

Coffee?

                                                Sure 30 mins?

**thumbs up* StandInRoom?*

                                                thumbs up*

While his prescription was filled, Josh walked around the corner to the pet shop. As he walked in, Martin Havelock walked out.

'Morning, Martin.'

'Good morning, Josh. Are you shopping today? Nice morning for it.' Martin looked flustered.

'Just some chores for Mum.' Josh nodded at the bag of cat food, food bowl and litter tray that Martin clutched against his chest. 'What's all this for? Have you bought yourself a cat?'

'Well, ah, yes. I've adopted a stray.'

'Is that the cat that Mrs Collins was feeding before she passed away?'

'What?' Martin had been collecting himself and now looked put out all over again. 'What cat?'

'Elizabeth Collins, in villa twenty-six. She passed away this week. She had a stray cat that she fed. Small. Grey tabby.'

'Well I don't know,' Martin hedged. 'How did you know about that?'

'Sometimes I clean for Molly and Elaine. They live next door. The cat sits on the fence and watches me through the window. Sometimes I give it some milk. It's pretty friendly when it gets to know you. I reckon if you feed it, it will let you pat it.'

'I thought Elaine did the cleaning. Isn't she Molly's carer?'

Josh paused. He didn't know what to say and could feel the heat rising up his neck. Martin could be a daft old bugger sometimes, he thought.

Martin frowned, as though he sensed he had slipped up somewhere, and made to leave. 'Well, I won't hold you up from your mum's chores. I'll see you on Tuesday.'

'Yeah, see you Tuesday, Martin. Oh, and Martin?' The tall man turned back to him. 'I wouldn't bother with the litter tray. They stink and he's probably used to pooping in the garden anyway.'

Inside the store, Josh walked past the rows of colourful pet toys and cutesy dog coats and turned left to find the pet food aisle. There were three different types of mouse food, all in pellet form. Josh selected the third brand and took it to the counter, where he asked for a three-month supply of Advocate flea treatment for medium-sized dogs. It was expensive, but his mum had given him cash to cover it this morning. He went back to the pharmacy with his purchases, collected his prescription and walked down the road to the café, where he leaned against the wall outside to wait for Emily.

'Hi babe!' Emily waved to him from across the road. She carried a backpack and one of her mum's cotton shopping bags. She also wore one of her mum's shirts.

'Hi babe, you look great. Is that your mum's shirt? Does she know you have it?' Emily had a habit of 'borrowing' and then 'forgetting to return' her mum's clothes. Most of the time, Emily's mum didn't seem to mind, but occasionally, when Emily's borrowing extended to more expensive items, the forgetting to return part got her into trouble. Worse, Josh had twice saved some of Emily's mum's white silk blouses from ruin after he had found Emily optimistically stuffing them into the washing machine with her jeans and running gear.

'Not sure.'

'So, no, then.'

'She loaned it to me last month, but I might have forgotten to give it back.' She linked her arm inside of his, gave it a squeeze and changed the subject. 'Have you ordered yet?'

Inside, they ordered two soy flat whites, using the keep cups that Emily kept in her backpack. As they waited for their order, Emily picked up the bag of mouse food at Josh's feet.

'What's this, babe? You haven't been feeding the mice in the shed, have you? Isn't that taking it a bit too far?' She poked him playfully.

Josh laughed and shook his head. His protection of the garden shed mice was a long running family joke that Emily had been let into last Christmas. When Josh was in primary school, so the story goes, he found a neighbour's cat stalking the house mice that lived in the shed at the back of the garden. Apparently, Josh had taken it upon himself to become the guardian of the mice and for a time would collect an old tennis racket from the garage after school each day and beat away any cat that approached the shed.

'Nah, I've left all of that behind me. I've moved on to loggerhead turtles.'

They collected their coffees and walked up the street to find a sunny spot to sit. She looked at him, waiting for the answer to her question. 'So …?'

There was no escaping it. 'I've acquired two mice.'

'Oh my God! No way, are you serious? Where are they? Are they cute? When can I see them?'

'Yes way. And, yeah, they are pretty cute. They have these little pink noses and their hair is really white.'

'Babe, you are adorable. Can we go see them now?'

HARLEY

Harley was disappointed. He had learned that it took time to train each resident to give him the food he liked, but today had been a long day and he was tired and hungry and Martin's balcony door was closed. At noon, after a late start and a doze on the footpath, Harley had left Harewood Hall, taken the steps down to the school, crossed the grounds, and purposefully made his way through the suburb to the railway line. Here, he had paused at the entrance to the darkened pedestrian underpass before trotting through to the other side. He waited with the other mourners until the traffic lights changed, then crossed the road into the cemetery. His presence went unnoticed by the small crowd. Most of them were elderly and looking at their own feet. Only one person, a teenage girl, saw him and elbowed the boy next to her. He scowled and complained to his mother, who in turn scolded the girl before turning back to her conversation with another woman.

It was a long way to travel for a cat. Harley rarely moved far from Harewood Hall and the nearby school these days and he was tired from the effort. He had been here before, though, many times, and positioned himself in a clump of agapanthus where he could watch the crowd without being disturbed. There was Paul, conspicuous with the large crucifix on his chest. Little Molly had lowered the seat on her walker and was sitting on it while Elaine chatted behind her to a man Harley didn't recognise. Both Molly and Elaine wore bright, loose clothes that stood out in the crowd of black and navy blue and Elaine's hands waved about as she talked. Meira sat on her own walker next to Molly, her face creased and her hands folded on her lap as she leaned forward. Martin was now crossing the road, his long face high above the other silver heads. Harley could see that he was walking with Pat, holding her arm as she clutched Bobby's leash in the other. Bobby had picked up Harley's scent and was intent on following it into the cemetery, straining at his collar. Harley shrank back into the strappy leaves. He was in no mood for an encounter with the dog. And there was the lady who fed the birds. Harley sometimes watched her from the fence on the other side of the tall trees. She hadn't fed him yet, but she would. In time.

A long black car turned into the gates and the crowd parted as it passed through at a walking pace. Harley could see the box underneath white and pink flowers. He stood up as the car and crowd passed by and then followed along behind them as they went ahead up the boulevard. There were children, lagging at the back. They wandered from side to side, the smaller ones picking up stones and stealing flowers. In their wake, Harley could smell soap and fresh clothes, not at all what he remembered of children. The teenage girl and her brother walked together, their heads bent towards each other and at one point the girl turned her head, caught sight of him and smiled.

For a while during the service, Harley sat at the open door. The box sat in front of a window on a platform that Harley knew would sink below the ground, taking the box with it. The flowers were still there. They would go too. There was a television, larger and higher than the residents had in their homes, on the wall to the right. Paul stood up at the front and spoke, and then other people took turns to do the same. When the crowd eased to their feet and started singing, Harley trotted around to the black car. It was out of sight of the people inside, its tailgate open towards the building. He sniffed at the tyres, paused at the open door. He could smell the flowers, the men's shoes, and the peppermint lollies that Molly and Elaine ate. The singing stopped and he felt the crowd deflate. He waited. Paul spoke again and the music started. Harley turned his back on the car and returned to the gardens to wait out the departure of the mourners.

One of the first people to leave was Josh, who set off in the opposite direction to the crowd. Curious, Harley followed him to a gate at the far side of the cemetery, smaller than the one he had entered earlier. He stopped as Josh passed through, then turned around and walked back through the cemetery. He had travelled far enough today and would start the long walk back to Harewood Hall.

Now, as the sky faded, Harley's paws hurt, and he was hungry. He had slept on Martin's balcony the night before, and found the rug acceptable but the balcony colder than he would have liked. He was starting to feel an ache in his legs. Standing in front of the closed door, it was plain that it would be some time before he might gain entry. He decided to try his luck with Meira.

7 · SUNDAY

JOSH

Josh ran his palm backwards and forwards over the blades of grass, enjoying the feel of the cool, supple new growth. He put down his book and turned his head to one side to look at Emily. The shade had shifted, and he covered his eyes with one hand.

'Have Marianne and Connell got back together yet?'

'No, and don't tell me. I don't want to know.'

He rolled onto his side and tapped her skin just above her hipbone where she was most ticklish.

'They do, but they break up again and Marianne moves to Germany to do a PhD,' he teased.

She wriggled away. 'Stop it. Or I'll tell you how *A Little Life* ends.'

Josh had borrowed a copy of *A Little Life* from Emily after he saw it resting on the seat of Meira's walker in the Harewood Hall café. Emily's copy was mangled from being carted around in her backpack and had coffee rings on the front cover. He was a third of the way in. It wasn't the happiest book he had ever read, but he had become invested in the main character and had been carrying the book around in his own backpack. His mum had given him an old pyjama bag to keep it from deteriorating any further. The bag was pink and white and covered with flowers, and he stuffed it in the bottom of the backpack whenever he took it out.

'I already know, I read the last chapter.'

Horrified, Emily put her own book down and gaped at him. 'You did not.' This was an unforgivable sin.

'I did. Jude quits law and writes a bestseller based on his life story.'

'Yeah, right, of course he does.' She rolled her eyes at him, picked up another piece of cheese and returned to her own book.

Josh thought about Meira. She had been his client for six months. He cleaned her apartment and they talked about politics. Meira seemed to know a lot about the world and had strong opinions on different political systems. She called herself Australian, but Josh knew that her family once lived in Vienna but had left Austria when the Anschluss was declared, when Meira was just a little girl. She hadn't been too keen to talk about her childhood. From what Josh could gather from Wikipedia, it wasn't a good thing to be an Austrian Jew during the civil war. He had read about signs painted on the windows of Jewish businesses and people forced to scrub the streets. There were stories of random house invasions, theft, beatings of old people, disappearances and the annexation of homes. Jewish people who left the country had to relinquish large sums of money, leaving them with nothing when they arrived, poor but safe, in England and America. Josh had read these stories before, of course, in history lessons at school, but these had seemed ancient, irrelevant in the world's most remote capital city at the start of the twenty-first century. Now, with Meira only a couple of kilometres away in her apartment, it was more uncomfortable to contemplate. What if his own country had secret histories hidden away?

Meira's family had moved to England when Meira was sixteen. Like Emily, she had finished her schooling in a second language and gone on to attend university in her new country. She had been one of the first students of electrophysiology under Professor Alan Hodgkin at Cambridge. There she had measured electrical currents in the nerves of giant squid. Emily had been wide-eyed when Josh relayed this news. Apparently, the great professor had been one of the fathers of neuroscience. He had developed action potential theory, which, according to Emily, was key to understanding how neurons talk to each other. She told him about the all-or-none law, drawing diagrams to explain, and wondered if Meira had been involved in developing voltage clamps. Josh had yet to make good on his promise to introduce them.

From what he could make out, Meira had lived a traditional life for a woman in the mid-late twentieth century. She met an Australian medical student studying at Cambridge on a scholarship. They married and moved back to Australia, where he became one of the world's leading neonatal care specialists and she raised their four children. Josh didn't know when or how Meira's husband died. He knew the sons lived abroad and her apartment was full of books and that she laid some sort of familial claim to Gustav Mahler. He also knew that Fiona was on a mission to get Meira to have more support hours. Good luck with that, he thought. His weekly cleaning was barely necessary in Meira's tidy apartment. Like many of his clients, Meira coped fine with life's daily tasks and he spent most of his time drinking tea and talking. Meira's apartment was stacked with books, and not just books that were bought twenty years ago and collecting dust on bookshelves. Each place where Meira sat or slept had a nearby table with an open book laid upside down to keep its reader's page. Their spines mirrored the local bookshop windows with their displays of literary prize winners, as well as a couple of gothic fiction novels that were being turned into horror movies. Josh thought he might like spending extra time with Meira if Fiona could convince her.

He checked his watch. 'Hey babe, we need to go if we want to stop at Harewood Hall on the way home.'

Emily put down her book and stretched. 'I can't decide if I like Marianne or not.'

'I didn't. I thought she was too self-absorbed.'

'That's a bit harsh, babe. She'd been abused and was traumatised.'

'Yeah, I know, but she played on it a bit.'

Emily raised her eyebrows. Sensing the potential for an argument, they left the conversation right there and busied themselves with packing up the picnic and loading it into the car. When they reached Harewood Hall, Josh had to manoeuvre the Golf around the back of a catering van that was jutting out into the road.

'Damn, I forgot that was on today.' The concert meant that he would almost certainly be seen and need to explain why he was at the village on a weekend. He drove around the heritage building and the outer ring of the west-end villas and parked on the southern side. There were two car bays there that were out of sight and he and Emily could walk down the residents' vehicle access ramp unseen instead of using the stairs.

Down in the basement, Josh unlocked the door to storage unit number five. He waved to the guy in the Tredwell Trades van. He hadn't expected to see them in here either on a Sunday. It looked like the guy had emptied out half of the storage unit.

'Working on the weekend, Josh?'

Josh flushed. 'I'm just collecting some tools from Martin Havelock. He said I could borrow them.'

'That's nice of him. Make sure you return them by the due date.'

They both laughed. Everyone, it seemed, knew Martin and his quirks.

'Isn't Martin in number seven, mate?'

'Um, yeah. But I also need to take some old photos up to Meira Jacobs.'

'Yeah, right. And that's a nice old couch she's got in there too. Make good use of it.' He smirked and threw a look at Emily. 'I'm out of here. You kids have fun while the grown-ups are upstairs enjoying the concert.'

He swung the van around and out of the basement and Josh led Emily to the back of Meira's storage unit, avoiding eye contact with the couch.

Emily pulled a face. 'What a creep. Who is he?'

'He's a painter or a carpenter or something for Tredwell Trades. They do all the refurbishments when residents leave. I don't know their names. There's a few of them and they're all good mates with the big boss. I saw them all once, getting off his boat at the yacht club. Best to stay on their good side.'

He pulled another stool down from the top shelf so they could both sit down.

'Close your eyes.' She sat and held her hands over her face.

'Ta-dah!' He pulled the blanket off with a flourish.

Emily looked at the mice and sighed. 'They're adorable. Can I touch them? Do they have names?' She put her fingers between the bars and both mice came over to sniff her. 'Look at their pink noses twitching.' She ran a single finger along each of their backs. 'They're so tiny!'

Josh reached into his backpack and pulled out a ziplock bag of vegetable sticks.

'Here, you can feed them these if you like.' He watched as his girlfriend held the pieces of carrot and celery steady for the mice to eat. He was relieved that she seemed to share his pleasure in his new dependants.

'Do they have names?'

'No. You can give them some if you like.'

'I'm calling this one Coco and the fat one Pudding.'

'Coco's a funny name for a white mouse.'

'But she's so elegant and sleek, like Coco Chanel. Can I hold her?'

Emily opened the door and reached into the cage. Coco dashed back under the newspaper, but Pudding waddled over to her open hand. Emily closed her fingers around the pudgy mouse and lifted her out and to her chest. She sighed again as she bent her nose down to breathe in the mousy smell. Josh felt an unexpected twinge of tenderness as he looked at them both, Emily's head bowed over the tiny animal as she perched on the stool. If he could find the right place, maybe it might be nice to move in together after all.

Emily looked up at him, frowning. 'Hey babe, you do realise the fat one's having babies, don't you?'

HARLEY

Dozing on the warm brick path on the western side of the heritage building, Harley half opened his eyes when Josh and Emily drove past. It had been a good day so far. Meira heard him last night when he called at her door and had obliged with a plate of chicken and a place to sleep. He remained curled up on her warm couch until midday when he was woken by the sound of a truck reversing in the staff carpark. He then spent a lazy and interesting couple of hours under the lemon-scented gums, watching people coming and going from the residents' dining room. One of the last to arrive was a sparkly woman with glossy black hair, and when she started to sing Harley relocated himself to the bushes near the café entrance so he could have a closer vantage point. From there, he could also observe the end of the food service and better time his arrival at the kitchen deliveries door.

When the singing finished and Joyce and two other women rose to clear away the plates, Harley made his move and relocated to the window ledge next to the delivery door. Here, he had a good view of the cleaning-up operations. The external catering staff, dressed in black trousers and white shirts, loaded the large silver dishwasher and stacked their orange trays. Joyce and the other residents arranged the uneaten food in plastic containers on the other side of the kitchen. Harley knew if just one of them looked up see him, he would receive a small plate of leftovers next to the door after the caterers had left. He hoped for the salmon. He'd been given the hummus last time and didn't need to try it again.

The delivery door opened, and the catering staff removed their trays and drove away in their truck. Joyce came into the kitchen from the dining room with another plate of food, filling the first plastic container and taking it to the fridge. Harley stood up in anticipation. The best time to be noticed would be when Joyce walked back towards him. But when Joyce had placed the container in the fridge, she walked in the opposite direction. After a moment, she walked back again, shaking her head, and he stood on his hind legs with his paws on the glass. She paused for a moment, then turned and walked back towards the fridge. Harley wondered if he should chance standing in front of the open door. He watched as she circled the island cooking bench, eyes scanning the walls, and then circled back again. She stood for a long moment a second time, looking at the food set out in its containers on the bench. A loud, jarring chord rang out on the piano in the dining room and Joyce abruptly turned her head towards the sound and the door. Walking quickly, she left the kitchen.

Harley raised his head from the warm bricks when he heard Josh's car door close and then another clunk immediately after it. He watched as Josh and Emily walked down the vehicle access ramp. He felt lethargic after his kitchen leftovers and disinclined to follow them. In the end, no-one had noticed him at the window, but he took advantage of the open door and a lull in activity after Joyce's departure to slip inside and claim all the salmon from the top of the remaining blinis.

PAUL

In the residents' dining room, the soprano twinkled and bobbed as she sang about being faithful to her lover. With her floor-length red dress and long shiny hair, she held the residents spellbound. She might look like an ingenue, but she has a voice older than her years, thought Paul. Her high notes rang like a young woman's should, but her middle register was round and full like a singer in her forties. One could only hope for what she would sound like when her voice matured, he mused.

Paul sat back, contented. He had to hand it to Joyce. She knew how to put on a show. Both the singer and the accompanist were final year students at the Academy of Performing Acts and Joyce had used her connections with the local Lieder Society to have them perform at Harewood Hall. The tables in the residents' dining room had been decorated with centrepiece roses, and the piano gleamed. There was sparkling wine, salmon on tiny pancakes, mushroom tarts and miniature beef wellingtons. Later, they would be served a selection of little cakes. Paul had seen them in the kitchen earlier. A choice of chocolate and almond. He would not need dinner tonight and the lamb chops he had defrosted this morning could be kept for tomorrow.

The song – *'Se Florindo è Fedele'* – finished and the audience clapped and murmured appreciatively to each other. As the singer took a sip of water and the accompanist announced a short break, Paul leaned across to his guest.

'She has a fine voice hasn't she, Jan?'

Jan was interested in buying into the village and she, like three other guests here today, had been invited to the concert to experience village life. As the guest most likely to be the next to become a village resident, Jan had been placed in Paul's care for the afternoon.

'She is gorgeous, Paul. She reminds me of a young Cecilia Bartoli. Quite the coquette.'

'Indeed.'

'And that piano is magnificent. How wonderful to have a Bösendorfer in the village.'

'Do you play yourself?'

'Yes, I do. I passed my grade eight exam when I was sixteen and I still practise every day. What about you?'

'Nothing, I'm afraid. I wasn't even allowed to sing with the worship team at church.'

'How unkind. Perhaps they could have just turned your mic down.'

He laughed. 'I wouldn't have been the first singer we'd done that to.'

Roy appeared above Jan's seated head. 'Paul,' he hissed. 'We need you now.'

Paul gave him a go-away look. Couldn't Roy see he was busy?

'It's about the water leak.'

Paul didn't want to talk about leaking village infrastructure in front of a potential new resident. Fortunately, Elaine was on the ball. 'I hear you are a musician, Jan,' she said, sliding seamlessly into the conversation and shooing him away. 'What type of music do you play?'

Roy shuffled Paul out of the residents' dining room and into the café. Jean and the three other committee members were already there.

'We've heard a rumour that the water bills are up because the ring main is leaking.'

'I've checked my bills and they are ten percent over.'

'I've checked mine too.'

'Apparently management are not going to do anything about it because the original plans have been lost and they can't find the leak.'

'I'm going to lodge a complaint with the State Administrative Tribunal.'

'I think we should take it to the local newspaper.'

Paul sat down at one of the café tables and gestured to the others to do the same. As usual, they had half the story and had made up the rest. A Tredwell Trades van trundled past the windows and he raised his hand in greeting at the driver. He feared he had eaten his last beef wellington for the day.

'Fiona briefed me about this on Friday,' he began, endeavouring to insert a measure of calm. 'The usage does seem to have increased since the end of summer. I reported it to Fiona last week after Roy kindly alerted me after the committee meeting.'

At this, Roy straightened a little and looked at the other committee members for acknowledgement.

'Last Thursday night, Gerry came back to the village at midnight to turn the water off and on again to each section of the village and check the water flow out of the meter. As you all know, he turned the water off again on Friday to replace each section's tap.'

'Yes, but it didn't work, did it?' challenged Roy. 'Good on him for coming in at midnight and all that, but if it didn't work, where does that leave us? We're just out of pocket for the cost of the taps.'

'I was coming to that, Roy,' Paul could feel his irritation rising. 'Gerry came in again on Friday night to check the meter and it seems most likely that the problem is in the ring main. Fiona called me to let me know yesterday.'

'And what is she doing about it?'

'Given that it is still the weekend, I would expect nothing yet.'

'While we pensioners pay for water to run into the sandhill.'

'You're self-funded, Roy, not a pensioner.'

'But I am,' said Jean.

'So am I.'

'I might be self-funded, but I still can't afford to pour my life savings into the ground.'

Paul waited until each committee member had claimed their poverty. 'The next step is to put a pipe inspection camera into the ring main.'

'How much will that cost? Management had better not think they can pay for it out of the Village Operating Budget.'

'Or the Reserve Fund.'

'The money has to come from somewhere,' protested Paul, exasperated.

'They can pay for it out of their own pockets. Why should we pay for management's incompetence?'

'It is hardly incompetent to have a leak in the plumbing system.' Paul paused. There was potential for a quick joke in there, but he decided now was not the time.

'Is it true that management have lost the plans for the village and that's why they can't find the leak? Gerry told me that the problem is most likely that the couplings have eroded or weren't installed properly in the first place. He said that he can't check them because management have lost the plans.' Roy looked triumphant. He had information that Paul didn't know.

Paul steeled himself for the huffs and groans and eye rolls of disapproval around the table. He wasn't disappointed.

'Obviously management don't know what they are doing, and we need to take it into our own hands.' Roy was on a roll now. 'I propose that we mark out where the ring main is and check the length of it ourselves.' The other committee members nodded enthusiastically.

Paul sat back. A pipe inspection camera would do exactly that but let them go ahead. Why not? It would keep Roy out of his hair for a good week or more, marking out the location of the ring main, turning taps on and off, checking the ground with torches in the middle of the night. He would be as happy as a clam. There was no need for Paul to get involved. He could hear the final song of the concert behind him and he switched off to indulge himself in the music while the other committee members made their water investigation plans.

Later that afternoon, after the plans had been agreed, the musicians had left, and the dining room cleared away, Paul stood with Molly and Elaine in the afternoon sun watching the magpies in the gum trees. He could see in the tops of the trees that the sea breeze had come in, but down here in the lee of the wind, he felt like a sun-warmed gecko and disinclined to take on much else in his day.

'Thanks for stepping in there with Jan, Elaine.'

'My pleasure, Paul. The last thing we needed was a Roy drama in front of a new prospect.'

'Do you think she's interested?'

'Yes, absolutely. She wants a villa so she can have space for her piano. I think she is looking at Elizabeth's.'

So soon, thought Paul a little sadly. Homes at Harewood Hall didn't stay vacant for long. There was always someone waiting for one of them to die.

'Look, Molly, there's Josh,' Elaine waved as Josh drove towards them in his little grey Golf. 'Hi Josh. Who's that you've got with you?'

Josh stopped and wound down the passenger side window. A smiley girl of Josh's age waved.

'Hi Molly. Hi Elaine. Hi Paul,' said Josh. 'This is Emily.'

Molly shuffled over to the car and reached through the window to take Emily's hand.

'Hello, Emily. Pleased to meet you. Josh, is this your sweetheart?'

Josh beamed. 'Yes she is, Molly.'

'She's so pretty. Does Josh look after you properly darling?'

Paul watched the young woman glow up at Molly. 'Yes, he does. He is very good to me.'

'Good. Keep up the excellent work, young man.' Molly looked pointedly at Josh and patted Emily's hand. 'Emily, you come and see me if he drops his standards.' She leaned into the car and whispered something in Emily's ear.

Emily giggled and colour spread across her cheeks. 'I will, Molly. I will.'

Paul shook his head. He didn't want to contemplate whatever advice Molly had given Emily to make her blush.

Josh waited until Elaine had steered Molly back away from the car before putting it into gear and continuing along the road. The two women waved goodbye to Paul and began their amble back to their villa. Paul looked thoughtful. What was Josh doing, bringing his girlfriend here on a Sunday? He wasn't due until Tuesday and both Martin and Meira had been attending the concert. He looked down at the basement entrance, intrigued, as he made his own walk back home.

MARTIN

Martin sat at a table with Meira, Pat and the Johnsons. No-one talked much: Pat because she couldn't hear above the general noise, and the Johnsons, because on the rare occasion that they did attend social events, just held hands and beamed at everyone. They were beaming at the singer now. And why shouldn't they, Martin thought to himself. The girl was done up like a Christmas present.

Earlier that morning, Martin had conducted his usual tour of the village and discovered two broken sprinkler heads on the verge outside the west-end villas. These had required a trip to Bunnings and an hour of repair work. Bobby joined him on the verge to supervise, sniffing the freshly dug and damp soil and then lying supportively in the shade. The bobtail lizard that lived in the garden bed in between the western end and the heritage building also came out to lie on the brick path in the sun. Martin couldn't tell if the dog didn't notice the lizard or was ignoring it. When he had finished replacing both sprinklers and tested them, giving both dog and lizard a light shower in the process, Martin escorted Bobby back to Pat's villa. He felt light-headed and short of breath after kneeling in the grass and took his time, calling to the dog to pay attention and stay with him. He must be careful, he thought, to pace himself while doing outside work these days. There was no point being useful if it meant that someone had to cart him off to hospital afterwards.

Martin had stopped to look in the windows at villa twenty-six on the way to Pat's. Elizabeth's curtains had been removed and the furniture taken away. There was new carpet on the living room floor and the walls were repainted in one of the many shades of white that dominated the paint cards at the hardware shop. Like Martin's apartment, the villa faced south, but was lower and didn't receive the views across the valley that Martin enjoyed. It had the advantage of a small garden, though, which

Martin sometimes missed. Elizabeth had a wedding bush in front of her living room window, underplanted with agapanthus. It was in bloom, the tiny white flowers casting a gentle scent. The round cast-iron table and chairs that used to sit on the small patch of lawn were gone now, but the roses that Elizabeth had planted were all flowering, giving an unrestrained display of pinks and reds and purples. Some of the blooms were quite blousy and Martin made a note to come back with his secateurs and deadhead them and prune back the longer canes. Squinting through the window, he was surprised to see a stack of packing boxes still in the living room. It was unusual for a refurbishment to start before removing a resident's belongings and Martin was certain Elizabeth's son had moved everything out last week. He stood there, thoughtful, then got his phone out of his pocket and took a photo through the glass.

Martin crossed the footpath to the villa that faced number twenty-six. This was Pat's home and it mirrored Elizabeth's rose display, similarly unconstrained by the pruning shears. He opened the gate and Bobby obediently shuffled through. Martin followed the dog up the path, knocked on the door and waited for Pat. When the door opened, she was holding a tea towel and had a surprised expression on her face.

'Martin, my goodness. What brings you here?'

'I have Bobby.' He nodded to the white dog who now made his way across the living room and turned in circles on his bed to find the best position in the sun.

'Oh dear, was he out again?' Pat looked unsurprised and unconcerned. 'Naughty boy. Would you like a cup of tea, Martin? You look like you've been busy.'

Martin looked down at his damp and muddy knees. His hands were still in their gardening gloves and he was carrying his toolbox. He remembered what Maureen had said about tea.

'Yes please, Pat, if it is not too much trouble,' he replied. 'Can I wash up first?' If he was truthful, he was grateful of the opportunity to sit before he walked back to the basement to return his tools. He was still a little light-headed and he could feel his heart hammering.

Now, four hours later at the concert, Martin felt much better. After his cup of tea with Pat, he returned his tools to the shed, cleaned up and had a lie down in front of the cricket. Australia was playing Pakistan in Brisbane, and Hazelwood was bowling to Shah. He watched as the ball took the leading edge and ballooned toward mid-off. Wade dived and he was out. Martin closed his eyes. By the time he woke up, Pakistan were all out for 335 and Australia had won by an innings and five runs. He'd switched off the television and come down to the concert.

The concert wasn't part of Martin's Action Plan, but it was consistent with goal number two. Unfortunately, the occasion didn't lend itself to conversation, but the food was excellent. He'd already eaten two sausage rolls, two salmon pancakes and one mini quiche. He kept missing the beef wellington and now they were bringing out the cupcakes, which at Harewood Hall signalled the imminent end of any event. He could see Joyce rising to thank the singer and the pianist. Like everyone else, she too beamed at the pretty girl and leaned over to kiss both of her cheeks. Everyone applauded.

'I don't understand why the young people want to sing all of these old songs.' Meira leaned across to him. 'Look at her, she is young and beautiful. She should sing happy songs written by people her own age. Not miserable ones written by dead people.'

'Were they miserable?' asked Martin. 'I couldn't tell.'

'It is a good thing you don't know your German,' Meira replied, mouth turned down. She didn't offer any more on the subject and stood to leave. 'Have you been feeding a cat by any chance, Martin?' she asked as she gathered her purse. 'Small, grey, muzzle starting to turn white.'

Caught out, Martin flushed. 'No, well, yes. Once. On Friday.'

'I thought so. He prefers chicken mince. No packaged cat food.' She turned her back and made her way back to her walker, holding onto the backs of chairs for support.

HARLEY

Harley could only manage half of his plate of minced chicken on the floor of Meira's kitchen that evening. He could feel the weight of his full belly as he returned to his spot between the couch and the television to clean himself. The last of the afternoon sun created a weak but still warm pool of light on the soft carpet. Meira continued to read her book.

Later that evening, after Meira had cleaned away her dishes and gone to bed, Harley wriggled through the partly open sliding door and jumped down from the balcony. He would return later to the rug Meira had left on the couch, but he was not ready for sleep yet. He trotted around the corner of Harewood Hall and inspected the stringline that had crept out from the water meter box late that afternoon. The box made a small ticking noise. Following the line through the garden bed, Harley could smell soil and the soles of boots. Two metres along, the line was held up by a thin metal spike with a yellow plastic flag. There was another spike the same distance further along, then another, and another. The line and the flags stopped at the access road to the resident's basement carpark. Here, Harley also stopped and surveyed the road up and down. Like all roads, it smelled unpleasant, of oil and grit and burnt plastic and he didn't trust it. After a time, when he was satisfied the road was safe, he trotted across and sat on the other side underneath a grevillea.

A beam of light flashed around the corner of the building and wobbled its way down the road. Harley could see three figures behind it and hear men's voices.

'You hang the microphone at ground level in front of you and you walk along the path of the pipe. The closer you get to the leak, the louder the sound picked up by the microphone.'

'How do you hear the sounds?'

'Through the headset.'

'It's that simple?'

'Yep.'

'What does the leak sound like?'

'Don't know. It could be a whooshing sort of sound. A bit like when your heart valves don't close properly anymore.'

'I wouldn't know about that.'

'Have you done this before?'

'No, but Jean's cousin has and he says it works really well.'

The three men passed by the unseen cat and walked through the garden bed along the stringline to the meter box. They discussed who should listen for the leak. Jean's husband Geoff was the temporary custodian of the microphone, so they decided it was right that he do it. They set up the instrument. Geoff inched along the stringline, the microphone dangling in front of him.

'It needs to be lower,' said Roy.

'What?' Geoff removed the headset.

'Lower. I watched a YouTube video. Like this.'

Geoff adjusted the microphone on its string until it almost brushed the ground and started from the beginning.

'And you need to go slower.' Roy again. 'The guy on YouTube walked really slow.'

'What?' Geoff removed the headset again.

'Slower.'

Geoff started again, shuffling forward through the groundcover. 'Shit.' He removed the headset for a third time.

'What's wrong?'

'It keeps catching in the bloody creeper.'

The three men put down the instrument and shone the torch on the groundcover.

'It won't work with that stuff in the way.'

'It needs to be cut back.'

'I'm not doing that tonight.'

'It won't take long. There's not much of it. You just need a pair of hedge cutters.'

'I'll get mine from the shed.'

'Get mine too, will you? It'll be quicker.'

Harley watched while one of the men collected keys from the others and walked back up the road. The other two wandered down to the rose garden and sat on a bench to wait. Harley decided that was enough for the night and took himself over to the villa where Bobby lived to see what the dog was doing.

8 · 2ND MONDAY

FIONA

Another day in paradise, thought Fiona as she drove northwards to work along the beachfront. The sea was flat, Rottnest Island was picked out on the horizon, and once again the sky was blue. No rain was forecast. On the street verges, capeweed was in flower and the winter grass was browning off. Unsettled weather in the north-west, where temperatures were already in the high thirties, was predicted to bring high winds early next week but you wouldn't know it today. Fiona hoped they weren't in for a hot summer. The residents in the heritage building tended to cope well in the heat; the thick walls, recessed windows and high ceilings made their apartments easy to cool. The west-end villas were modern buildings, mostly standalone and, although they were well insulated and air-conditioned, their size and the tendency of their occupants to leave the windows open made them heat up during long periods of hot weather. Many west-end residents spent their summer days in the cooler common areas of the heritage building, but the less mobile avoided the walk from their villas.

After her first summer at Harewood Hall, Fiona had proposed a covered walkway from the villas to the café, but this had failed after residents couldn't agree on whether the walkway should have a hard or vine-covered roof. Opponents of the hard roof (mostly residents of the heritage building) objected that the roof would block their view of the gardens. Opponents of the vines (the west-end residents) said that the debris from the plants would create a trip hazard. In the end, nothing had been done. Fiona made a note to check the air-conditioning service records and book a service for the heritage building before December.

Fiona's weekend had been disappointingly uneventful. Football season was over so there were no games to watch and no children to drive to and from training. Sam and Jack had disappeared into their bedrooms to study for exams. She wouldn't know they existed anymore if it weren't for the fridge emptying every six hours. Her husband had gone to Karrinyup to play eighteen holes on Saturday and had followed that up by spending all of Sunday on the boat. Her friends were also hunkered down feeding studying teenagers. Aside from a fiftieth at Crown on Saturday, the weekend had been something of a non-event. Still, she was starting the week with fresh laundry, a clean house and a full fridge (topped up by an extra visit to Coles on Sunday afternoon). She supposed she couldn't complain.

At the northern end of Marine Parade, Fiona turned left and pulled into a ten-minute car bay outside the Kirkwood Deli. The corner door was crowded with bunches of flowers, dogs, and women in active wear. Underneath the café windows, vegetable boxes signalled organically grown abundance. A woman wearing a dark-blue mining company cap and colour-blocked running tights stood in front of boxes of cherries. She looked up and waved as Fiona negotiated her way inside. Forsaking the racks of fresh bread, newspapers and yoga magazines on her right, Fiona went left and inspected the ready-made lunch offerings. She picked out a roast pumpkin, feta and rocket sandwich on sourdough, a chocolate nut bar, collected the flat white that she'd pre-ordered by text when she left home, paid at the counter and returned to her car.

As she navigated her way through the school-run traffic, Fiona ran through the empty villas and apartments in her mind. It wasn't strictly true what she'd told Bill Collins Jnr about the waiting list. It was true that there had been a waiting list for Harewood Hall – a long one – but it had dwindled over the past three years. Now she had only a few prospective buyers and they all wanted north-facing apartments in the heritage building. New inquiries were becoming rare and the marketing and sales team had to work hard hosting events and open days. Today she would need to review her client database and come up with some creative ideas to attract interest. She wondered if Vincent would agree to offering an incentive to new buyers. Some of her competitors were advertising cashbacks and even overseas holidays. She couldn't see her clientele being won over by the prospect of a free trip to Bali though. Maybe she would call marketing and get their thoughts.

Ten minutes later, Fiona turned left up the tree-lined approach to Harewood Hall. As the front of the building came into view, she took in the solidity of the edifice and the spring planting in the garden beds. It was true what they said, a retirement village manager needed to be a jack-of-all-trades, but she loved Harewood Hall and her residents and wouldn't exchange her job for anything. Gerry waved to her as she drove across the front of the building. He was standing at the southern garden beds near the water meter. He walked over to the car and she pulled up to let him lean in the window.

'When you get settled, Mrs Boston, you might want to come out and have a look at this.'

Another ten minutes later, Fiona and Gerry stood side by side looking down at the garden bed. Fiona held one hand across her mouth, suppressing a smile, and holding her mobile phone in the other. She tapped the phone against her thigh as she shook her head. Gerry stood silently. She could feel his uncertainty as he waited for her reaction.

'What were they thinking?' Fiona now asked, breaking the silence.

'I think they had a ground microphone, so they were probably trying to get it close to the surface.'

'A ground microphone? Where on earth did they get a ground microphone? Aren't they expensive?'

'I think one of the resident's cousins is a leak detection contractor.'

Fiona snorted. 'Why does that not surprise me?' She chuckled as she surveyed the garden bed. She had to give them credit: they had done a neat job. The African daisy which gave the south-eastern garden bed a soft grey blanket now had a perfectly straight and even-edged path running through the middle from the meter box to the road. The nocturnal landscape architects had taken care to level the path and sweep it clean of cuttings, which Fiona guessed they had distributed among various residents' compost bins. The stringline that ran down the centre of the path was tight and the yellow flags evenly spaced.

'I suppose if you put yourself in their shoes, it makes perfect sense.'

Gerry grinned, relieved. 'This stuff grows pretty quick, Mrs Boston, and I can transplant some from the back of the bed to give it a head start.'

'Thanks, Gerry. I take it they are going to continue all of the way around the ring main?'

'I expect they will, Mrs Boston.'

'In that case, please find the gentlemen and give them a copy of the site plan showing the location of the ring main. At least they will get their stringline in the right place first off.'

'Are you sure?' Gerry frowned at her. 'I thought we weren't giving those out anymore.'

Fiona eyed her residents' moonlight efforts. Gerry was right, she had ducked all resident requests for village schematic diagrams since Roy attempted to disconnect his villa from the electricity network. She shrugged. 'What could go wrong? It's only water.' She gave the garden bed one last look before turning back to the heritage building, still shaking her head. And all in the middle of the night, unseen and unheard, Fiona presumed. Bravo.

Later in the afternoon, Melissa came to the doorway of Fiona's office.

'Excuse me, Fiona, Mr Allen would like to see you if you are available.'

Is that so, thought Fiona. Roy was her choice of resident most likely to be the ringleader of last night's path-clearing.

'Yes of course I am, Melissa. Please show him in.'

Roy, it seemed, was not here to discuss water leaks or impromptu garden paths, but another long-standing gardening matter.

'I've been speaking with Martin,' he announced as he sat down in one of the tub chairs with a thump.

Have you indeed, thought Fiona. You've had a busy weekend. She gave what she hoped was an interested but non-committal smile.

'He thinks I might have got the wrong end of the stick on the gardening decisions. He said I shouldn't jump to conclusions without first examining the facts.'

This was unexpected. She would have thought Martin would be a ready ear for complaints about management decisions. Or perhaps not. Knowing Martin as she did, it would make sense that he would be reluctant to draw conclusions without solid evidence. She waited for Roy's apology.

'So, what Martin suggested I do,' he continued, 'is examine the records of gardening decisions dating back' – here he referred to his notes – 'at least five years and determine if there are any systemic differences according to gender.'

Fiona sat back in her chair.

'Martin will help me with the statistical analysis,' he added.

Fiona considered him. Roy was sitting on the edge of his chair, leaning forward, his notes in front of him in both hands, and the glasses he had put on to refer to them now set down on the table. He looked like a schoolboy asking for something he knew he wouldn't get, but hopeful of a favourable response regardless. It was, in fact, a sensible request, she thought, especially given that she had done the same thing two weeks ago and knew what the result would be. It might put the matter to bed once and for all, and it would have the added benefit of occupying Roy and Martin for a few days. She had no doubt they would spend hours together designing a spreadsheet, inputting data and running the stats. They would have a lovely time. Residents had made 510 gardening requests in the last five years and each of them, including Fiona's decision on each matter, were recorded on neat pink forms in a file behind her desk. They were also recorded on a spreadsheet on Fiona's computer, which would make Roy's task easier. She reached behind her and pulled down the file. for him.

'That is such a good idea, Roy. Let me know what you find.'

JOSH

Josh pressed the bell to stop the bus outside the university even though ten other students were already standing ready to get off at the same stop. He left the car at home on uni days because students who live within a three-kilometre radius of campus didn't qualify for student parking permits and the casual parking rates were too high. He walked with the group of students, most of them people he already knew from local high schools, through the pedestrian underpass and entered the top of the Great Walk that traversed the campus from the highway to the river. At the highway end, the walkway was shaded by Moreton Bay fig trees that hung heavy branches overhead and gave the campus a sweet figgy smell at the end of each summer. Beyond their trunks, Josh could see the ducks in the reflection pool and the sandstone arches of the Winthrop Hall Undercroft. Being one of the largest spaces on campus, the Undercroft was where most students had taken at least one exam in first year, and Josh and his friends could all tell stories of gazing at the ducks while they tried to recall the content of their Biology 101 courses during their three-hour allotted time.

Passing the sandstone Arts Building on his left and then the library on his right, Josh came to the cricket ground, where two teams were warming up. Each set of players had laid out their coffin-shaped bags along opposite sides of the weatherboard pavilion. Some of Josh's friends were playing today and later he would take his lunch out to the edge of the ground and watch for a while.

Opposite the oval, Josh found himself a table and pulled out his textbook for his 3pm tutorial. He hadn't finished the required reading yet and wanted to get it done before lunch. He was halfway through the final pages on the properties of geographical information systems when a tall, thin man in a dark suit with a takeaway coffee sat down at the next table. He was joined by an equally tall and thin young man in jeans. Supervisor and research student, thought Josh. They were discussing the research design and statistical methods the student would need to use. Josh had no interest in research statistics. He intended to go straight from his bachelor's degree to the workplace. But he could see the student in profile, and he looked familiar. Not that this was startling. Most people on this campus were friends or friends of friends or people he had bumped into at parties, so many faces were familiar. He couldn't place this guy though.

Josh went back to his reading – he had to fit in a two-hour lab at 10am – with the occasional glance at the student at the next table. He read for a few minutes, then opened up his browser and typed *pregnant mice* into the search bar. He got 34,300,000 results and clicked on the second one, *how can I tell when my female mouse is pregnant?* Here, he learned that a typical mouse will give birth to forty-two to sixty offspring per year and that gestation usually lasts nineteen to twenty-one days. Josh counted backwards. Assuming Emily was right, and assuming Pudding had done the dirty the day before she and Coco were freed, that meant she would give birth anytime now and there would be another five mice in Josh's care.

Shit, he thought. He had to move them. The Harewood Hall basement was no place for Pudding to raise her babies and keep a whole family of mice. Maybe he could return the mice to the lab. If he went there in the middle of the night and timed it right, between security patrols, he could leave the cage at the front door. The blanket would keep them warm. But that would mean returning them to the horrors of laboratory experiments. Maybe he could leave a note saying they had been in a contaminated environment and weren't useful for research anymore. Would the research centre care? Josh imagined serious, white-coated scientists standing over the note and discussing the origins and integrity of the author while the cage sat neglected on the cold floor. But would that mean they would be euthanised instead? Josh couldn't see a way out that wouldn't involve the premature death of his two dependents and their babies. Perhaps a kind-hearted junior research assistant would volunteer to adopt them? They would push their way through the group, read the note over the professor's shoulder and, with tears in their eyes, offer to rescue the mice and avert their imminent deaths in the gas chamber that Josh now imagined at the far end of the laboratory.

But maybe Emily was wrong. Maybe Pudding was just fat. Josh continued reading. He got partway through the *All Plugged Up* section of the webpage and pushed the lid of the laptop closed in disgust. There was no way he was going to search through the cage for a lump of mouse semen. He would wait and see.

The two men at the table next to him appeared to reach an agreement and, smiling at each other, stood up to leave. As the student turned to leave, Josh saw his face in full and placed him. He was Fiona's son, of course. Josh nodded at him and stood up as he came over to his table, knocking over his water.

'Hey, Sam, how's things?' he asked as he mopped up.

'Yeah, good, Josh, how's things with you?'

'Good, yeah. Looking forward to summer.'

'You still working for my mum?'

'Yep. Still there. How's your thesis going?'

'Good now. I got stuck on the stats and I was pretty stressed, but I think I've got it sorted.'

'Was that your supervisor just then?'

'Yeah, Professor Graves.'

'Cool name.'

'I know, right? He's a legend. Does all of this awesome stuff with mice.'

'Right,' said Josh, stuffing his hands in his pockets and looking down at his feet.

'He exposes them to all of these viruses and parasites so he can study how their immune systems respond.'

'Isn't that a bit, you know, unethical?' Josh returned to his visions of Coco and Pudding wasting away in pain and fear from a deadly viral infection.

'Not if he eliminates diseases that kill millions of people. Anyway, it's all humane and cleared by the ethics committee. You're not one of these mad greenies who trash research labs are you?'

'Nah, mate, not me. I'm all for science.'

'Good man. If you're interested, he's giving a talk to Mum's residents next Tuesday. You could go and listen. Maybe take one of your oldies along with you. They'll love it.'

JOYCE

Joyce could still remember the time when Harewood Hall was a psychiatric hospital. It was known as the Hospital for the Insane when she was a girl and the neighbourhood children were perpetually in terror of being sent there by their parents if they were naughty. The building that now housed its residents in a mantle of respectability had been a brooding and formidable presence on the other side of the swamp. When Joyce and her sisters went exploring, it had to be either circumnavigated or spied on with caution. It was rumoured that a mad man lived there who ate children and was kept in chains. Joyce knew now that the hospital had in fact been progressive for its time. It had adopted the York model, was run by a qualified medical practitioner, and definitely did not use chains to restrain patients. Most relevant to the children of the district, however, was the absence of high perimeter walls and the encouragement of patients to enjoy the gardens. This made them readily visible and perfect subjects for spying.

When Joyce and her sisters were children, they could approach the grounds from the south, where the coastal bushland was still undeveloped.

Now, the hill was cut away and access blocked by a high retaining wall and oversized houses with swimming pools and tennis courts. Screened by the bush, Joyce had once watched a female patient in a white dress walk backwards and forwards across the lawn cradling a swaddled baby in her arms, her head inclined and her left hand patting the baby's nappy-clad bottom. Joyce and her sisters had giggled, nervous at being seen, as she had paced closer and closer to the low fence. As she approached, they could just catch the melody of a song she was singing, low and lilting. Just when the girls were ready to flee, the woman stopped, hurled the infant away against the wire, and ran back into the shadow of the building, her skirt tangling in her legs. From behind the fence, Joyce could see the little bundle lying on the grass, a crack running through its porcelain face from forehead to nose.

By the time the hospital was decommissioned, Joyce was in her twenties and living abroad with her own two small boys. Psychiatric patients in modern medical systems were being transferred out of institutional care and into smaller, more intimate homes, where they took part in the daily activities of life, cleaning, gardening, cooking meals and even shopping for groceries. When she returned to Australia, she was shocked to find that one such home had been built in her own suburb. Apart from the minibus parked outside and the obvious mobility concessions, it looked like every other house on the street, residents and their carers coming and going like any other person would, the community apparently either oblivious or reconciled. It would be another two decades, Joyce mused, before the community became as sympathetic to women with postnatal depression. Joyce had her own trials in childbirth and motherhood, and she wondered what the woman in the white dress had endured, locked up away from her family.

Joyce picked up another forkful of quinoa and salmon salad and considered the two quotes on her laptop screen. Today she was having a late multitasking lunch in the Harewood Hall café. The caterers for Christmas lunch had responded this morning and she wanted to check their quotes before making a recommendation to the Social Club Committee. As she worked, Paul arrived and ordered a toasted sandwich and a coffee. She looked up at him in surprise.

'It's not like you to be in the café on a Monday, Paul.'

'I thought I'd treat myself today, Joyce.'

Joyce appraised him as he fitted himself into a chair at the adjacent table. He had a hard, rounded stomach, heavy legs, and the thick hands and wrists of a man who has laboured. She wondered how a parish priest came to have hands like that.

'You weren't always in the church, Paul, were you?' she asked.

'Since my thirties, yes I was,' he replied. 'But I left school at fifteen and trained as a plumber first. Then I spent twenty years as a trade union chaplain. That's where I got this.' He patted his stomach.

Joyce blushed, caught out. 'I didn't know there was any call for chaplaincy in unions. I thought socialists don't believe in God.'

Paul laughed. He'd had this conversation before. 'The union movement is quite prepared to use scripture to support the cause, and the Bible has a lot to say about workers' rights. *Masters, treat your slaves justly and fairly, knowing that you also have a Master in heaven.*'

Joyce thought for a moment. 'Colossians?'

'Well done.'

Joyce checked the time and closed her laptop. If she left now, she could get to the local butcher and buy one of his small lamb racks for dinner. Yesterday, she had seen a recipe for pistachio-crusted lamb, and she wanted to make it for dinner tonight. Before heading up the stairs, she stopped at reception.

'Melissa, would you be a darling and put Mr Kelly's lunch on my account?'

'Yes of course, Mrs Wise. That is exceedingly kind of you.'

MARTIN

'So, you are back then,' Martin said to the small grey cat sitting at the open balcony door. The cat didn't reply and turned to rub his head against the doorframe.

'Don't even think about that. I know what you are doing.'

Martin had read a lot about domestic cat behaviour in the past two days. Aside from learning about how cats mark their territory, he now also knew they were fussy eaters who didn't like changes to their accustomed diet. And he also had Meira's tip from the concert yesterday.

'I take it you don't like Advance Ocean Fish pellets then.'

The cat rubbed his head on the other side of the door and then sat to look at him.

'I've heard that you didn't mind the chicken though.'

They both sat and looked at each other. Martin levered himself off the couch with a sigh and went to the kitchen.

'I suppose it's a good thing I bought extra.'

The cat kept himself on the balcony side of the door while Martin emptied a small mound of minced chicken into a bowl and carried it outside. Setting it down, he stood back and motioned to the cat.

'Go on then, help yourself.'

Martin went back to his couch and the evening news while the cat ate.

HARLEY

Harley did indeed prefer the chicken and was pleased to see it appear in the bowl. He had spent the day asleep in the basement, tired from his night-time adventures. Last night, he had found Bobby asleep next to the window, but a few strategic turns past the door had woken him up. Harley watched as the dog stretched and then eased himself through his round portal into the garden. Bobby snuffled around the pot plants, lifted his leg against an agapanthus and wriggled his way under the gate.

The dog had trotted with a sense of urgency but not so fast that Harley needed to make an effort to follow him. The temperature was dropping under the clear night-time sky, but Harley still had his winter coat. He expected that Bobby would head for the school playground, intending to forage among the discarded sandwiches and yoghurt pots. He followed him past the café and the entrance to the kitchen and under the lemon-scented gums that were now still. Small creatures rustled in the leaf litter under the gums, but Harley ignored them. After the concert treats and Meira's chicken, he wasn't in need of food himself. To his surprise, Bobby continued down the road instead of turning down the steps into the school grounds. He sat and watched the dog's curly white back for a moment as it trundled down the road. Just before he was out of sight, Harley jumped up and loped after him, ready for an adventure.

Tonight, Harley licked up the last scraps in his bowl, washed and walked over to the balcony door. It was closed but he was used to this and he kept his composure as he sat looking at Martin, waiting for him to notice and let him in. He hadn't been allowed into Martin's apartment yet. From the balcony, he could see the long couch that Martin only ever appeared to use at one end. He sat there now and although the couch appeared to be quite comfortable, he was fidgeting and shuffling. He rolled his shoulders back and forth and tipped his neck from side to side. With one hand, he squeezed under his other armpit, rubbed his throat and grimaced. He reached towards the end table and took a sip from a glass of water, sighed and settled back down.

The cushion at the other end of the couch looked soft. Like Meira, Martin had a deep carpet on his floor. Unlike Meira's apartment, the carpet did not, as far as Harley could see, receive any warm sunlight. Martin compensated for this by running the air-conditioning at a higher temperature. Harley could feel the warmth through the glass door. He was quite ready now to come inside and stood up. As he had hoped, the movement caught Martin's eye. He watched as the man frowned and then winced. He put his hand to his chest again and then his throat. His skin paled. He stood up and, instead of coming over to the door, went into the kitchen with the glass of water, popped two tablets out of a silver packet and dropped them into the glass. Harley watched, intrigued, as the water fizzed upwards and turned cloudy. When it had settled, Martin sipped from the glass and returned to his place on the couch.

Harley sat back down too. He watched Martin for a while, willing him to look over again, but he only had eyes for the television and the glass of discoloured water. In Harley's experience of humans, this could go on for a while. Disappointed, he stood up and made his way off the balcony to try his luck at Meira's.

9 · 2ND TUESDAY

FIONA

Fiona stood in the deep shade of the southern wall of the heritage building inspecting the second phase of the residents' night-time water leak investigations. This side of the building received little sun and seemed always to be damp. She wrapped her scarf closer around her neck and looked up at the residents' balconies. Although they didn't get the sun and weren't as favoured as the apartments on the northern side, they had views across the leafy suburb to the lake and didn't stay vacant for long. Martin was out on his balcony, carrying a small red plastic dish that looked awfully like a pet-food bowl. She waved up at him.

'Good morning, Martin.'

'Good morning, Fiona. Are you inspecting the, err, inspections?'

'Yes, we are.'

'They are doing it all wrong, you know that don't you?'

Fiona smiled to herself. She should have expected this.

'A ground microphone is all well and good, but it is old technology and they could do it in less than half the time if they'd used tracer gas. I suppose you don't know what that is.'

Fiona had learned to humour Martin. A few minutes of listening to his advice could save months of lengthy email exchanges about how there was a better way.

'No, I don't, Martin. What is it?'

Gerry, who had not yet learned to be as diplomatic, huffed and shoved his hands in his pockets. He walked to the end of the building and back while Martin explained the use of tracer gas to detect leaks in water pipes.

'Well, I didn't know that,' said Fiona when he finished. 'Perhaps you should let Roy know.'

'Roy? Roy can't even set up a spreadsheet. I had to explain to him the difference between dependent and independent variables yesterday. How did he get to his age without understanding the basic principles of data analysis?'

Fiona smiled but she wasn't going to bite. They both turned and waved as the Tredwell Trades van drove past and descended the vehicle access ramp to the basement.

'You'd think they were running Multiplex, the number of times they are in that basement each week,' Martin grumbled, frowning at the van.

'What's that you've got there?' she asked, ignoring him and nodding towards the plastic bowl in Martin's hand. 'Have you got yourself a pet?' This was a loaded question as all pets needed to be registered with management.

'No,' he replied, his tone rather sharp. 'It's water for the birds. In urban environments they need water sources when it gets hot.'

Fiona looked about herself at the absence of birdlife on this cold, southern side of the building. When she looked back, Martin had retreated inside.

Gerry returned from his unnecessary walk, but then Fiona's mobile phone rang. It was Melissa.

'Hi, Fiona, sorry to bother you. Solar Solutions have just called. They can start next week but they haven't received the payment.'

'Maybe it hasn't landed in their account yet. Can you call finance and ask if it was paid?'

'Already done. They said they put it through on Friday.'

'Thank you. Can you call Solar Solutions back and let them know? Perhaps suggest that they give us a call if it hasn't arrived tomorrow. I don't want to delay the project.'

'Will do, thanks.'

Fiona turned her attention back to Gerry, who was now pointing westward, indicating an imaginary line running parallel to the building.

'The ring main turns here and does a loop around the heritage building.'

'So that's where our sleuthing friends will be investigating tonight.'

'Yeah. They might have some trouble getting the microphone close to the ground when they get to the section with the camellias.'

'Can we prune the lower branches without harming the plants?'

'Yes, we can, no problem. They'll bounce back in no time.'

'Let's do that today then.'

Fiona decided to walk back to her office via the west side and check on the refurbishment of Elizabeth's villa. It would give her a chance to warm up in the sun. As she turned, a movement at the base of the building caught her eye. A low, grey shape paused behind a camellia bush. Fiona bent low to see through the ill-fated branches. It was a cat – the well-fed stray she presumed – and it looked guarded and tense.

'Hi puss,' she crooned, 'it's OK, I'm friendly.'

The cat flattened its ears. Fiona bent lower and the cat growled, its lips pressed firmly together.

'What do you have there, puss?' She took a step forward and the cat backed against the wall. Fiona thought she could see something pale hanging out of the corner of its mouth. 'Oh, I see, you're earning your keep. Well, I'll leave you alone then. Keep up the good work.'

Fiona retreated and the cat settled onto its haunches. She knew it would watch her until she rounded the corner of the building before attending to its meal.

PAUL

Paul was back at his favourite table. It was warm in the north-facing café and he could see the magpies in the gum trees as they swooped and hopped about the leaf litter in the garden. The café sound system was tuned to a classical music station and Arvo Pärt played overhead. Two students in school uniform walked along the public footpath on the other side of the trees. The bell had already sounded but they didn't seem to be anxious to make up for lost time. Gerry drove past, going the other way, on his quad bike. He saw Paul and held up a hand in greeting. Paul waved back. He returned his attention to his food. Being a Tuesday, it was savoury morning-tea day. This morning, the kitchen had made sausage rolls. They were large, fat and porky, studded with cranberries and wrapped in a deep yellow, buttery pastry. Paul sliced off another piece and sat chewing, contented.

He thought about Joyce and their conversation on Friday night. He recalled how, later that evening, she got lost mid-sentence and the way Elaine had intervened and put her back on track without Joyce noticing. Later, he had watched as Joyce walked up the staircase with her husband, Peter, his hand resting at the small of her back in case she stumbled. We look after each other, he thought, even the difficult ones.

He reached across to the adjacent table and picked up the copy of the day's newspaper. The front page had run with a story on a methamphetamine epidemic in the state's south-west and featured a picture of a sad-faced mother holding an old school photo of her addicted son. The boy in the photo grinned at the camera, his eyes sparkling, and his teeth even and white. He wore an open-necked blue polo shirt with the logo of his primary school on the pocket and his throat evidenced a summer spent playing cricket on the beach. The article included an inset of a recent police head-and-shoulders photo of the boy. Here, his cheeks were sucked in and his neck scrawny under large, sad, staring eyes. There was no smile to show off the teeth, but Paul had seen enough addiction to know that they would no longer be white and perhaps not even all there. It was a world away from Harewood Hall and the young people who worked here. He thought of Melissa and Josh and Gerry and wondered if they had ever crossed paths with the drug and if they had, what miracle had kept them away from it.

Page three had a photo of the premier standing in front of a gift-wrapped minibus and shaking hands with the CEO of a disability services organisation. Below the fold was a report on a theft from the prestigious university by the river. Mice used for important research on transmissible diseases had been stolen from the university's secretive medical research centre, according to an unnamed source. The university wouldn't comment on the theft, which was said to have happened three weeks ago, but the president of the Student Guild claimed it was common knowledge on campus. An animal rights activist group said that it was only a matter of time before universities using animals for research would be held to account by a public that was disgusted by their inhumane practices. A representative from the Department of Health said it was unlikely the stolen mice were a biosecurity risk, but the department would review the university's containment policies as a precaution. The department recommended that households use sensible rodent control practices and report any infestations of white mice.

As he scraped up the last of the pastry crumbs, Paul saw Josh drive past in his grey Golf. He parked in his customary bay under the banksia, took his backpack out of the car and headed towards the building, chewing on the side of his thumb.

JOSH

Josh arrived early for his shift at Harewood Hall so he could feed the mice. He'd skipped his morning run, opting for an extra half hour of sleep after lying awake the night before, turning over the implications of the professor's imminent visit to the village. Would Fiona want to give him a tour of the village while he was here? What if she brought him down here to the basement? The professor would know straight away that his missing mice were here. Josh pictured him, nose in the air, striding toward Meira's storage unit. *Here they are!* he would proclaim, extending a long, thin finger. And everyone would turn and look at Josh.

Flicking on the light switch at the top of the stairs, Josh was startled to see how much light had been thrown, then realised that a second fluorescent tube had been fixed to the ceiling above the residents' storage units. He rubbed his eyes, wishing he was still in bed, and walked around to the back wall and used his key to open the door for number five.

The two stools were where he and Emily left them on the weekend. Emily had wanted to know where Josh had got the mice and what he was going to do with them. He told her he was babysitting them for a friend.

'Why don't you keep them at home? It'd be nicer than keeping them down here.'

'I think Stan would freak them out. And Mum wouldn't let me anyway.'

Emily had nodded. 'Fair enough.'

'What about your place?'

'Are you kidding? With Dadi and Nani here?' She rolled her eyes. Emily's grandparents were visiting from Singapore and her grandpa disapproved of Emily's dog coming in the house. He said the house smelled of animal and complained that his clothes were now covered in dog hair. She was right, he'd lose it if she brought home two mice.

'What about if you kept them in your dad's shed?' he asked.

Emily gave him a look. 'Who is this friend of yours anyway? It's not Mike is it?'

Josh had changed the subject. He was already mortified by the lie and didn't want to dig himself into a deeper hole.

In the basement, Josh topped up the feeder with mouse pellets and refilled the water from a plastic bottle in his backpack. He sat on the stool and stroked Coco's back while she ate.

'Where's your sister?' he murmured. With the other hand, he poked the pile of shredded paper in the corner of the cage and was rewarded with a pale pink nose poking back. 'What are you doing in there girl? It's time for breakfast.' Pudding waddled out to the mouse pellets, which she ate methodically before waddling back again. Josh figured even mice need a sleep in from time to time.

Later that morning, he cleaned Martin's apartment. He figured this was just about the easiest job in the world. The apartment was already cleaned to a clinical standard, and after Josh had finished, it looked and smelled the same as it had when he started. Nevertheless, Martin insisted on Josh vacuuming, mopping and dusting to a schedule each week, and Josh was required to mark off each item as he worked, indicating that it was complete. The A4 list on the kitchen bench had to be worked through in order, so that Josh worked from high to low, clean to dirty. First, he stripped the bed, sorted and started the laundry, then dusted the living room and bedrooms. He cleaned the windows, wiped down the surfaces in the kitchen and bathroom, then vacuumed and mopped the floors and took out the bins. While the floors were drying, he put the first load of washing in the dryer and loaded the second into the washing machine. It was Martin's habit to visit his basement workshop at some point in the routine, and Josh took the opportunity to check that he was up-to-date in his medication and the food in the kitchen was fresh and within the expiry dates on the labels. He would text Martin's daughter from the staffroom later to confirm. Today, as he checked the fridge, he noticed a row of plastic sandwich bags lined up in the freezer section and labelled by day of the week. They appeared to be minced chicken. Josh smiled to himself. Of course, they were for the cat. The cat eats better than some of the residents, he thought. The litter tray, he noticed, had been repurposed as a drip tray for Martin's potted peace lily.

Back in the staffroom, Josh completed his visit record and heated up his mum's leftover lamb curry for his own lunch. He sent a text to Martin's daughter confirming that Martin's medication was up-to-date and all the food in the pantry and refrigerator was fresh. He didn't mention the chicken in the freezer. Josh had never met Elise, although he understood that she lived locally and, like her dad, worked as an engineer. He imagined a female version of Martin. A tall, lanky woman, with a long face and large hands. In his mind, she wore a calf-length navy blue skirt – not the floaty, pleated ones that Emily wore, but a solid, straight skirt that would withstand a stiff wind – and a matching jacket with a sensible white shirt underneath. Her hair would be tied back in a bun and she would hold her hands together as she talked to prevent them from contradicting her words. She texted back promptly. *Thank you.*

Fiona and two other support workers had also stopped for a break and were eating their lunch at the staffroom table. Anwesha patted the chair next to her. She'd been his mentor when he'd started at Harewood Hall and still looked out for him.

'How did you go with Martin this morning?' she asked.

'Fine, the usual cleaning routine.'

'Is he still giving you the list to mark off?'

Josh laughed. 'Why is he so pedantic? Doesn't he drive you crazy sometimes? The way he goes on about that retaining wall.'

'It's just his way. You can work with it. Are you still in touch with Elise?'

'Yes, I've sent her a text just now.'

'Have you noticed anything unusual?' asked Fiona over her salad.

'No, what sort of unusual?'

'I saw him with a pet-food bowl.'

'I think he keeps one on the balcony filled with water for the birds.' The second lie in three days.

'Yes, that's what he told me too.' He watched her frown into her salad. 'What are you doing for Meira this afternoon?'

'Just the usual cleaning.'

'How is she?'

'She seems fine.' He squirmed a bit. He knew the questioning was meant to keep residents safe, but it still felt like he was reporting on them, and he didn't want to get Martin into trouble. He hurried the rest of his lunch and got himself ready for his afternoon shift.

Later, in Meira's apartment, Josh straightened up the newspapers on the side table next to the couch. The weekend edition of the national broadsheet was folded open to a lengthy article on rising nationalism in the United States. Meira saw him eyeing it.

'What do you think of it, Josh?' she asked him. 'Is the president right? Should they put tariffs on imports?'

'I think he understands that people are frightened of losing their jobs. They want America to produce things at home instead of in China.'

'He's a smart man. People are frightened and will vote for him if they think he will save their jobs.'

Josh wasn't so sure about the smart man part, but he agreed with her about the jobs.

'But do working people understand that they are losing their jobs to automation, not China?' she challenged him.

Josh thought about this. 'I don't know. Is it really automation? There is a lot of stuff made in China now.'

'Yes, it's true. Technology is responsible for eighty-five percent of job losses in the last ten years. Only a small number of jobs have gone offshore. It makes sense, Josh. A robot welder costs eight dollars an hour to run but you have to pay a human welder twenty-five dollars.'

'Seriously? But isn't being a welder a pretty rubbish job anyway? Wouldn't people rather do something else?'

'Not if a welder is all you can be. Not everyone can go to university and become an environmental scientist.'

Josh thought about this as he dusted and straightened up the cushions on the couch. That was fair enough if it was true. She was smart, Meira, and still concerned about the world. He lifted the throw rug to shake it out and created a shower of cat hair. He sneezed.

'Where did the cat hair come from? Meira, when did you get a cat?'

She tutted. 'No, he is just a stray. Sometimes he comes, sometimes he doesn't. When he does, I feed him, and he sleeps on the couch. I call him George, after the composer.'

Josh thought for a moment. 'Gershwin.'

'Well done. Do you like his music?'

'Mum has him on her iPad. I like the one with the cool clarinet solo.'

'*Rhapsody in Blue.*'

'That's it. But you should be careful. He might have fleas or worms. What does he look like?'

'Gershwin or the cat?'

Josh laughed.

Meira shrugged. 'Small, grey, black markings. He likes chicken mince.'

I bet he does, thought Josh.

HARLEY

The backyard was littered with evidence of children. Bicycles, helmets and basketballs were lying on the lawn. Five tennis balls clustered in the middle of a trampoline and a dark blue jumper with a school crest soaked up the dew underneath. A large tree hosted a wooden platform and a rope swing. A wide, covered veranda ran the length of the house and on it next to the back door was a hessian dog bed, a dish of water and a full bowl of dog biscuits. This had been Bobby's destination on Sunday night. Harley had followed him along the road, across the intersection in front of the school, and down a narrower street lined with jacaranda trees, curly iron fences and white rosebushes. Bobby had turned into the bitumen driveway of a red-brick house and trotted through an open side gate and into the backyard. Reluctant to enter the narrow space at the side of the house, Harley chose to follow him along the top of the fence. From here, he watched Bobby help himself to the food and the water, climb into the dog bed, and fall asleep.

The fence was where Harley sat tonight. It was earlier than it had been two nights ago, when all the lights in the house were already switched off. That night, Bobby had slept until dawn, lifted his leg on the veranda post, and then without fuss exited the same way he had come in. Harley had spent the night under the veranda, and followed him back to Harewood Hall, where Bobby let himself back into Pat's villa and curled up on his bed for another couple of hours until Pat woke and gave him breakfast.

Tonight, the lights were on, making the inside of the house visible from Harley's position on the fence. Bobby was back at Harewood Hall, but Harley could see a yellow dog sitting at the feet of a boy watching the television. The boy pulled at the dog's ears while the dog gazed up at his face. The room looked warm. The boy crossed one ankle over a knee and the dog shuffled to get a better position. A girl walked in from a hallway door between the sitting room and the kitchen and scooped a cat up off the floor behind the boy. On the fence, Harley stood up, alert. The girl looked smaller than the boy and wore long pyjamas, not at all like the nightdress that Elizabeth had slept in, but more like the matching pants and shirt that Martin wore. He watched her carry the cat into the kitchen, cradled like a baby, its paws in the air. She bent her head down to its face and tapped its nose with her finger. Harley jumped off the fence and onto the veranda to get a better look. The cat was grey, like Harley, but with no markings. It had a round face and small, folded ears. It looked fat. The girl transferred it to one arm, took an orange-coloured bottle from the fridge and, with a quick glance back at the boy, drained it. She put it back on the shelf and closed the fridge door. She hoisted the cat onto her shoulder and left the room, flicking the boy on the back of his head with her fingers as she walked past. The boy rubbed his head with his free hand but otherwise ignored her.

A voice called out from somewhere inside the house and the boy stretched and turned off the television. He put his face down to the dog's and rubbed his hands over the dog's ears. The dog stood up and wagged its tail. Together they walked out the back door. The boy was thin, with long arms and legs. He wore shiny, baggy shorts and, when he stepped outside onto the veranda, Harley could smell boy-sweat. He wanted to cross the veranda boards and rub himself against his legs. The boy sat on the steps and watched the dog do its rounds of the garden.

'Good boy, Frankie.'

Neither of them noticed Harley on the veranda post.

Harley watched Frankie follow his nose. Harley shared his own name with a toy horse. This was before Martin, and Meira, and Elizabeth and long before Harewood Hall. There was a boy like this one – his name was Michael – who used to feed him and cuddle him when he was a kitten. Harley had his own bed then, and a special box where Michael had taught him to poop. The bed and the box were both in the laundry of the house where Michael lived. Michael understood that it was not nice to sleep in the same room as your own poop and would let him into his bedroom when the rest of the family had gone to bed at night. Harley would curl against the back of Michael's knees, careful only to move to readjust himself when Michael shuffled in his sleep. Harley would stay there until morning, deep in the fug of stale school bags and clean pyjamas. The other Harley, stiff and unmoving, stood on a shelf with the other animal toys.

Harley didn't remember how he came to live at Harewood Hall or why he didn't live with Michael anymore, just that Harewood Hall was different to Michael's house. Here, there were more people and not as many animals. At Michael's house, the only humans were Michael's family. Harley sometimes thought he could smell the smell of Michael's house when the easterly wind blew in the morning. Harley didn't mind being George. At Harewood Hall, he had safe places to sleep and regular food. The people who lived there soon worked out that he preferred fresh chicken instead of dry cat-food pellets and he had warm places to lie in the sun undisturbed if Pat remembered to keep her gate closed. Sometimes, the residents' grandchildren came to visit, and Harley would watch the boy children as they played ball games. Their sports bags smelled like the boy on the veranda and the wardrobe in Michael's bedroom.

Finishing his garden inspection, Frankie came back to the veranda and lifted his leg against the same post that Bobby had marked. He put his head into the boy's lap.

'Sorry, buddy,' the boy told him. 'I have to go finish my homework. You need to go to bed.'

Frankie climbed onto the dog bed and curled into a circle, resting his nose on his paws with a sigh. Harley watched him, unconvinced. He was reluctant to move until he was certain the dog was sleeping. He settled in to wait. After a time, the house also stilled and there was no more light spilling into the back room. Harley had judged that it was almost safe to go, when Frankie grunted and levered himself off the bed. Harley watched as the dog squeezed back through the dog door, jumped onto the couch and fell asleep.

10 · 2ND WEDNESDAY

MARTIN

At seven, Martin walked through the front doors of Harewood Hall and out into another warm easterly wind. He had read on the Bureau of Meteorology website that the high pressure dominating the west of the continent would remain where it was until at least the weekend, when it would begin to move east and be replaced by unsettled weather developing in the north-west. Just in time to spoil the crops, he thought.

Martin walked down the limestone steps to the school, around the school buildings, and out to the sports fields. The golden retriever investigated the rugby posts off the leash in the middle of the oval, his owner ignoring him while he paced out his lap counter-clockwise at the edge. Martin followed him in the same direction. The younger man walked fast and was drawing away. What age could he be? In his sixties, that was obvious, but early or late? His hair was thinning, and he was clearly heavier than he had been in his younger days, but not so heavy that Martin would describe him as overweight. Martin himself weighed 78.5 kilograms, depending on the time of day. At 186 centimetres, that made his body mass index 22.5, which was in the middle of the healthy weight range according to the Heart Foundation. Martin picked up his own pace. The younger man looked like he had a BMI much higher than Martin's and could only be fifteen years younger at the most.

Martin swung his arms, taking care not to dislodge the plastic bags from his pocket and started to puff a little. It felt good. He thought about the walking races he sometimes watched when the Commonwealth or

Olympic Games were on television and how those competitors appeared to be much older than other athletes. He didn't think of himself as the competitive type, but perhaps he could have done this when he was younger. He wondered about senior competitions. What did they call them? Masters Games. Perhaps he could look them up online and see if they had an upper age limit.

Martin surprised himself by rounding the last corner of the oval earlier than he expected and found himself powerwalking towards the man with the retriever. He was sitting on the grass and had been joined by a small white dog.

'You were moving there, mate,' the man said. 'I thought you were going to catch me.'

Martin huffed with embarrassment at having been seen competing with a stranger. 'An old fellow like me? Not a chance.' Still, he felt not at all out of breath and a little pleased with himself.

'I've seen you down here before. It's a great spot isn't it? My kids used go to school here. We live on the other side of the playing fields.'

'I walk here every day.' The retriever came over to sniff him, curious and tail thumping. Martin reached out to pat his head and he shied away before coming back in, cautious nose out in front to sniff the back of his hand.

'Good boy, Frankie,' said his owner. 'My grandson's dog. You know what it's like. They're all too busy to walk him. Hey, you're the guy who picks up the lost property. I don't know how many Tupperware containers we lost at this school back in the day. My wife was always going nuts at the kids for leaving them behind. You live in the aged-care place at the top of the hill.'

'Retirement village,' Martin corrected, annoyed at the misperception of Harewood Hall and disconcerted that this man knew so much about him. 'Aged care is for people who can't look after themselves. We all have our own apartments.'

The younger man grunted.

'I do my own cooking,' Martin added.

'I've heard it is pretty flash,' said the man, ignoring the correction. 'I bet Vincent Tredwell is raking it in. I did business with him once. He beat me down on price something cruel.'

Late sixties, thought Martin. And fatter than he looked from a distance.

Not getting a response from Martin on Vincent, the younger man changed the subject. 'Hey, you don't know who that white dog belongs to, do you?'

Martin did indeed know who owned the dog, now that he could see it up close. It was Bobby, off the leash and roaming free as usual. He called him, and Bobby trotted over. He would have to take him back. His new acquaintance took his leave, and Martin looped the handles of one of his plastic bags through Bobby's collar. He punched his thumb through the bottom of the bag, looped the handles of the second bag through the hole and tied them off, giving him a plastic-bag leash. It was a little too short for Martin to stand up straight but would have to do. He wasn't going to carry the dog. The lunchtime rubbish would have to stay where it was today.

Dog in tow, Martin climbed back up the limestone steps to Harewood Hall and walked around to the northern side. The wind was stronger up here than down on the sheltered school grounds and the bags began to fill with air and thrum. This made Bobby dance about in alarm. Unequal to the task, the bags began to tear, and Martin hurried along, awkwardly bending to the right. Departing from his usual circumnavigation of the village, he turned left at the north-western corner of the heritage building to return Bobby to Pat's villa. Here the high stone walls sheltered them from the wind and the bags deflated and went silent. But Bobby's adventure was not finished yet. Ahead of them, basking on the sheltered footpath, sat the cat. Bobby gave the plastic bags one last tug, tearing apart the makeshift leash and raced off, barking at the cat, which softened into the shadow of the building, leaving him rushing around the vacated space, unable to work out where it had gone. Martin swore in annoyance, recaptured the confused dog, pocketed the destroyed plastic bags, and returned him to his owner.

After leaving Bobby with Pat, Martin returned to the western face of the heritage building and inspected the stringline that marked out the path of the ring main buried below the ground. The resident inspectors were making slow progress and had arrived halfway along the wall. He shook his head in irritation. He couldn't understand why people wouldn't see sense. He had explained tracer gas to Roy, who had disregarded him out of hand. At this rate, it they would be well into next week before they discovered the leak. He thought it was time to write a letter to management.

JOYCE

Dear Mrs Wise

RE: APPROVAL TO PRUNE LEMON-SCENTED EUCALYPTUS

I refer to our meeting last Friday and your subsequent letter objecting to our approval to conduct maintenance pruning of the five lemon-scented eucalyptus (Corymbia citriodora) trees on the northern boundary of Lot 24601, being the site of the Harewood Hall Retirement Village. I appreciate you taking the time to write to Council and thank you for your commitment to Council's Greenway Policy and protection of local fauna.

As magpies are not recognised on Council's register as a protected species, their use of the trees on your site is not a material consideration in approving maintenance pruning of the trees. I note that Corymbia citriodora are particularly large trees that are not native to the western suburbs and are considered pests in some parts of the metropolitan area. They are prone to drop branches during dry spells, creating a risk of damage to property and potential injury to people if located in high traffic areas. Council has considered this risk in granting approval for the trees to be pruned before the start of summer. An officer of the Council will inspect the trees during and after pruning to ensure that the health of each tree is not compromised.

If you have any queries regarding this letter, please telephone Council offices between the hours of 8.30am and 4.30pm Monday to Friday quoting reference number ENV-2019-229.

Yours sincerely
Michael D'Souza BSc (Hons)
Senior Environmental Officer

We'll see about that, thought Joyce. She picked up her phone, typed *Bevan* and pressed dial.

'Good morning, Amy darling, it's Joyce Wise here. Can you put me through to Mayor Worth?' She waited. 'Yes, I know, darling, but it is an urgent matter and I know Bevan will want the opportunity to respond. Thank you, Amy, I'll hold.'

Peter and Bevan had been good friends since they were sat together as W surnames in grade one in primary school. They had gone on to attend high school together, competed in Head of the River together, played drinking games at law school together and took the bus into the city together every day for a year during their internships. Bevan had hosted their farewell party, and Joyce and Peter had travelled back from South Africa for Bevan's wedding.

One important thing that Joyce knew about Bevan was that he never missed an opportunity to represent his community, especially when food and drink was involved. And the grey vote would be an important factor in next year's council elections. Joyce had a feeling Bevan would be delighted to come to the residents' fish and chips night this Friday. If he happened to have a few drinks at sunset under the beautiful and doomed lemon-scented gums, so much the better.

Take that Michael, thought Joyce. My generation is still in charge.

JOSH

The ground floor of the university library opened onto a pond that spanned the width of the building. It looked north across the library lawn and the ring of trees that provided homes for the campus magpies and kookaburras. It was a suntrap and a good place for students to study and doze if they weren't squeamish about duck poo or the kookaburras who carried off the occasional duckling. Josh had heard friends describe how other friends of friends had found tiny, dried-out webbed feet under the trees. He didn't know if that was true or not. He'd never seen any himself. There were plenty of ducks and duck poo today, but no kookaburras or ducklings. He pushed aside his fringe with his fingers and re-read the last page of the paper on geographical information systems. He wasn't taking anything in.

Josh marked his page and logged out of his assigned readings. He opened Google and typed in *mouse adoption*. He got 21,000,000 hits and all the top results were for the United States. He tried *mouse adoption western australia*. The top result was for the Department of Child Protection and the second was for the RSPCA. He clicked on the RSPCA site, where he got lost down a rabbit hole reading about the impact of domestic violence on family pets. The third result was Bandit Rodentry, a local rat breeder offering *healthy, bold, happy rats with a wide variety of interesting colours and patterns*. Scrolling down past another Department of Child Protection entry, a link to the Rentokil webpage, and Puppies for Adoption Australia, Josh arrived at the Related Searches list, clicked on *mouse adoption near me* and found himself back in America.

Josh rolled his shoulders backwards and stretched. He needed to stop this and get back to his reading. He typed in *where can I sell pet mice*, which gave him 49,400,000 results, at the top of which was Gumtree. Scrolling down to Yahoo Answers, he read *if you give them to a pet store, they will probably be sold as snake food*. He slapped the laptop closed in alarm and groaned. He was stuck with two mice, one of them about to give birth. He had no-one to give them to and selling them meant registering on Gumtree, taking calls, and showing buyers the mice and that was all just too hard. He wondered if he should just release them into the back shed at home. It was warm in the shed, and dry, and the other mice seemed to find plenty to eat. He wondered if Coco and Pudding would get along with the other mice. What if the other mice already had their own mouse society with hierarchies and allocated sleeping places? Would Coco and Pudding fit in? Or would the other mice kill them and eat Pudding's babies? Isn't that what lions do? He visualised finding their pink disembodied tails, discarded like the duckling feet, on the floor of the shed in amongst the wood shavings and fallen screws from IKEA. No, they could stay where they were for now.

'Hey, babe.' Emily put her hands on his shoulders and bent over, kissing him on the top of his head. Josh reached his arms up to wrap around her neck and tilted his face up to return the kiss.

'Hey. How did you find me?'

'Sarah said you were down here. I saw her at the student guild after my lecture.'

'Sarah needs to apply for an internship with ASIO. How was the lecture?'

'Boring. I am so not going to become an organisational psychologist.'

Josh laughed. 'Are you sure? Dad says there are plenty of psychopaths at his work.'

She wrinkled her nose. 'I really hope there aren't. How's your assignment going?'

'Slowly. I can't take any more in today. How about we go get ice-cream?'

'At the beach?'

'Done.'

PAUL

Pat's roses had not been pruned last winter. Long canes arced overhead and rubbed together near the centre of each plant. Some spilled over the fence, swinging close to the footpath with their heavy thorns. Paul pulled on his gardening gloves and opened his secateurs. Starting from the top of the end bush, he cut off the overhead canes in fifty-centimetre lengths and dropped them into the green waste bin that he had wheeled out from Pat's back garden. Then he opened out the centre of the bush, removing the dead, spindly and crosscutting stems. When he had cut the first bush back by a half, he rolled the bin forward and started on the next. Across the path, Martin did the same for the roses against Elizabeth's fence. The fence lines would look bare when they finished, but the plants would recover soon enough and by late summer would be in bloom again.

Martin had caught him yesterday in the café, preventing Paul from following Josh down into the basement.

'Are you handy with a pair of secateurs, Paul?' he'd asked. Paul was indeed. The church at his parish had a thirty-metre fence line planted out with red Mr Lincolns. Each winter he had pruned them back by one third and deadheaded them each summer.

'Are you free to prune Pat's and Elizabeth's roses this week? I know they are blooming, but they were missed in winter and the thorns are a risk to people on the footpath.'

The two men agreed to meet midafternoon the following day.

Despite the long spell of warm weather, it was pleasant in the garden, late enough in the day for a gentle breeze to have picked up from the west. It was too early for school children to be walking home and the suburb was quiet. Most residents were having their afternoon naps. The test match in Adelaide didn't start until tomorrow. Paul and Martin snipped away in companionable silence. Paul finished the second bush and put down his secateurs for a break and a drink. Taking his water bottle with him, he crossed the footpath to where Martin was pruning a large Just Joey. The big, ruffled apricot petals floated off the overblown buds as he took hold of the stems.

'Time for a break, mate.'

'Good idea.'

Martin retrieved his own water bottle and they surveyed their work while they drank. They waved at Jean and Geoff as they circled past in their dark blue Volvo.

'I don't think we'll get it all in the bins,' Martin observed.

'I'll bring mine over,' Paul offered. 'I won't be putting anything in it this fortnight.'

'Elizabeth's son has left some packing boxes behind,' said Martin, nodding towards the villa after taking another swig of water. 'They're stacked up in the living room. Fiona won't be happy.'

Paul frowned. 'That's not like Bill. Are you sure they're not leftover tiles or something belonging to Tredwells?'

'If they are, the boys badly over-ordered.' Martin gave him a look. 'Go see for yourself.'

Paul let himself through the gate and walked up the neat, brick-paved path. Through the uncurtained window he could see ten packing boxes, each secured with masking tape, stacked in the middle of the room. Some were battered at the corners. They didn't look the right shape for tile boxes. Taking care not to walk on the agapanthus, Paul edged over to the corner of the window to look across the whole room and through to the kitchen. The boys had done a decent job. The walls were well coated and cut in, the edges straight against the architraves. The carpet had no obvious ridges and he could see the tracks where it had been vacuumed after being laid. The kitchen hadn't been re-tiled but the grouting had been cleaned. If it weren't for the boxes and the empty plastic lunch bags left on the floor of the kitchen, the villa was ready for viewing.

Paul and Martin went back to work and continued along their respective lines of roses. Paul missed being on worksites in the company of teams of tradesmen, working alongside each other with their own jobs to do. It was a visceral environment, a construction site. The kind that defines tribes. A different world to the gentle gardens of a retirement village. The hard sunlight reflecting off glass and steel, the heat in summer, the smell of cement dust and the brick saw, thumps and crashes of steel being delivered, yells from overhead, the weight of his boots and the afternoon stickiness of sweat and sunscreen. The walk back to wherever he was able to park the car – there was never enough parking for the tradies – and stopping for a cold drink at the service station on the way home. Paul envied the Tredwell boys when he saw them at the village in their dual-cab utes and high-vis work shirts.

It wasn't all guts and glory. Paul learned that the hard way when he finished his theology degree and started working as the union chaplain. Workplace accidents were the worst, of course. The bobcat operator who was crushed when the floor above him collapsed. The twenty-tonne, pre-cast concrete wall panel that was not braced and fell on three construction workers who were having lunch in its shade. The tiler who fell from a second-storey roof that had no tie-down points installed. The many, many motor vehicle accidents. The big, hard men who wouldn't stop shaking days after they held bandages around a mate's pulped hand waiting for the ambulance to arrive. The bewildered wives at the front doors of mortgaged houses, whose brains couldn't process the message that their husbands were not coming home. There were protocols for contacting the families of people who died at work. No contact until death has been certified by a medical practitioner. No notification of death by telephone. Do not visit the next of kin alone. Do not speculate on the cause of the accident. Never admit fault. Tell the next of kin where the deceased's body has been taken and when they can visit. Offer to go with them. Paul had seen and done all these things and while he was pleased to have been there for the hard men and their wives, it was a part of the job that he did not wish to do again.

FIONA

It was 4.45pm and Fiona was almost at the end of her day. She had just finished reading Professor Graves' summary of his proposed presentation to the village residents next week. She wasn't convinced of the appropriateness of the subject matter, but Joyce had contacted Vincent after reading about the research in the paper, and Vincent had contacted the professor, and it all seemed to be arranged before Fiona knew about it. She typed a thank-you email back to Professor Graves, confirming the time and date (next Tuesday at 5.30pm) and the availability of a screen for the PowerPoint presentation.

Melissa knocked on the open door. 'Is it still OK if I go a few minutes early today?'

'Of course it is.'

Melissa was attending her boyfriend's football club wind-up tonight and had an appointment to have her hair done.

'Before you go, do you know if that solar payment went through?'

'Oh goodness, I completely forgot to tell you. They called earlier. Apparently, they haven't received it yet.'

Fiona frowned. 'Never mind, I'll call head office now.'

'Sorry.'

'That's alright. Have a nice evening. Which dress did you decide on?'

'The red one with the pleats.'

'Good choice, you'll knock them dead.'

Melissa bounced out the door and Fiona called head office, hoping to catch the finance team before they went home.

'Hi Jessica, yes, it's Fiona here.

'I'm well thank you. I'm calling about that solar payment. Solar Solutions tell us they haven't received it yet. I know you put it through last week, but they have checked their account again today and it's not there.

'Yes, I know payments sometimes take a few days, but this one seems to have gone missing. Do you think you could call the bank and follow it up?'

'Yes, I know they won't be there right now. Tomorrow will be fine.

'That's great. Thanks Jessica.'

She ended the call, put her fingers to her temples and breathed in and out again. It had been a long day. She'd had a stream of residents through her office since she arrived. Roy had come back with questions about her gardening records. He believed that some of them were incorrect. (They weren't.) And that some were missing. (They were all there.) He had also discovered an inconsistency in the gardening policy and his contract. One referred to *front garden* and the other to *lettable area*. Which one was correct and where were the boundaries for each defined? (Both were correct, and the boundaries were set out in the gardening policy and Roy's contract respectively.) Joyce had come in to advise that the mayor – a close personal friend to her and Peter, she reminded Fiona – would be attending Friday night fish and chips and would Fiona like to stay back that day and join them? (She would.) Also, Bobby was off the leash again this morning: could Fiona have another word with Pat please? (She would do that too.) The light globe in Elaine's and Molly's living room had blown (she sent Gerry to replace it) and someone thought there were possums in the roof of the heritage building (unlikely, but Fiona would send Gerry up there to check). And then, as she had been hoping, Meira would like Josh to visit for one extra day each week: could he come tomorrow? (Yes, he could; she confirmed and booked him in.)

She was done. Fiona checked her inbox, switched off her computer, and gathered up her bags. She locked her office door and the main entrance door, activated the security system, and left through the staffroom. Outside in the staff carpark, she lifted her face to the sea breeze and stretched her back. It was stiff after a long day of sitting. Paul and Martin walked along the access road towards her, holding gardening tools.

'You look like you've had a hard day,' said Paul as they got closer.

'Nothing to complain about,' she smiled. 'You two look like you've been busy.'

'We've pruned Pat's and Elizabeth's roses,' replied Martin. 'They were dangerous. They could have taken someone's eye out.'

'Goodness.' One less potential crisis for her to deal with. 'Thank you for doing that. I think you both deserve a beer.'

'Exactly what we had planned after we put the tools away. You should do the same.'

'I prefer a wine myself, but yes, I think I will stop and get myself a nice rosé on the way home.' She turned towards her car.

'Oh Fiona, one more thing before I forget.'

Fiona turned back again. There was always one more thing.

'Bill Collins has left a stack of packing boxes in villa twenty-six. I suppose you know about them already?'

'He has?' Fiona wasn't convinced. 'I'll check with him tomorrow. Thanks.' She climbed into her car and kept the windows up. She would get that bottle of wine, and some cheese. And she might order takeaway tonight too.

11 · 2ND THURSDAY

PAUL

'That's right,' said Fiona into her phone, 'the first progress payment of fifty thousand dollars.'

This would be the money for the PV array, thought Paul. They had fought hard to get the project approved and now Fiona was anxious to get it started.

'I don't understand,' said Fiona after a moment. 'The balance in the Reserve Fund was $850,511 at the end of the last month. How is it possible that the current balance can't cover the payment?'

Paul looked up. What was this? The balance was indeed $850,511 and with the projected income and expenditure for this financial year, was not budgeted to fall below $550,000. He caught Fiona's eye and raised his eyebrows.

'It's OK,' she mouthed at him, with a quick glance out into the hallway to ensure that no other passing residents could hear.

'Yes, that would be helpful, Jessica. If you could give me access to Dynamics, I'll check it myself.'

She put down the phone.

'Problems?' asked Paul.

'Nothing that can't be solved,' replied Fiona. 'We had a payment that didn't clear due to insufficient funds in the Reserve Fund. Head office is always mixing up the accounts.'

'That's a lot of money to mix up,' Paul observed.

'Yes,' she agreed. 'But Jessica has given me access to the accounting system and I'll check it myself and make sure all the transactions are accurate. I'm sure there will be nothing to worry about.'

Paul was not so sure, but let it pass. 'How did you go with Roy?'

'He and Martin have discovered what we knew all along. Male and female residents get treated just the same when it comes to what they can and can't do in their front gardens.'

'Thank goodness for that.'

'He still wants to change the policy though,' she added.

'Of course he does.'

'In some ways I feel for him, you know. It can't be easy, coming into retirement from a job like Roy's. He was probably quite powerful.'

'He was in mining, wasn't he? CEO?'

'Chief finance officer. He never quite made it to the top.'

'Ahh, I see. What do you know about this talk on Tuesday night?' Paul asked, changing the subject. 'I understand Joyce organised it.'

'She went over my head and straight to Vincent, I'm afraid. But the professor sent me his presentation today.' She handed him the hard copy that she had been reading the day before.

Paul flipped through the document. It looked like a brochure for a safe European car, all navy blue and white, the gold logo of the research centre featuring on the top left corner of each page. There were dot points, referenced statistics and detailed diagrams. A biography of the professor featured on the second page and included a smiling photo of a man in his fifties with neat hair wearing a blue suit under a white lab coat. The lab coat featured the gold research centre logo on its pocket. Paul stopped at a complicated diagram featuring pictures of rodents and cats and humans linked in two red and blue circles. The red line carried purple triangles through the mouth of the human shape and into its stomach.

'I read in the paper that his discovery will save millions of lives,' he said. 'Something to do with mice. But I don't think theological college equipped me to understand this. Do you know what it's all about?'

'It is all a bit beyond me too. But you know how pregnant women are supposed to avoid cats?'

Paul shook his head. 'No.'

'Cats carry a parasite that is normally harmless but can cause pregnant women to miscarry.'

'Horrible.' Paul eyed the diagram. 'How do people catch the parasites from the cats?'

'The cats shed the cysts through their poo, and the cysts can get onto their hair. People stroke their cats, don't wash their hands correctly, and ingest the cysts with their food.'

'Delightful.' Paul made a mental note to top up the hand sanitiser in his bathroom. 'And how do the cats get the parasites?'

'Eating infected mice.'

'Good grief.' He rolled his eyes. 'Every resident will be at Bunnings on Wednesday morning buying mouse traps.'

Fiona laughed. 'The weird thing about it though, is that mice are instinctively averse to the smell of cat urine. They hate it. It smells like ammonia and helps them keep away from places where cats live. But the parasite makes them attracted to the smell.'

'So, it lures them to the cats.'

'Who eat them, allowing the parasite to get into the cat's intestines where it reproduces again.'

'Clever parasite. How do people know if they are infected?'

'Usually they don't, but they can develop flu symptoms. Body aches, fatigue, fever.'

'So, it's not dangerous to most people, just pregnant women. I don't think we have any of them here.' Paul laughed.

'Not normally, no, but Professor Graves is studying a variant of the parasite that also causes internal bleeding. If a person with a compromised immune system is infected, the inflammation can cause cells in blood vessels to break down. The person can bleed to death.'

'Seriously? I'm not sure we want this guy giving a talk at the village. He's going to create a panic.'

'No, but Vincent funds his research and stopping it now would be …'

'A career-limiting move?'

'You got it.'

Meira moved her queen to e2, fencing in Josh's king, his one surviving piece.

Josh considered the board. Meira had progressively and calmly taken each of his pieces over the last forty minutes. He had started the game in high spirits, moving his pieces around the board at whim, advancing his pawns and making bold moves with his queen. He captured more of Meira's own pieces than he expected, sometimes losing his own in the process, including his queen to a knight that he had failed to see. As the game went ahead, he had understood that there was a method in Meira's apparent lapses of judgement, and he felt his heart rate rise in panic. By the time she took his third last piece, a rook, he knew he wouldn't win.

Josh moved his king to b3.

Meira moved her queen to d3.

Josh retreated to a2.

Meira moved her queen to d2, putting Josh's king in check and forcing him into the corner.

Meira moved her king to a4, bringing it closer into the action with her attacking queen. Josh realised what was happening. He moved his king to b1 but had no idea where he would go next.

Meira moved her king to b3. Josh knew it was all over and hid his king back in the corner.

Meira moved her queen to c1. 'Checkmate, Josh.'

Josh stretched and puffed out his tension with a laugh. He had learned to play chess with his dad when he was ten but had lost interest, unable to see more than two or three moves ahead. Now, at the end of his first game with Meira, he could see that she deployed a strategy to destroy him from the start. He'd like to learn to do the same thing. He put the pieces back in their starting positions while Meira got up and switched the kettle on.

After his shift on Tuesday, Meira had asked Fiona if Josh could come back on Thursday 'for some company'. As he expected, the afternoon had been more like hanging out with a genial, if ruthless, auntie than actual work. This morning, after Meira had returned from morning tea downstairs in the cafe, they sorted through a box of photos that they would later scan and send to her children, and then she suggested the chess game.

'Why did you bring your king out into the open like that at the end?' he asked. 'I thought you were supposed to protect your king in chess.'

'You had no key pieces left that could attack him without being caught first by my queen,' Meira replied from the kitchen. She poured their tea and fetched the milk from the fridge. 'And I needed his help to checkmate your king. Remember, the king moves one square at a time and takes a long time to cross the board. I had to bring him out early so he would get there when I needed him.'

Josh took the chessboard back to its place on the bookshelf. As Meira stirred the tea, he surveyed the titles, twisting his shoulders backwards and forwards. He could feel an ache starting in his back and neck.

'Are you sore, Josh?' asked Meira. 'I'm sorry. My chairs are not so comfortable.'

'No, I'm fine,' he replied. 'It is just from soccer last night.'

'You play soccer at night?'

'Indoor soccer. Five a side. We won. Emily came to watch.'

She brought the tea to the table and returned for a plate of biscuits.

'Would Emily play chess with you?'

'I'm sure she would, but I don't know if I want her to.'

Meira chuckled. 'Will she beat you?'

'Yes.'

'I have another board. Not a nice one like this one, just a fold-up board for travelling. It is in the basement. You can have it.'

'I'd love to, Meira, but I'm not allowed to accept gifts.'

'You can borrow it then. We can say I asked you to practise so you can be better company for me.'

Josh drank his tea while Meira instructed him in the basic principles of chess strategy. Josh's dad had already taught him some of these. Control the centre. Protect your pieces. He had not learned how to castle and brought the board back to the table so Meira could demonstrate. When she had finished showing how the king and rook move together to place the king behind a row of pawns, she declared that she was tired and sent him downstairs to fetch the travel board.

Walking down the steps to the basement, Josh felt himself getting out of breath. The overhead lights were already on and he put his hand to his forehead to protect his eyes. His head felt warm and his hand came away wet with sweat. The ache in his shoulders was developing into a headache. At the bottom of the stairs, he waved to the Tredwell Trades guy unloading more boxes into the storage unit and asked if he wanted a hand.

'No thanks, mate, I got this,' the man replied. He glanced over at him. 'You OK? You look like shit.'

'Yeah, I think I might be coming down with something.'

'You're as white as a ghost and there's enough of those here. Here, take some of these and go home.' The man reached into the cab of the van, rummaged around and tossed him a white and orange box. 'Drugs fix everything.'

'Thanks.' Josh caught the box with both hands and stuffed it into his backpack. 'Will do.'

It didn't take him long to find the chessboard. His labelling system paid off and he found it in the box in top back corner. The board was wooden, but smaller and lighter than the one he had just played on with Meira and folded in half to create a fabric-lined nest for the pieces. The pawns were tiny. A gold sticker on the inside lip announced that it was *Made In Turkey*.

Josh shivered. It seemed cold inside the basement today. He worried about his mice. They'd seemed unsettled in the past two days and the shredded newspaper had been tossed around. Some was even hanging through the bars of the cage. There was a blanket underneath the chess box in the packing box, and Josh took it out and draped it over the cage, tucking the corners under. He wondered if he should get them a heater.

HARLEY

Harley was sleeping on Meira's couch when he was woken by sounds from the bedroom. Something wasn't right. He felt the hairs on his back prickle as they stood upright. Harewood Hall was silent except for intermittent noises that might have been a voice but sounded somehow reduced. Light from the clear night-time sky spilled through the glass balcony door across the carpet. Harley jumped to the floor and crept to the hallway that led to the bathroom and two bedrooms, his body low and his ears twitching. The smaller room had a single bed with a bedside table and chest of drawers. He swivelled his head to peer inside. It was never used, and nothing moved. The larger bedroom had a king-size bed, bedside tables, a dressing table and a wall of built-in robes. Like the living room, it opened onto the balcony through large glass doors and looked out over the suburban valley to the north-west. There was a large painting above the bedhead and the dressing table was crowded with photos in silver frames. Next to the door, the trousers and button-down shirt that Meira had worn that day were folded on a chair. Her grey slippers were on the floor next to the bed.

From the open doorway, Harley could see Meira in the moonlight, a small shape tucked into the side of the huge bed. She was twitching and muttering in her sleep. Harley had never been into Meira's bedroom and he was reluctant to cross the threshold now. He leapt up onto the dressing table next to the door and stood, ready to flee if she woke and saw him. From here, he could see that she was, in fact, only twitching her right arm and leg. The left arm and leg were limp and one side of her face was slack, her lower lip hanging. He walked across the dressing table, stepping in between the photos, and leapt the short distance to the bedside table. Nose forward and twitching, he inched across and eased himself onto the white plastic box that sat on the bedside table so he could get a closer look.

'This is Blueforce. How can I help you, Mrs Jacobs?'

Harley leapt off the table and bolted to a corner of the room in alarm. He crouched, hackles raised, ready to fly out of the room and if necessary, out of the apartment.

'Hello? Mrs Jacobs? Meira? Are you there? Are you alright? Do you need assistance?

The voice came from the white plastic box. Harley stayed watchful. He waited and listened to the voice.

'Mrs Jacobs, you have activated your emergency call system and we are sending an ambulance to you now. It will be there in ten minutes.'

FIONA

The call came at 10.36pm as Fiona put the last of the teacups in the dishwasher. The screen on her mobile phone said Blueforce, the emergency call contractor for the village.

'Good evening, Blueforce, this is Fiona Boston. What's up?'

'Good evening, Fiona, this is Steve from the call centre. We've had an alert from apartment five at Harewood Hall and we can't raise the resident, Mrs Meira Jacobs, on the phone. Our records indicate that Mrs Jacobs lives alone and had a stroke six months ago. We've called for an ambulance to attend.'

Fiona's heart sank. It was the worst part of her job.

'Thanks, Steve. I'll be there in ten minutes to assist.'

The ambulance service held a copy of the master key for the village, but Fiona still needed to attend and lock up Harewood Hall after the paramedics had left. She slipped her feet into her loafers, grabbed her bag from the hallstand and called upstairs to her husband.

'It's work, love, I need to go to the village for the ambulance.'

12 · 2ND FRIDAY

JOSH

Josh opened his eyes and lay still for a few minutes. He stretched his neck from side to side and shifted his shoulders. Groaning, he rolled away from the morning light streaming in through the window. He was sick. His head hurt and his face felt hot, and the large muscles in his thighs had a deep ache. He filled his lungs and collapsed the air out again. It hurt. And he was thirsty. He remembered the glass of water on his bedside table and, without lifting his head off the pillow, reached for it and pulled it to his lips. He tried to drink sideways, spilling water onto the sheet, which became cold and clammy. He lay there for another moment, the glass resting on the bed and held the right way up by his hand. His whole body felt weak. He needed drugs. Propping himself on his elbow and sliding the glass back onto the bedside table, he levered himself upright. He rested again. There was Codral in his backpack from yesterday, from the Tredwell Trades guy. The backpack leaned against the wardrobe on the other side of the room. He wondered if he should call his mum.

He swung his legs over the side of the bed and the room swam. He sat until he regained his balance. Easing himself to his feet, he took four steps across the room, and lowered himself to the floor next to the bag. He leaned against the wardrobe, closed his eyes, and took another deep breath. This is shit, he thought. He'd never felt like this before. Josh hadn't had a cold or a virus since, well, since he could remember. He'd had a runny nose and a cough now and again, but nothing like this. Each year, his mum took them all to have their flu shots and Josh had powered through successive winters virus-free. Surely this is not what it is like every time people get the flu, he thought.

He rummaged through the bag and found the box with its two blister packs inside. He would need to get back to the bedside table for the water. Stan came into the room while he contemplated whether to crawl or walk back to the bed. Crawling seemed a bit too pathetic, but he didn't want to be vertical again. Stan helpfully licked his face and put his head down on Josh's lap.

'Hey buddy,' Josh croaked, and then coughed from the effort. Stan lifted his head at the movement and sat up, looking into his face.

'Come on, let's go back to bed.' Josh opted for crawling. Intrigued, the dog followed behind. When he reached the bedside table, Josh leaned against the bed, popped the blister pack and swallowed two white daytime tablets with water. He put the glass and the box on the table and crawled his way back into bed. Stan jumped up beside him and Josh cuddled him closer for warmth. It was ridiculous how cold he felt.

Later that morning, Josh woke with a start. Stan was gone and he was really, really hungry. Cautious from his earlier experience, he edged his feet off the bed and sat for a moment. His muscles ached and his head hurt but at least he wasn't sweating. He shuffled to the door of his bedroom, one arm reaching for the wall, and propped himself against the doorframe, resting and listening. The house was silent, and he figured no-one was home. Still cautious, he made his way downstairs and into the kitchen, taking the box of tablets with him. He loaded six Weet-Bix into a bowl, added milk and turned on the coffee machine. Stan was at the back door, tail wagging in expectation, and Josh let him back inside. They sat down on the couch together, Josh with his breakfast and his coffee. He popped another two tablets out of the blister pack, wrapped a blanket around himself, and found the Adelaide test match on Foxtel.

FIONA

Fiona finalised the settlement calculations for Mrs Collins' villa and now she just needed to send them to finance for confirmation and she would be done. The villa refurbishment had finished yesterday, in record time thanks to Bill Collins Jnr and Tredwell Trades, and she had an appointment with a prospective buyer at 10am. She picked up the application form and read it through again. Doctor George Godden, retired general practitioner and widower, currently living locally in his own home. He would be coming in with his two daughters, Simone and Sallyanne. An online search of Doctor Godden showed that he also played violin in the local community orchestra and was tall, blue-eyed and had a full head of hair.

'Aren't you going to cause a stir amongst the ladies,' Fiona said aloud to his LinkedIn profile photo. Dr Godden had not been able to attend the concert last Sunday due to a prior musical commitment of his own, but he planned to attend Friday fish and chips tonight. Fiona herself would stay back to introduce him to his future neighbours.

Fiona rubbed her eyes and went out to the kitchen to fix herself a cup of coffee. It had been past midnight when she returned home last night and although she fell asleep straight away, she was still tired. She had beaten the ambulance to Harewood Hall, unlocked the building and deactivated the alarm system herself. Late at night under a clear sky, the stone edifice had been stern and cold and she had hurried inside. With the lights on, the gardens outside were thrown into hard shadows and she was discomforted rather than reassured. It was too easy to imagine the shadowy shapes shifting and separating into otherworldly beings. Perhaps the ghosts of past patients. Maybe the man in chains who ate children would clank around the corner if she waited too long. Fiona shook herself out of it. It was ridiculous to indulge in ghost stories when there was a real live person needing her help. She turned her back on the windows and went straight upstairs rather than wait for the ambulance. The first floor was silent as she walked down the hallway, past the Wises' apartment on her right. The nightlights spaced along the walls were designed not to throw shadows, but made an even, indistinct light, like a fading photograph. At the last apartment, she swiped her access key over the lock and pushed the door open into a small vestibule through which she looked out to the open-plan living area and balcony. Through the uncurtained glass doors, she could see the night sky to the west and the streetlights marking the main thoroughfare north across the valley. The orange roofs of the west-end villas shone in the moonlight, dew already wet on the tiles. The suburb was otherwise dark and silent.

As she stood there, flashing red-and-blue ambulance lights bounced off the trees on the western side. Fiona walked straight to the master bedroom where she found Meira still in bed and checked for breathing and a pulse. She sat on the quilt and took her hand, still warm, and waited for the paramedics to arrive. She didn't notice the shadow move in the corner until it slipped by her. Already spooked by the night, she jumped in alarm as she caught a glimpse of two hind legs and a tail as a cat shot through the door and escaped out of the apartment and down the hallway. Her heart was hammering when the two paramedics arrived with their resuscitation box and a gurney.

'Cat's spooked,' the first had said. 'But I guess there can't be too many places to hide. It shouldn't be too hard to catch him.'

Fiona took her cup of coffee back to her office and logged into Dynamics, the corporate accounting system. Later that day, she was still deep in the accounts, trying to understand the transactions she could see on the screen. Melissa joined her.

'From what I can see, there have been three payments from residents into the Reserve Fund this month.'

'That's right. But the system says they are for villa fifty-four, apartment seven and apartment nine.'

'That doesn't make sense. Mrs Barrie has lived in villa fifty-four since two thousand and four and isn't leaving us anytime soon. Apartment seven is Martin Havelock and apartment nine is Joyce and Peter Wise.'

'All of whom are alive and still living here.'

'And none of those payments could have been for another village and put in here by mistake?'

'No, I called the other village managers and checked.'

'Well they still don't explain why there wasn't enough money in the account to cover the solar payment.'

'But this does.' Melissa pointed to a withdrawal from the account of eight hundred thousand dollars one day before the solar payment was approved.

'What the hell?'

'And it was put back again yesterday.' She was right. There was a corresponding payment into the account.

'I don't get it. There must be a mistake.'

She dialled head office to ask Jessica, and Melissa ducked out to the office to take a call at reception. While she waited for head office to pick up, her phone pinged. It was a text from Josh.

Flu symptoms. Fever, sweats, weak, aching. Can you check Martin and Meira OK? Will let you know if still sick on Tuesday.

Melissa put her head back through the office door. The hospital had called. Meira hadn't had a stroke after all; she had hypoglycaemia that was identified on arrival at the hospital emergency department. Other than an elevated temperature, her symptoms had cleared after receiving a glucose infusion. The hospital wanted her to remain on the ward for observation over the weekend and Fiona could expect her to return to the village on Monday.

Fiona put down the phone. Head office was ringing out; she would have to try again on Monday. She switched off her computer and tidied her desk, figuring the news about Meira was a good enough note to finish the day. She would freshen up and have a drink with the residents while she waited for Dr Godden to return. She could check on Martin's health over a wine.

MARTIN

Martin arrived in the resident's dining room at exactly 6.30pm for Friday fish and chips night. Like the previous two weeks, the room was already half full and some of the residents were well through their first drinks. Why did people arrive early when the newsletter clearly said 6.30pm? He made a mental note to check his own newsletter as well as the noticeboard.

As he entered the room, he could see Molly, Elaine, and Pat at a table near the windows. Bobby sat at Pat's feet, red leash tangled on the floor next to him. Paul and Fiona, glasses of wine in hand, stood near the reception desk with a slim man with abundant, wavy hair. Joyce shuffled her feet and wrung her hands at the entrance door. Roy, Jean, Geoff, and Peter Wise were having an animated conversation as they stood next to the bar. Martin went to the bar and the group shuffled aside to let him in. Roy was describing how he, Geoff, and Don Baxter from villa thirty-five had been searching for the water leak when the ambulance arrived the previous night.

'... and then that damn cat – you know the one that Elizabeth used to feed – came bolting around the side of the building like its tail was on fire.'

'You know what I think?' said Geoff. 'I think it was in Meira's apartment when she had the stroke.'

'Don't tell me she was feeding it too,' said Peter. 'Joyce has started leaving –'

'And it hightailed it out of there when the ambos arrived,' finished Roy, reclaiming his story.

Martin ordered himself a beer, noting that the other men were already a third of the way through their glasses.

'It sits on the fence under the gum trees. You know, outside the café,' said Peter. 'I can see it from our balcony. Waiting.'

'We should tell the council. They'll trap it and have it taken to the Cat Haven,' said Roy. 'Stray cats kill the native birds and spread disease.'

'They'll just put it down, poor thing,' protested Jean. 'And I don't think that's true about spreading disease, is it?'

Martin coughed and looked down at the floor. 'If it's not doing anyone any harm, we should just leave it alone.' He looked up at the others, who stared at him in surprise. 'Cats keep the mice down,' he added.

Jean changed the subject and the group spent the next fifteen minutes enquiring after each other's children. When the dinner service was due to start, Martin left the group and turned to find a seat with the ladies by the window. On his way through, he noticed that Joyce was still peering anxiously down the road. Always a well-presented woman, she looked more put together than usual tonight, he thought. He wondered who she hoped to impress.

'Good evening, ladies.'

'Good evening, Martin, how lovely to see you here again.'

'What's Joyce doing there by the door?'

The question was answered when a large sedan pulled into the circular driveway and parked directly outside the entrance door in the universal parking bay. Martin saw Fiona frown. A large, middle-aged man climbed out of the driver's seat and Martin recognised him at once as the dog walker from the school playing fields. Definitely late, not early, sixties, he thought. Through the windows, he saw him make a show of running up the three steps and embracing Joyce. Peter followed behind Joyce and the two men exchanged hearty handshakes before Joyce directed the arrival's attention to Fiona and Paul and the wavy-haired man, who had now joined them outside. Joyce's guest leaned towards her as she asked him a question, and then raised a pantomime finger before turning around to rummage in the back seat of the car. He turned back to them holding a broad gold chain, which he hoisted over his head with a flourish and draped around his shoulders. The group laughed silently behind the glass.

'Goodness,' exclaimed Jean, walking over to the window next to them. 'Who invited the mayor?'

'Joyce did, of course,' replied Elaine, choosing not to treat Jean's question as rhetorical. 'He's here to see the trees and stop them from being pruned.'

'But Fiona doesn't know that,' stage-whispered Molly.

'Who's here?' asked Pat.

'The mayor, darling.'

'That's why the floodlights are on outside. So he can see the lovely trees.'

'Who's the other man?'

'The famous Dr Godden.'

'Why is he here?'

'He's looking for a wife, I expect.'

The party made their way inside and Martin lost sight of them for a few moments until they entered the dining room and the mayor started his rounds.

'Hello, Mr Mayor,' said Elaine, as the large man loomed over them. 'How nice of you to join us.'

'Call me Bevan, please.' Mayor Worth went around the table and shook everyone's hand.

Molly twinkled at him. 'I'm ninety-seven.'

'Goodness gracious, that's an achievement. I hope you'll invite me to your one hundredth birthday party in three years.'

'Oh, you are much too young to come to an old lady's birthday party. You look seventy if you are a day.'

'I'm sixty-five actually.'

Molly patted his hand. 'Never mind.'

Martin smirked and sipped his beer.

When the mayor got to Pat, he bent down to talk to Bobby. 'And what's your name?'

'He's Bobby,' replied Pat on Bobby's behalf. Bobby pulled back his lips in a grimace, accentuating his overbite.

'It's alright, fella,' said the mayor. 'I'm friendly.' He looked up at Pat while he put out his hand to pat Bobby's head. 'I'm great with dogs.'

Bobby growled another warning and bit him.

'Oh dear,' said Pat. 'I'm afraid he doesn't like men.'

The mayor looked at Martin, who was handfeeding Bobby a liver treat.

Martin looked back. Maureen hadn't told him how to respond when an elected representative gets bitten by a dog that you are feeding. Two drops of bright red blood welled from the back of the mayor's hand. Martin offered him a napkin.

'It doesn't seem to be too deep. He's an old dog and his teeth are quite blunt. You'd better put some antiseptic on it when you get home though.'

The mayor accepted the napkin, which he wrapped around his hand, and moved on. He hadn't appeared to recognise Martin, and Martin was disinclined to remind him. The dinner service started. As they ate, Martin spent ten minutes repeating his story about fixing the occasional tables. The ladies were appreciative. Roy joined them and they then spent twenty minutes discussing the solar project and agreed that they needed to recheck the figures for the payback period. Roy would ask Fiona for the figures on Monday.

When Martin returned to his apartment, it was later than he intended. He was also overly full from the beer and large portion sizes sent out by the kitchen. He put his hand to his chest, swallowed with a grimace and fetched his reflux tablets from the kitchen. He would have a word to the chef. Most residents left food on their plates and if Harewood Hall could reduce the portion sizes, perhaps they could also reduce the price.

HARLEY

Harley spent most of his day in storage unit number eight, recovering from his exit from Meira's apartment in the middle of the night. The paramedics with their boots and wheeled bed had smelled of something sharp and urgent. The hallway was unknown territory but gave him only one way to run, so he took it. Downstairs, there was no way out, but the smell of the paramedics and the waiting ambulance made it clear which door would open and Harley waited in a dark corner then slipped through unseen when they left, taking Meira with them.

Today had not been uneventful either. Midmorning, Fiona had come down to the basement with three visitors, two women and a slim man who gripped the handrail and took the steps one by one. They had walked around the parking bays and then inspected the storage unit two down from where Harley slept. He opened one eye and caught Fiona looking at him but was otherwise undisturbed. In the late afternoon, he had sat on the northern fence for a while watching Joyce on her balcony, and then when the sun shifted he moved himself to Pat's villa where he inspected the roses and sat on the fence, watching Bobby sleeping and twitching on his bed.

While Harley sat, the Tredwell Trades van arrived at Elizabeth's villa and two men removed some boxes that looked and smelled like the ones in the basement. They went in and out several times before one of the men came out of the front door waving two plastic bags. He shouted at the other man, who shouted back and poked his finger hard into the first man's shoulder. Harley stood, wary, and watched as the first man used both hands to shove the second man in the chest, dropping the bags into the garden and causing the second man to stagger backwards into the pruned rosebushes. Harley heard a tearing sound as he righted himself and ran at the first man, grabbing him around the waist and driving him into the ground. The two men rolled over each other on the patch of grass. The second man levered himself above the first man and swung his elbow backwards, driving his fist at the first man's face. Just before fist and face connected, the first man wrenched his head away and the fist ploughed into the brick paving. The second man howled, and Harley crouched, ready to flee. The first man scrambled backwards and came to a rest underneath the wedding bush, flattening the agapanthus.

At that moment, Paul came striding, fast and loud, up the path.

'What the hell is going on here?' he shouted.

Harley dropped back onto his haunches and watched as Paul entered the yard and gestured for the two men to stand. He held up his palm to the second man as the first one spoke, and then pointed to the second man. Then Paul spoke and the two men shook hands. Paul pointed at the second man's fist, which had been dripping blood into the grass, and gestured with his head towards the van. One after the other, the two men left the yard, climbed back into their seats, and drove away, Paul watching them until the van was out of sight.

Paul went into Elizabeth's villa, and then came out and locked the front door. Harley watched him collect the two plastic bags from the garden, sniff them, put them in his pocket and return down the path the way he came.

13 · 2ᴺᴰ SATURDAY

JOSH

Josh hadn't managed to watch much of the cricket before the fever returned yesterday. He'd sent a text to Fiona to let her know his symptoms in case any of his clients became unwell and had remained in bed all of Friday and into Saturday morning. On Friday afternoon, he texted Emily and asked her to pick him up some more cold and flu tablets. As it turned out, the Tredwell Trades guy was right. Drugs did make everything better. Today, they would keep him upright for long enough to go to Harewood Hall and check on the mice. He was worried that Pudding might have given birth. Maybe it was time to return them to the lab, he thought. He could do it tonight. He'd tell his mum he was going out to buy more meds. There was a party at the student guild, so there would be people on campus. If security saw him, he could say he was walking home. But what if someone else from the party saw the cage and took it? The engineering students club was holding the party, and he didn't like the idea of a couple of engineers adopting Coco and Pudding. Engineering students had no idea about anything except beer and concrete. If he went at four in the morning, the mice would be safe from the engineers, but then how would explain it to his mum? Were pharmacies even open at four? It was all too hard. Josh curled into his pillows and went back to sleep.

In the afternoon, he was drugged up and back in the Harewood Hall basement wearing his thickest woollen jumper and his head covered in a beanie. Coco and Pudding were burrowed under their shredded paper and came out to sniff his hands and be fed carrot sticks. There was no sign of any baby mice. Maybe Emily had been wrong. He hoped she was; it would buy him some more time. Josh stayed long enough to change the paper and their water and top up the mouse food. He was picking Emily up from work on his way home and didn't want her to have to wait.

Josh parked his car on the street outside the bookstore. He could see Emily behind the counter and waved to her from the driver's seat. The shop looked busy. A slim woman in jeans and white trainers browsed the Christmas displays and a small girl wearing a pink tutu hopped from one foot to another while she waited with her dad at the counter. She held a green picture book in both hands. Her father lifted her up to choose a birthday card and Josh watched as Emily bent towards her and then leaned backwards to reach the rolls of wrapping paper behind the counter. She smiled and chatted to the little girl while she wrapped the book. Outside on the street, people having late lunches sat at the tables for the small bar next door. The dining area was marked off with black canvas and shaded by a tree. Three men in button-down shirts focussed on carving their steaks, their beers half full, not speaking. A waitress in a long black skirt brought out a pizza to a group of four young women, holding it on one hand above the heads of the diners. She walked with an easy stride, her hips rocking and the skirt swishing, and Josh watched her as she delivered the food and retreated into the dark of the bar. She returned with a bottle of rosé, which she opened and poured into the women's glasses. They toasted themselves, giggling, their mouths full of pizza. The father from the bookstore walked past, the little girl on his hip and clutching the book, now wrapped in multicoloured paper and tied with an extravagant red bow.

Emily opened the passenger door and climbed in, chuckling to herself.

'What's so funny?' He leaned over to kiss her but she ducked her head, fiddling in her bag.

'The old lady that was in here just now. The one before the little girl? With the hat? She's ninety-eight and she still lives alone.'

'Wow, what's her secret?'

'That's why I was laughing. She gave me life advice.'

'Are you going to share?'

'Have a glass of wine every day and don't be skinny. She said all her skinny friends are dead.'

Josh laughed as he reversed the car back out into the street. 'I guess we'd better pick up a couple of burgers on the way home then.'

'I'm good with that.' Emily patted his head as he drove. 'Look at you all rugged up. You're so warm. How are you feeling? Guess who I saw today?'

'Sarah.'

'How did you know?'

'Sarah is everywhere. See that guy at the bus stop over there? He's really Sarah, but in disguise. And that mum with the pram? She's also Sarah.'

She laughed again and poked him in the ribs, making him swerve the car. 'Stop it. You can't be that sick if you can still make fun of my friends. She said to say hi.'

'I don't know why; I just saw her at Harewood Hall.'

Emily looked at him, a blank expression on her face.

'I'm joking, Em.'

'Oh, I get it. OK, joke's finished now. What about the mice, how are they?'

'They're fine. I didn't stay long. No baby mice yet.'

'That's good. Maybe Pudding is just fat after all. Are they both well? Not sick at all?'

'No. Why would they?'

'No reason.'

Back at Josh's house, Josh made popcorn and Emily selected a movie. She chose *Jasper Jones*. They had both read the book but had never found the time to see the movie. They curled up together on the couch, Stan squashed between them, licking salt off their hands. When Jeffrey hit a six, they cheered and when Eliza packed away the photo of her dead sister, they both cried.

'Who was your favourite character?' Emily asked when the credits rolled.

'Definitely Jeffrey,' he replied. 'I don't need a superpower!' Josh stretched out his arms and pretended to fly to the kitchen where he started making hot chocolates. 'Who was yours?'

'Jasper's dad. Hugo Weaving is the best.'

Josh put on a pair of sunglasses from the kitchen bench and pretended to slick back his hair. 'Mr Anderson,' he said in a rasping, drawling voice.

'Wasn't he brilliant in *The Matrix*? But I preferred him as Elrond.'

'You must destroy the ring.' Josh tossed the hem of an imaginary robe as he turned back to the stove to get the heated milk.

'Babe, you're hilarious and a total nerd. You should keep taking those drugs.' Emily took her laptop out of her backpack, pulling out receipts, lollies and hair ties with it. Josh brought the hot chocolates back to the living room. Amongst the detritus was a recent copy of the daily newspaper. It was folded open at 'University Disease Outbreak Fears'. He picked it up and read through the article. When he finished, he looked up and saw that Emily was watching him.

'Coco and Pudding don't belong to a friend, do they babe?' she said.

'Ahh, no.' He didn't see any point in trying to wriggle out of it. 'No, they don't.'

'Are they the mice in the paper?'

'Yeah.' Josh steeled himself. He knew Emily would want to know why he lied to her, but he didn't know what to say. He didn't even know why he did it himself. She would be so disappointed in him. He could see it on her face already. She would never trust him again. He'd have to tiptoe around her from now on and account for his every movement. Eventually the distrust would get to them both and they would break up. He'd never meet anyone like her again in his life. Maybe he should get a job out in the mines where there were no women at all, and he could work and drink beer until he died. Rich but alone.

'So, what are you going to do? Josh? Hey, Josh? Over here, babe.'

Josh refocussed on her. He'd been staring out at the garden, at the shed that was doubtless full of happy, free mice.

'I don't know,' he replied.

'Do you think maybe you should take them back to the lab? What if they are infected with this parasite?'

He hadn't thought of that. 'Oh shit, what if I've been infected? Maybe that's why I'm sick.'

'Babe, it's not you I'm worried about. You've got a virus, not a mouse parasite.'

'You don't know that. I could be seriously sick. I could die.'

'What did your mum say?'

'That I have the common cold and need to rest and drink lots of water.'

'There you go then.'

PAUL

Paul sat in his garden in the sun. He could hear Sibelius' fourth symphony through his open window and on the table in front of him he had a copy of the weekend newspapers, a cup of tea, some fresh bread and some jam. Earlier in the morning, he had walked down to the nearby primary school, which hosted a farmers market each Saturday. He took a trolley with him – the type that little old ladies use – and bought fruit and vegetables, a loaf of sourdough, and the paper. He was tempted by the jars of pickles, but he had to be careful these days not to put too much in the trolley. While it was easy to pull along flat ground, the walk back up the hill could be challenging if he weighed it down. The market had been busy. Full of happy people and dogs. Paul wandered the stalls, tasting some smoked bacon (delicious), a turmeric drink (not so) and the local feta (too salty, and eye-wateringly expensive). He put some coins in the violin case of a student raising money for a school music tour and sat for a while on a bench in the sun, enjoying the contented murmur of the crowd and the smell of fresh coffee. In front of him at a baker's stall, two dogs circled each other until their owners, laughing, untangled the crossed leashes before collecting their bread and going their separate ways. His walk home had been easy and slow.

Paul folded the broadsheet in half and then half again to read a column on freedom of speech. He spread a slice of bread with butter and jam, and took a mouthful of tea. A famous rugby player was suing his club which had sacked him after he publicly said that homosexuals must repent or go to hell. The columnist argued that the rugby player should be free to express his beliefs and that the shutting down of politically incorrect views was dangerous. Paul took another mouthful of tea. He was unconvinced; he didn't know what God thought about homosexuality, but the rugby player could have thought more about the impact of his words before he spoke them. He turned the page. Loud voices interrupted Paul's thoughts for the second time in twenty-four hours. This time it was women's voices. Older women. A dog was barking, indignant and protective. Paul waited for a moment, considering his breakfast. He decided to take it with him.

He walked up the path where he and Martin had pruned the roses earlier in the week and saw the source of the ruckus. Outside villa twenty-five, Joyce waved her arms at Pat, who stood at her front door with her own arms folded and feet planted. Elaine was at the front gate and Molly was in her own front garden next door, leaning on her walker next to the fence. Bobby danced and barked around Joyce, excited by the waving and the loud voices. Paul watched him dive in towards her ankles, teeth bared, and then heard him yelp as her toe connected with his shoulder. The dog retreated behind Pat, where he planted his feet like his owner, tense and grumbling. As Paul got closer, he could make out the conversation.

'That is exactly what I'm talking about, Pat. You can't control him.'

'Joyce, you are in his territory. He is only doing his job,' said Elaine, from the front gate.

'I have a right to access the front door.'

'And now you've done that and been asked to leave,' pointed out Elaine.

'I don't see why we can't have a civil conversation about controlling your dog, Pat.'

'Because you are carrying on like a pork chop, that's why, Joyce.' Elaine, from the gate again.

Paul positioned himself next to Elaine at the gate. He too could see the wisdom in keeping the fence between his ankles and the dog.

'Good morning, ladies. Joyce, is there a problem?'

Joyce repeated her grievance. Bobby had bitten the mayor, a distinguished visitor to the village, and lifelong friend of the Wises. It was disgraceful. The mayor might never visit Harewood Hall again. They should all be ashamed, especially Pat. She knew Pat had her troubles, but she had a responsibility to keep the dog on a leash and under control. If she couldn't do that, then Bobby should be rehomed.

Paul hadn't seen the mayor-biting incident himself, but the story had passed from table to table last night. He took a bite out of his bread and jam and waited for Joyce to run out of steam. Bobby took the opportunity to come to the gate and focus on the bread, bottom planted on the ground. Paul looked down at him. Butter wouldn't melt in your mouth now, he thought. He tore off a corner and passed it over the gate. Bobby picked it from his hand with care then swallowed it down whole. A waste of good sourdough.

'How about we go down to the café and talk about it, Joyce? We can have a coffee and fill out an incident report for Fiona to deal with on Monday.'

Reluctant to let go of her anger, but visibly tiring, Joyce obliged with one last shot.

'I'll call the ranger the next time I see him off the lead, Pat.'

Paul opened the gate and picked up Bobby to let Joyce pass. The proximity to the bread was too tempting, though, and Bobby snatched the rest out of his hand in two quick bites.

'Oh dear,' said Pat. 'Naughty Bobby.'

FIONA

The crowd was thinning out at the Active Aging Expo and there were fewer passers-by to accept showbags. Fiona handed one to a couple who looked to be in their seventies, smiling and asking them if they had enjoyed their day. The man looked through her, focussed on getting back to his car and home again, but the woman took it with a weak return smile and a thank you. They didn't stop. I hear you, Fiona thought, wishing she could retreat to her own car. The day had been warm and humid, and through the afternoon the elderly crowd had looked more and more weathered. The Tai Chi club and the Energetic Eighties line dancers had long ago climbed back into their minibuses and driven away. The sea breeze was making a late appearance, ruffling the treetops, but it was yet to send some air past the front of the tented stand. Three members of the St John Ambulance team strode past at a brisk pace. Their day was also done. Each year she attended the expo, Fiona gave thanks that she lived in the western suburbs and not to the east of the city where the afternoons sweltered away from the sea. At least the expo was next to the river and stood half a chance of getting some relief. Today was not that day.

Fiona looked across to the facing stand, where her competitors counted their remaining bags. Fiona was a member of Aged Care Australia, the industry member association, and each year she volunteered to run their stand at the expo. The facing stand was run by Church and Charitable Aged Services Australia, which was also an aged care industry association but whose members were, as their name indicated, restricted to church and charitable organisations. Some years ago, Fiona had driven a campaign to merge the two associations. Joint forces, she had reasoned, would have better chance of influencing government. The campaign had been waged over two years, with numberless hours spent by both sides negotiating joint policy positions and arranging travelling roadshows to convince their respective members. To their dismay, it had failed over bitter debates about tax policy. It turned out that Vincent Tredwell was opposed to tax exemptions for his not-for-profit competitors and, as a principal sponsor of ACA (as well as both of the major political parties), had refused to include the exemptions in ACA's advocacy platform. CCASA's membership had insisted on ACA abandoning this position as a condition of the merger. Vincent, and therefore the ACA, had held his ground and negotiations were aborted. Fiona recalled assembling the disheartened negotiating teams from both sides at a bar one night in the city where they lamented what was lost and drank too many bottles of New Zealand sauvignon blanc.

'How many do we have left?' she asked her own bag-counter.

'Five. So that's one hundred and ninety-five bags we have handed out today.' Toni stood up from the near-empty box of bags and stretched her back. 'Shall we pack up? I'm hot and I'm thirsty.'

'Yes, it's time.' Fiona turned back to the CCASA tent. Despite their differences on tax policy, the two associations still worked shoulder to shoulder to promote the industry. 'How about you, Lisa? How many bags did you hand out?'

'Almost one hundred and eight, I think.'

'Well done. Are you coming for a drink?'

'Not this time, sorry. I'll see you at the seminar next month.'

Fiona and Toni packed down the stand and walked across the park to the hotel on the riverbank. Toni was the manager of Vincent's Seaview Retirement Village and they were meeting Lidia and Priya, who ran two more of Vincent's villages. Like most businesses in the industry, theirs was dominated by women, mostly former nurses in their forties and fifties. Fiona wouldn't say they were a tight-knit group. They didn't get the chance to meet often enough for that, with work and husbands and children, but they enjoyed each other's company when they got the chance. They selected a table for four on a terrace overlooking the river and ordered a bottle of pinot grigio.

'How are your sales going?' Fiona asked.

'So-so,' Toni replied with a grimace and long gulp of her wine. 'There's been more interest since the start of spring, but I've still only got eighty-five percent occupancy.'

Fiona grimaced in sympathy. Toni's village was larger than Fiona's and eighty-five percent occupancy meant she had fifteen apartments to fill. Harewood Hall was running at ninety percent, which was good compared to the industry average, but lower than her target of ninety-five. Fiona needed to fill three vacancies to get there and hoped Dr Godden and Pam Herbener would get her two thirds of the way next week.

'How's head office taking that?'

'Not well. Vincent grumbles every month when he has to top up the operating account.'

They both chuckled.

'Poor Vincent. He might have to buy his next pair of shoes from Windsor Smith instead of Louis Vuitton.'

'Breaks my heart.'

'Who's broken your heart now?' Lidia asked as she walked up to the table with Priya. She put a red leather handbag on one of the two empty chairs and leaned across to embrace both women. 'He's obviously not worth it, seeing as how you are laughing so much.'

'Vincent and his shoes. Is that a new bag?'

Lidia laughed out loud. 'Did I tell you about the time he stepped in a pothole at my village in his Louis Vuittons?' She sat down and poured herself a full glass of wine. 'I didn't think I was ever going to hear the end of it. But he found the money to fix the road.' She snorted as she laughed again and clasped her hand across her mouth.

Priya rolled her eyes. 'Can you send him down to Mandurah? I need him to walk through some potholes in my own roads. Give me that bottle before you empty it, Lidia.'

They all took long silent mouthfuls of their wine and looked out over the river. Despite the afternoon breeze, the water was mirrored and reflected the city towers on the opposite bank. Families rode past on pushbikes and fit women jogged. In suburbs all around them, Fiona reflected, the oldies would be waking up from their afternoon naps and thinking about what was for dinner.

'What's going on with head office at the moment?' she asked her colleagues.

'Who knows?'

'Who cares?'

'Why, what have they done this time?'

'I was following up a payment for the solar project – the one Roy campaigned for – and Jessica gave me access to Dynamics. I found incorrect payments everywhere.'

'Wait a minute,' Lidia opened her eyes wide, 'you lost me at "Jessica gave me access to Dynamics". How much did you pay her? None of us have ever been allowed to look at the accounting system.'

'She's new. She might not know that we aren't allowed to have access.'

'Anyway,' continued Fiona, 'I've had three payments into my Reserve Fund since the last statements were produced, all from residents that I never had.'

'Nice work if you can get it,' laughed Lidia.

'They were probably meant to be for me,' said Priya. She had the largest village and had residents 'departing' every month.

'No, they weren't yours, I checked,' said Fiona. 'And it gets worse. Almost the entire balance was taken out of the account two weeks ago and then the same amount put back in yesterday.'

'No way.'

'Yes way.'

'It sounds like a certain businessman might have cashflow problems,' observed Lidia, raising her eyebrows as she poured herself another glass of wine. She turned the empty bottle upside down in the wine cooler and signalled the waiter.

'He'll be in trouble if he gets caught raiding the Reserve Funds.'

'I thought of that too,' said Fiona, 'but it doesn't explain why he's been putting money in.'

The four women looked at each other.

'He'd better not be doing that sort of nonsense in my village,' said Lidia. 'My residents are as sharp as tacks and they'll take him to the State Administrative Tribunal as soon as look at him.'

'But they wouldn't find out though, would they?' replied Fiona. 'Like us, they just get the monthly statements produced by head office. They won't see any of these transactions if head office doesn't include them in the statements.'

Lidia shrugged. 'As long as he doesn't send us broke, I think I'd rather not know. I assume you can pay for the solar project now that the money is back in the account?'

'Yes,' replied Fiona. 'Yes, I can.'

'There you go. Nothing to worry about.' Lidia opened the fresh bottle of wine and refreshed everyone's glasses. 'Does anyone have a menu? I'm starving.'

HARLEY

The blanket on the chair had been moved to a cushion on the carpet just inside the balcony door. The cushion was large and quite flat, providing an acceptable base for sleeping, washing and observing. The blanket had started to smell familiar. From his allocated position on the floor, Harley could see Martin over the arm of the couch as well as the television screen. Usually a warm and humming presence, the television tonight was unsettling. Discordant notes droned continuously, interspersed with sharp, unexpected sounds that made Harley flinch and Martin frown. The figures on the screen were stiff and moved with a tension that Harley felt rising along his own back. He finished his toilette and curled into a circle, facing away from the television. Martin looked down at him.

'Don't you like this program? Sensible cat.'

Martin paused the television, went to the kitchen and made a cup of tea. From his cushion, Harley could hear the water boiling. He put his head up when he heard the fridge open and tucked it back in again when he saw that the only item to come out was a bottle of milk.

'They covered it up, you see,' said Martin as he returned to the couch. 'They wouldn't admit that the State could be wrong, so they refused to evacuate the people. Even when the evidence was in front of them, they wouldn't believe it. It was impossible, they said. There must be another explanation.'

Martin drank his tea, contemplating the paused screen. A litter of rocks and concrete covered the flat roof of a tall building. 'And then they lied to the Germans about the radiation levels and sent those poor men up there to clean the roof.' He ran the palms of his hands over the fabric of the couch and sighed. 'The Americans. They think they invented fake news, but the Russians beat them to it by thirty years.'

Martin drained his cup and switched off the television. 'You are a nice cat, but cats don't sleep inside.' He opened the door and motioned with his hand.

Disappointed but unsurprised, Harley took himself out to the balcony, where his blanket and cushion followed.

14 · 2ND SUNDAY

FIONA

To: fiona.boston@tredwellforresthall.com
From: georgegodden@hotmail.com

Subject: villa 26

Dear Fiona, thank you for sending me the disclosure documents and purchase information for villa 26 at Harewood Hall. While the villa is well located and presented, I have considered other options and decided to purchase an apartment at The Residence in Dalkeith. The Residence, I feel, offers superior views and facilities and, on balance, better value for money. I also believe that the resident population at The Residence, being somewhat younger than the Harewood Hall residents, is a better fit with my own age and way of life.

Please thank the Residents' Committee for their hospitality at the fish and chips night on Friday. I hope the Mayor's hand recovers soon.

Best, (Dr) George Godden.

Fiona had heard her phone ping inside the house. Sam was in the kitchen and she called for him to bring it out to her. She leaned back in her chair and adjusted her sunglasses. They were not usually necessary on her deck in the morning, but today she was a little sensitive to the light. Lidia had taken it on herself to keep the pinot grigio flowing and Fiona suspected they had drunk a whole bottle each by the time the night ended. She sipped some more coffee and gave Sam a weak smile as he passed her the phone.

'I've got some Berocca in my backpack if you want some, Mum,' he offered.

'I don't know what you mean.'

'How about I get it for you anyway?'

'Bring me some paracetamol too.'

'Will do.'

Fiona read the email, angling the screen away from the sun. She groaned. It was the daughter's doing, she was sure. The older one. Simone. The younger one – Sallyanne – had asked all the questions, but the older daughter had probed deeper when she didn't like what she'd heard. Which was fair enough, Fiona thought. Their dad would spend a lot of money to buy into the village and his children didn't want him to make an unwise decision. Nevertheless, the older daughter had seemed to have made up her mind before she arrived. Fiona sighed. And the Bobby incident on Friday night wouldn't have helped. She would need to talk with Pat about that on Monday. At least she still had Pam Herbener. Two weeks ago, Pam had taken home the disclosure documents to read before signing the lease and now was the right time to call and see how she was going. Eight years of working in retirement living had taught Fiona not to push her clients, but now that Dr Godden had pulled out, she couldn't afford to lose Pam as well. She was confident she could get Pam to sign her lease this week, meaning that Fiona would still have two more vacancies to fill. She would call her tomorrow.

Sam returned with the Berocca and two paracetamols. Fiona swallowed the tablets and drained the glass, the orange water cooling her head. She was going to the art market on the university campus later that morning and would need all the pharmaceutical help available. Leaning back and closing her eyes, she thought back to the conversation around the table earlier last night. What she hadn't told her colleagues was that she had discovered a pattern of payments into the village Reserve Fund dating back as far as the accounting system would go. Every month, there were two or three entries that corresponded to the amounts she would normally expect to see for a resident's end-of-lease payment. She had not been able to find matching records showing that the leases had been terminated. In addition, for the last two years, the Fund had been all but cleared out every quarter, only for the money to be returned two weeks later. None of these transactions were in the monthly statements that head office sent to the village. Whatever Vincent was up to, he'd done it for a long time. If they were audited, they would be in serious trouble. She flexed and pointed her feet to get the blood moving. The paracetamol had kicked in and she would have to get up and get dressed soon. She wondered what her own liability would be if Vincent was found out. She could easily demonstrate that she had known nothing about it. But now that she did know, did she have an obligation to report it to the regulator? She would need to find out. At the very least, she should advise Vincent of the transactions and give him an opportunity to explain them away. Fiona sighed and levered herself off the chair and went inside to shower.

JOSH

Josh woke up at dawn and lay in bed wondering if he was still sick. He wasn't sweating, which he figured was a good sign, and nothing hurt. Emily had stayed over and was asleep beside him. She made tiny girl-snores when she slept on her back, and he stroked her arm until she snuffled and rolled over. Last night he had agreed that he would take the mice back to the research centre when he recovered. Emily had worn down each of his excuses and objections. She couldn't understand what had driven him to take the mice in the first place, she said. Neither did he, if he was honest. Like he told Sam, he was no anti-science ecowarrior and he didn't like to think of himself as a common thief. All he could come up with was that it was meant to be. An act of destiny. Emily had laughed at that and told him he wasn't the Crown Prince of Denmark and the mice were not a letter from his father. He got huffy, but then she promised to stay the night and he forgot the jibe. The plan for today, assuming he was no longer sick, was that he would drop Emily at the train station so she could go to work and then he would take the mice to the university and drop them at the front door of the research centre. Some overworked postdoctoral student was certain to come in on a Sunday. They would find the mice and take them inside. Josh would leave them to their fate.

Josh and Emily had breakfast then drove to Harewood Hall to spend one last morning with Coco and Pudding. They cut up some carrots and celery and ran some blank paper through Josh's dad's shredder. When they arrived at Harewood Hall, they parked around the back, let themselves into Meira's storage unit, and sat with their charges, feeding them and drinking takeaway coffee from their keep cups. Emily held the two mice on her lap, whispering reassurances while Josh changed their paper. She'd told him what a great job he'd done, caring for them, that they were calm and alert and their coats shiny. Pudding was even looking lighter on her feet.

After dropping her at the train station, Josh headed up the highway towards the university, Coco and Pudding strapped into the back seat with the blue dog blanket secured over the top of the cage. Josh put some music on to distract his thoughts. Maybe when this was done, he and Emily should move in together. Then maybe they could get a dog. It would compensate for giving up the mice. He imagined Emily with a puppy. It could be a surprise. He would go to the Shenton Park Dogs' Refuge and bring it home while she was at work. She would squeal and cuddle it and then she would hug him and tell him he was the best boyfriend ever. The puppy would be black and white and fluffy and would do little piddles on the floor until it was toilet-trained. Or maybe they would adopt an old dog who needed someone to love. They would give it a bed in their living room, and it would sleep there all day, thumping its tail gratefully when they walked past and patted its head. Josh would take him for walks, and eventually would carry him home when he could no longer make the distance. They would relocate him to their bedroom in his last days and sit with him, his head in Emily's lap when he drew his final breath.

Josh brushed the tears away from his eyes and refocussed on the road. The traffic became heavier as he approached the campus. Cresting the last hill, he could see it was backed up two blocks. He moved into the right-hand lane and joined the queue. It took two light changes to turn right across the traffic and then another five minutes to arrive at the carpark entrance closest to the research centre. He turned in and was gridlocked after five metres. The carpark was full, and vehicles waited in the lanes for people to leave, their indicators flashing. Families with prams and bags and picnic chairs wandered between the cars and couples walked hand in hand towards the centre of the campus where a blue-and-white banner welcomed them to the art market.

Josh slumped forward and put his head on the steering wheel. He had forgotten. Emily had taken him to the last art market in March. It was huge. They had walked the stalls alongside hundreds of people, looking at ceramics, silver and leather made by local craftsmen. Josh had worn his Daniel (ink.) owl t-shirt that day and the artist gave him a thumbs up as he walked past the stall. Emily bought a fruit bowl the colour of the sea for her sister's birthday and he bought Emily a baby succulent in a handpainted pot. She could put it on her windowsill with all her other babies. When they had seen everything, they queued for okonomiyaki. They ate it on the grass and drank locally brewed kombucha. Sarah was there – of course – and had spied them from across the lawn and told them about a band about to play on the other side of campus. They joined her and some other students and spent the rest of the afternoon drinking wine and listening to music in the sun. They had taken a box of macarons home for Josh's mum.

It took Josh twenty minutes to circle the carpark and get back to the exit. There were no empty bays. He turned left and joined the traffic crawling along the campus perimeter road towards the river. A car in front of him, a red Corolla, stopped suddenly then reversed as the tail-lights on a parked car flashed and a family with a pram loaded themselves inside. One of the two children had had enough of market day and sobbed, his mouth downturned and his face red and sweaty. Josh watched the boy raise his arms to be lifted into the car and then flop against his dad's shoulder, defeated, his face turned to the ground. I get you buddy, thought Josh, market day wasn't part of my plan either. He waited while the family collapsed the pram and reversed out, letting the lucky Corolla driver in, and then continued his crawl down the road.

At the bottom of the campus, he indicated to turn right and away from the university, causing the car behind to honk in annoyance.

'Settle, petal,' he said out loud with a glance in the rear-view mirror. He blinked in alarm. The driver was Fiona's son, Sam. Josh glanced over his shoulder at the cage in the back seat. It was still covered, but the yellow plastic base poked out from a fold that had worked loose. He reached behind to tuck it in, then pushed the nose of his car out into the intersection, making hopeful eye contact with the slow-moving traffic coming towards him. A woman in a low, white sports car stopped and waved him through. He raised his hand in acknowledgement, smiled and waited for someone in the opposite lane to do the same. He avoided looking back at Sam, hoping he would turn left. He tapped his fingers on the steering wheel. The woman in the sports car, now blocked by his Golf, gave him an encouraging smile. Then there was a break in the traffic, and he was free to go.

Josh drove two blocks and then turned into the smaller residential streets around the university. Here, the roads were shaded on both sides by an avenue of trees. The verges were wide, and provided plenty of parking space. On a weekday, these streets were out of bounds for students, but Josh hoped that the council rangers weren't patrolling on a Sunday. He was wrong. Two rangers came towards him on foot on both sides of the road, issuing fines as they went. He pulled over, his engine running, and wondered what to do. He could park in a driveway, make a dash for it, and hope that no-one would come home in the fifteen minutes it took to get to the research centre and back again. He looked up the road for a likely target. There were commercial offices at the end of the street with car bays that he could use if no-one else had got there first. He indicated to pull out, but at that moment, a car pulled up next to him and the driver leaned over.

'Hey, Josh, I thought that was you.' It was Sam. 'Sorry to honk at you like that. The traffic got to me.'

'Hey, Sam. No worries. It's madness here today.'

'I know, right? I've just dropped Mum off.' Sam waited for Josh to respond with his own explanation of why he was in market traffic.

'Cool, she'll like it. Em and I went to the last one.'

'Nice move in front of the Porsche, by the way. I wouldn't have pulled out in traffic like that.'

Josh didn't think he'd been that aggressive but laughed anyway.

'Anyway, she let me through too, so thanks. Are you and Emily free tonight?'

'I think so, yeah.'

'Sarah's brother is having drinks at his place. Come along. We'll order some pizza. You know the place, right?'

'On the hill near Harewood Hall?'

'Yeah, I'll message you the address. Six o'clock.'

'Thanks, I'll check with Em.'

'See you then.'

Sam drove on. Josh felt sick. The rangers passed him, pointing to the No Parking sign as they went by. Josh nodded and gave them the thumbs up. He couldn't risk it. He pulled out and drove back to Harewood Hall.

PAUL

The tea in the plastic cup was weak and lukewarm but Paul drank it down anyway. He grimaced and looked at Meira. Her bed looked about as comfortable as his vinyl chair and there was nothing on the bedside table except her packed overnight bag.

'I know, I know. I didn't come here for the five-star food,' she said. She reached inside the bag for the book he had brought her on Friday. 'Here. You should read this. It doesn't do your profession any favours and it's miserable, but a good read.'

'You're not exactly talking it up,' Paul observed as he took the heavy paperback from her hand. 'What's it about?'

She waved her hand as though dismissing the book from her life. 'If I tell you, you won't read it.'

Paul opened the front cover and read the synopsis. '... *an increasingly broken man, his mind and body scarred by an unspeakable childhood, and haunted by a degree of trauma,*' he read out loud. 'Good grief, Meira, what are you trying to do to me?'

She pursed her lips and shrugged. 'Put it in the library if you don't want to read it.'

Paul had brought the book and a bag of Meira's things from her apartment to the hospital on the day after she was admitted. She had been bored already and was impatient with the medical staff who wanted to keep her in for observation over the weekend. She insisted that she would only stay until Sunday and was dismissive of the nurses' protests that her doctor would not be able to discharge her until Monday morning.

'Then I will discharge myself.'

Paul had offered to collect her and take her back to Harewood Hall. He promised the medical team that he would see she was settled and look in on her daily. When he arrived, she was already dressed and ready to leave, disconnected from the intravenous drip (Paul had been informed by the nurse that she pulled it out herself) and the monitors turned off. Eventually, the ward clerk returned with the discharge papers and Paul gathered up Meira and her belongings. He had forgotten to bring her walker and, despite her protests, took her back to his car in a hospital wheelchair, her bag on her lap. She waited, strapped in the car, while he returned it.

Back in her apartment at Harewood Hall, Meira insisted on making Paul a cup of tea. While she busied herself in the kitchen, he looked about the open-plan kitchen and living room, taking in the books, the chess set, and the old photos. There was a side plate on the floor of the kitchen and Meira picked up and put it in the sink.

'I heard there was a cat in village,' said Paul. 'Are you the one who has been feeding it?'

'And Martin,' she replied.

'Martin Havelock?'

Meira looked at him, eyebrows lifted and an amused smile on her face. 'Yes, Martin.'

'I never would have guessed.'

'No? He has a kind heart. Look at what he did for me.' Meira nodded at the dining chair at the end of her table. 'He fixed it. The leg broke when I moved here; the removal company was so rough. Now you can't tell unless you know where the crack was. He wouldn't take any payment.'

Paul inspected the mended chair. Typical of Martin, the repair was almost invisible, and the chair took his weight without protest. He stayed there while they drank their tea.

Instead of returning to his villa, Paul took the stairs down to the basement carpark. He fished his master key out of his pocket and slotted it into the Tredwell Trades storage unit door. As he suspected, it was the only door in the village that they didn't fit. He looked through the bars and could see the packing boxes stacked against the back wall, partly obscured by painting materials. He walked over to Martin's unit, where he let himself in with the master key and helped himself to a torch, which he took back to the Tredwell unit and trained on the boxes. He took the plastic bags he had retrieved from Elizabeth's villa out of his pocket. He couldn't be sure, but they looked to have the same blue bar running across the bottom as the plastic sticking out of the torn boxes.

Paul tucked the bags back into his pocket and returned the torch to its designated place on Martin's tidy shelf. He put his hands on his hips and surveyed the tools on the pegboard. They were clean and oiled. Everything was in its place. The workbench underneath was dust-free, ready for use. A yellow notebook sat on the top right-hand corner, squared off to the edges. Paul opened it to the first page. Here, Martin had marked out a table with four columns. Each row was dated and against the dates were degree markings. The third column, titled *Observations* contained short notes – *No obvious cracking* and *Moisture evident, course three, RHS*. As he placed it back on the bench, taking care to realign it with the edge, he fumbled and as he caught the book to prevent it from falling to the floor, it opened to the back page. Here, Martin had marked out another table, also with dated rows and a column marked *Observations*. Paul read through them. *Eight boxes delivered. Eight boxes removed. Ten boxes delivered. Ten boxes removed.* The records dated back for the past two years. Last Sunday, Martin had written *Ten boxes delivered (villa 26?).* Paul took out his phone and took a photo of the last two pages and then returned the notebook to its place on the bench.

The vehicle access gate rumbled and slid open. Josh's grey Golf pulled in, did a circuit of the carpark, and stopped three metres away. Uneasy about being seen snooping, Paul eased himself into the back wall. He watched as Josh opened the door to unit five, returned to the car and fetched a large object covered in a blue blanket. He took it inside, lifting it by a hook on the top and supporting the bottom with a careful hand. Paul listened, straining to hear, as Josh murmured something indistinct and then heard him lock the door and restart the car. When the access gate closed, Paul locked Martin's storage unit and walked over to where Josh had just been. Once again, he peered through bars. The light was not as good here, but he could make out the blue shape. He went to fetch the key out of his pocket for the third time when the gate once again rumbled. Deciding he had snooped enough for the day, he jogged to the open gate before it closed again, waved to Peter Wise on the way and walked up the ramp to his villa.

'It is completely unacceptable, Peter,' said Joyce, putting down her knife and fork to emphasise the point. 'Dogs should not be allowed in the dining room whether they are on or off a leash. It is unhygienic. Who knows what diseases he might have? I don't care if he is vaccinated, wormed, or deloused or whatever. She fed him food off her plate. Did you see her? It was disgusting. She can do that kind of thing at home if she must, but not in the residents' dining room.'

She paused to drink from her wine glass.

'And it is a trip hazard. He might have been under her chair, but that leash was all over the floor. What if a resident had tripped on it and broken a hip? Then where would she be? Of course, it won't be her problem at all. It is the village that will be at fault and then our insurance premiums will go up. We are the ones who pay for it in the end. I bet Fiona doesn't think about that when she gives Pat her gentle little reminders. I've overheard them, you know. She doesn't think anyone can hear but they talk right under our balcony. It's all *please* this and *we all love Bobby* that. She's too soft and one day she'll be sorry.'

Joyce huffed in exasperation and drank some more wine.

Peter tried for placation. 'I agree with you, love. There is no place for pets in the residents' dining room. Especially when food is being served.'

'And another thing,' Joyce tilted her wine glass at him. 'Who in their right mind allows an eighty-six-year-old woman in a retirement village to have a dog? Didn't they think of the poor animal's welfare?'

'I think Pat brought Bobby with her when she moved in. It would be a bit cruel to force her to let go of him just because she's coming to live here.'

'That's not the point, Peter, and you know it.' Joyce raised her voice. 'We all know she can hardly look after herself, let alone a dog. It was obvious to everyone that she had dementia from the day she moved in here. Look at the way she walks for heaven's sake. It's a wonder she can leave her villa.'

Peter thumped his glass on the table and she jumped.

'I can't see why this bothers you so much, Joyce,' he exclaimed. 'Why can't you leave the poor woman alone? It doesn't hurt you. For goodness sake!'

Joyce had no answer. She felt her certainty collapse as if it was a physical thing inside her, scaffolding that couldn't hold under the weight of her husband's reasonableness. She felt her chin tremble. Mortified, she couldn't meet his eyes. She was a bad person, mean and judgemental. She looked at her plate and put down her glass.

'But what if it happens to me?' The words came out as a croak.

'Oh, love. Come here.' Peter stood up and walked around the table and put his arms around his wife. He kissed the top of her head and put his own head down, so they were cheek to cheek. 'If you are that worried, why don't we go see someone?'

HARLEY

Later that night, Harley returned to the northern side of the village. Instead of walking around the heritage building, he took a short cut through the basement, and wriggled through the hole in the limestone footings onto the top of the internal wall. Walking along the tops of the various sideboards, fridges and packing boxes, he passed the smell of the mice under their blanket, pausing only briefly to register the presence of just two bodies, crossed the basement floor and trotted up the steps. As usual, the door was propped open and Harley exited through the staff entrance without fuss. He paused before crossing the access road to the staff carpark. There were no sounds or movement to the east or west and the sky was clear. Above him, the lights in Joyce and Peter's apartment were still on but there was no sound of people inside. The sea breeze had faded to nothing.

Harley ambled across the road and explored the ground under the gum trees. He could smell the birds that had been foraging earlier in the day and Bobby and the brown labrador that walked past each morning. Tonight, there was also a strong scent of tomcat, and Harley re-marked each tree. He crouched at the edge of the hole that the residents had dug earlier that evening. The resident garden inspectors had turned the corner of the heritage building on Friday and proceeded along the northern side. Two hours ago, they reached the garden bed under the lemon-scented gum trees. Harley had been watching them from Joyce's balcony when the ground microphone started beeping.

'What's that noise?' Roy asked. He was the one with the headphones this evening.

'What noise?' replied Geoff.

'This one.' Roy gave Geoff the headphones. Geoff looked at him in disbelief.

'That's the signal, you idiot. It's picked up the leak!'

The three men ran the microphone back over the path they were following.

'I can't hear anything.'

'You need to go slower.'

'Go back over it again.'

'You've got it too high now.'

'I can hear it. Right here.' Roy stamped his foot on the wet soil.

'Stay right there.'

Roy stood his ground and Geoff sunk a metal stake into the ground next to his foot.

'Right. Now what do we do?'

'We dig it up.'

'What, right now?'

'I haven't been out in the cold lugging this shovel around night after night just to find it and leave it. We're digging it up.'

Roy scraped away the mulch and sunk his blade into the soft, damp soil. Harley heard a crack.

'Shit.'

'Be careful.'

'It's not my fault if they didn't bury it deep enough.'

Working with a little less force, Roy dug the soil away, uncovering a plastic pipe. Getting down on his hands and knees, he loosened the soil away from the sides and underneath the pipe. Harley smelled clean water.

'Gotcha.'

Roy straightened up. 'I'll tell Fiona in the morning.'

'What do we do about the hole?'

'Nothing, we leave it here.'

'What if someone falls in?'

'Who?' asked Roy, laughing. 'It's the middle of the night.'

'Early morning people. Dog walkers. Martin. Gerry. We should put up a barrier at least.'

'Fair enough.'

They used the garden stakes and stringline to mark off a barrier around the hole and, in good spirits, went home to bed.

There was water at the bottom of the hole. Harley could see a slow trickle from the side of the exposed pipe. A cat yowled nearby, and Harley tensed and crouched lower. He was happy to mark his territory against newcomers but had no appetite for a confrontation. He stilled, on guard, alert for any potential company to proceed in another direction. Suddenly and quite unexpectedly, he saw movement at the western corner of the building and a small white shape appeared. Harley remained where he was at the side of the hole while Bobby trotted towards him, nose high and on a mission. Harley silently arched his back, until he was as tall as the dog, a warning growl ready in his chest. Bobby paid him no attention and continued on. Harley watched him head down the road towards the street with the boy and the red-brick house. He deflated and returned to his contemplation of the hole.

The water got deeper, and the trickle became more solid. No longer supported by surrounding soil and encouraged by the impact from Roy's shovel, the crack in the pipe stretched and widened. Harley watched as the water rose and began to seep through the looser soil at ground level. It spilled over and started a dark track through the garden bed. When it reached the bitumen road, it moved faster, heading towards the staff entrance. Curious, Harley moved with it, and when it reached the top of the basement stairs, he sat there watching it pour, step by step, to the basement floor. Eventually, the little stream became wide enough that Harley could no longer stay where he was without getting wet. He decided he would sleep on Martin's balcony rather than risk the basement and took the long way back around the building.

15 · 3ᴿᴰ MONDAY

MARTIN

Martin woke at six thirty and ate his breakfast on the balcony. He was surprised at the temperature, even allowing for the south-facing aspect. The cat was still asleep on the cushion. Perhaps he could let it sleep inside tonight. It would mean filling the litter tray, but there were big winds forecast and the cushion might blow away if it was left out on the balcony.

Last night for dinner, Martin had crumbed and fried some chicken breasts, roasted half a dozen potatoes, and made a salad of green leaves, red onion, and cherry tomatoes with a honey and mustard dressing. When the chicken and the potatoes were done, he put them in a baking dish, covered it with alfoil, and put the dish in an old picnic basket. He covered the dish again with a clean tea towel, placed the salad bowl on top, and covered that with a second tea towel. He retrieved the half full container of stewed apricots from the fridge and, after a small hesitation, added the ice-cream from the freezer. His basket full, he locked the door to his apartment and set off down the hall to apartment five. This morning, he felt pleased that he had successfully cooked a meal for another person and could mark off another achievement against his goal of *finding a sense of purpose* in his Action Plan. The dinner had the added and unexpected benefits of being enjoyable and showing the cat that he knew what he was up to. Martin took his presence on the balcony overnight as an admission of duplicity. He cleared away his breakfast dishes, brushed his teeth and set off for his morning walk.

Of course, he had been the first person to find the burst water pipe and discover the flood in the basement this morning. He couldn't expect anyone else to be up and about at this time on a Monday. Martin had followed his usual path around the school playing fields and when he got back to Harewood Hall, he turned right to circumnavigate the village. He'd walked past the gum trees with their unsightly and ineffective concrete plugs and felt the dirty water underfoot before he'd seen the river that flowed across the road and down to the basement. The water was not deep, but it moved fast and carried with it the mulch, leaf litter, and soil from a hole in the garden bed. Garden stakes and flagging were strewn across the road. Martin wasn't inclined to test the depth of the hole itself but, guessing that the water came from the ring main, he estimated it to be at least half a metre. He tracked the water's path across the road, into the staff entrance of the heritage building and down the steps. He didn't bother to switch on the light. It didn't matter how much water was in there, no-one could do anything now but turn the water off at the mains and wait for it to recede.

Fortunately, Martin had had the foresight to store all the staff members' telephone numbers in his contacts list. He had entered them in when he first arrived at the village and updated them each time a revised village telephone list was issued. He took out his mobile phone and notified Gerry on the spot. He then strode around the front façade of the building to the mains tap, turned it off and returned to the burst water pipe. The site needed to be secured to mitigate the risk of any residents or passing dog walkers falling into the hole and, barred from access to his own materials in the basement, Martin would use the remains of the stringline.

FIONA

Driving to work along the beachfront, Fiona could see the beginnings of the cloud that had been forecast to come down from the north over the next two days. Expect unsettled weather, said the Bureau of Meteorology, but Fiona didn't hold her breath. Spring storms were not uncommon, but in Fiona's experience often only brought rainless thunder and lightning. She decided to forego the Kirkwood Deli today. She had leftover biriyani from the market yesterday and would heat it up in the staff kitchen. As she drove to work, she ran through her tasks for the week. First and most importantly, she needed to call Pam Herbener about apartment six. Perhaps she should also revisit the people she had invited to the concert last Sunday. Paul had reported that one lady in particular – Jan – had been keen, but Fiona had yet to catch her on the phone despite calling her twice. She would try again today. She still smarted from the 'value for money' and 'somewhat younger' comments in George Godden's email, and wondered if she should have another talk with Marketing about their pricing.

Her second priority was to make sure head office processed the missed progress payment for the solar project. If the project didn't get started soon, it wouldn't be completed before the Christmas shutdown and the village would miss out on the benefits of a full summer of free electricity. She would also need to write to Vincent about the unexplained payments in and out of the Reserve Fund. Despite Lidia's advice, she was worried about her own liability and couldn't let it pass. Third, the tree-pruning contractors would arrive tomorrow morning and she needed to check their Working At Heights certifications and online site inductions. Finally, there was the disgraceful altercation on Friday afternoon between the Tredwell Trades workers at Elizabeth's villa that couldn't be ignored. She would have to complete an incident report and notify Vincent. Then there was the usual routine of the gardens, resident bills, meal plans, staff rosters, scheduled maintenance and any other matter that the week threw at her.

She circled around the front of the building, taking in the honey-coloured stone edifice and, as she did every day, gave thanks for her good fortune. She continued around under the gum trees, where she came to a stop, confused. The road to the staff carpark was blocked. Garden stakes and pink flagging blocked the access road, and dirt and garden debris was scattered across the ground from the garden bed to the staff entrance. A group of residents gesticulated at Melissa, who appeared to be blocking them from going into the basement. Gerry knocked on her driver's side window, which she wound down so he could talk.

'It's alright, Martin turned the water off at the mains and the plumber is on his way.'

Fiona's phone rang. It was Vincent.

Joyce sat on her balcony and watched the magpies swoop at the workmen digging out the garden bed below. She had heard that a water pipe burst overnight and flooded the basement, and now the water was turned off until lunchtime. The staff had been required to drive around the southern side of the building to get to the carpark. It was rumoured that the access road might collapse. The residents' vehicle access to the basement carpark, including for Joyce and Peter, was on the other side of the building and unobstructed, but no-one knew at this point whether there was any damage to the vehicles parked inside. Joyce was not concerned. Their own cars were fully insured, and their excess was minimal. Peter had simply taken an Uber to golf and would hire a set of clubs for the day.

Joyce went back inside and filled a kettle for tea. She had a man deliver filtered water each week for tea and coffee so the temporary outage didn't concern her. While the water boiled, she fetched her laptop and opened it up on the kitchen bench. Her browser was open to the Alzheimer's Association website and she scrolled down to the 'Understanding Dementia' link. She was still a bit shaken from last night. She had known something was wrong for a while now but hoped it would go away. Three months ago, she had searched for half an hour for a book she was reading at breakfast, only to find it in the refrigerator after she gave up looking. That had been strange and embarrassing and Joyce was thankful that Peter had been at golf at the time. Last week she was mortified when she went to pay for a new blouse in David Jones and had stared at her wallet, unable to work out which card was her credit card. To her shame, the shop assistant in her fitted black-and-white dress took it out and processed the payment for her. 'It happens all the time,' she had said, her voice low and gentle.

Joyce didn't know what to make of these incidents. Peter was supportive last night, of course. She couldn't ask for a better husband. When she'd had Ben, their second, Peter was so attentive, taking time off work and staying at home with her. She hadn't needed his help, with the nanny and everything, but she understood that he was concerned, especially after Jason. They were their golden days. She and Peter would load the baby and all his things into the car and drive out to Gordon's Bay or

Stellenbosch. They would sit on the beach or visit a wine farm. Joyce would take a magazine and they would go for long walks with Ben in his pram. Then he would sleep all the way home.

It was different when Alison was born. They were in Hong Kong by then and Peter worked longer days and often on weekends. Joyce had another nanny, who was such a treasure and wonderful with the two children, but she missed Peter and her friends from Cape Town. It had been hard to fit in with a new expatriate community – her third – and although she had found a competent doctor and saw her once a fortnight, she had few people to talk to about the joys and frustrations of new motherhood. There had been getting-lost incidents back then too, and once Joyce had left Alison in a department store after trying on a dress for the company Christmas party. After that, she had spent a week in hospital. Her doctor said she needed to get some rest.

Joyce finished her tea and went out to the balcony to check on the plumbing repairs. The van was still there but it looked as though the workmen were packing up. Gerry was talking with them, leaning on a rake. She would go down to morning tea with the girls and hear all about it soon.

PAUL

Downstairs in Fiona's office, the residents' committee members who could be gathered at short notice waited for Fiona to get off the phone. Paul composed himself. He knew how this would play out and guessed that the only thing he could do would be to sit through it and mop up afterwards. Out of the corner of his eye, Roy's heel bobbed up and down while he clutched a sheaf of papers in his left hand. Paul could see the muscles knotted in his arm. He knew that Fiona's mobile phone would barely touch the desk before Roy would lean forward and demand answers.

'Yes, that's right, the two hundred and sixty-four thousand dollar Reserve Fund payment from villa fifty-four, made on thirty April,' said Fiona into the phone.

'No, it's not ours.

'No, it is not Priya's either. I checked. Neither are the other two payments.

'And the eight hundred thousand withdrawal from the Reserve Fund at the start of the month.

'Yes, I know the money has been returned to the account.

'Yes, I know that means there are now sufficient funds for the solar payment.

'Yes, it is still a problem actually, Jessica. There are rules about what money can be paid into the Reserve Fund and how it can be used.'

Paul looked at the other committee members, concerned that they would pick up on the conversation. They weren't paying attention anyway. Roy was looking at his lap and tapping his papers, rehearsing his opening lines, and Jean was texting someone on her phone. Paul sat back in his chair and waited.

When Fiona put the phone down with a rueful look at Paul, Roy jumped straight in.

'Our water was turned off without notice this morning.'

Paul looked at Roy in disappointment. They had talked about this. He leaned forward to rein him in, but Roy put up his hand.

'Just a minute, Paul. Let me have my say. My wife was in the shower, washing her hair, when the water stopped.' He clicked his fingers in Fiona's face. 'Just like that. Can you imagine what that is like, for a seventy-two-year-old woman, left wet and soapy on a cold morning? You've got some explaining to do.'

'It was an emergency, Roy, what was Fiona supposed to do?' protested Jean.

'That's management's problem, not mine. It says here,' Roy jabbed his finger at the lease contract open on his lap, 'that you are required to give us six hours of notice in the event of a shutdown of essential services.'

'Would you rather have the water pouring into the basement for another six hours than have Bronwyn suffer a bit of soap on her skin? Goodness, Roy, be reasonable.'

'Like I said, Jean, that's management's problem, not mine. And speaking of the wasted water, I don't know how many thousands of litres you have just poured down the basement, Fiona, but you'd better not think that we will be paying for it.'

Jean sighed and rolled her eyes. Paul figured it was time to intervene.

'I think our immediate concern is to secure the site and get the pipe fixed. We can deal with those other matters later.'

Roy opened his mouth to object and this time it was Paul's turn to put his hand up.

'Fiona, can you give us the current status?'

He was rewarded with a grateful smile. 'Of course. Martin Havelock kindly roped off the area this morning and staff have been directed to drive around the southern side to access the staff carpark.'

'Which means that the residents on the western side will have a continuous stream of traffic past our living rooms until it gets fixed,' pointed out Roy.

'A plumber from Tredwell Trades is already on site,' Fiona continued, 'and expects to have the pipe fixed and the water reconnected by lunchtime. Gerry has swept the footpaths clear, so there is no falls risk for residents who want to access the café from the northern side. The basement is draining faster than we hoped and I expect will be accessible so we can assess the damage to residents' property from late this afternoon.'

'And who's going to pay for the damage? The poor residents in the heritage building apartments I suppose?' Roy again. Paul gave him a look. He'd heard about the pipe excavation and the sound the shovel made as Roy sunk the blade into the wet soil. Roy avoided his eye. Paul let it go. Gerry and Fiona had assumed the hole opened up because it was no longer supported in the ground. He figured it was best left that way.

'The corporate insurance policy has limited coverage for residents' property, and I expect it to cover this incident. Of course, I need to confirm that with the insurance company first.'

'So you haven't done that yet,' Roy rolled his eyes and looked around at Paul and Jean.

'Well,' said Paul, slapping his hands on his thighs and avoiding Roy's gaze, 'I think that just about covers it. Fiona, will you send out a notice when the water is back on? Excellent.'

Fifteen minutes later, Paul left the building through the café doors and walked back to the western side of the village. The sky was still clear, but the air was thick ahead of the forecasted storm. The workmen had finished fixing the water pipe and Gerry was sweeping away the dirt and leaves from the access road.

'All done now, Gerry?'

'Good as gold, Paul.'

'Water back on then?'

'Yep, you can go shower for as long as you like.'

'Good to hear.'

Paul continued as far as the staff entrance then, looking behind him to make sure Gerry had moved on, he lifted the security tape and, taking care on the wet steps, descended into the basement.

Downstairs, the air was cold and damp and smelled of ammonia, making Paul think about his conversation with Fiona earlier the previous week. The water had all but drained away, but the concrete was stained dark and shallow puddles revealed where the floor was uneven. The basement walls were wet up to the second course, which Paul hoped would mean that the residents' vehicles were all undamaged. Residents who used shelving to store their belongings away from the floor would also escape too much loss. Not so the bookcases, sideboards and other pieces of furniture that had not won a place upstairs. Various wooden legs were stained dark with water and over the next few days would swell and crack. On the floor of storage unit sixteen, Paul could see where Richard and Mary Johnson stored their personal papers – probably a lifetime of tax records – in suspension files in plastic tubs on the floor, the type you buy in Officeworks. By the looks of them, they could still satisfy the taxman.

As Paul walked across the basement towards the storage units, he could feel grit under his shoes from the soil that had been washed from the garden bed and down the stairs. Leaves and pieces of bark lay scattered about the floor, but the bulk of the debris was made up of dozens of plastic bags. They were the type that were once used by parents to keep sandwiches fresh in children's school bags, before they were abandoned by the younger, eco-conscious mummies in favour of reusable sandwich boxes. They were also the type that Paul had retrieved from Elizabeth's unit and, he suspected, had caused the fight in Elizabeth's garden last week. Paul picked one up. It had a blue band across the bottom. The ziplock had come apart and it was empty. Paul sniffed it and jerked his head back, inhaling a heady whiff of cat pee. Gagging, he dropped it onto the floor and picked his way through the mess. Closer to the storage units were bags that were less damaged. These contained gluey white lumps. Paul wasn't game to sniff them; they were not the purpose of his mission this morning. He'd deal with that matter later. He continued to storage unit number five.

Using his master key, Paul unlocked the door. The cardboard boxes inside were soggy, and some had spilled their contents onto the floor. White sticky labels had fallen off and made small papery blobs. The stink of ammonia was not as heavy inside the storage unit, taken over by the musty smell of wet linen. Paul could pick out the animal smell cutting through it. Despite the tumbling mess, the path through the boxes to the back of the unit was still clear and Paul made his way through until he saw the blue blanket on a waist high shelf next to two bar stools. He checked underneath the blanket, lifted the cage keeping it covered and, picking up one of the plastic bags on the way, carried it back up the stairs. As he left, the vehicle access gate trundled open, letting in the Tredwell Trades van. Good luck lads, he thought, you've got a hell of a clean-up in front of you.

FIONA

To the Village Manager

RE: APPROVAL TO PRUNE LEMON-SCENTED EUCALYPTUS

I refer to our approval to conduct maintenance pruning of the five lemon-scented eucalyptus (Corymbia citriodora) trees on the northern boundary of your site (Lot 24601) dated 2 October 2019. You are instructed to immediately cease all work until further notice. An officer of the Council will contact you to make a suitable time to inspect the site.

If you have any queries regarding this instruction, please telephone Council offices between the hours of 8.30am and

4.30pm Monday to Friday quoting reference number ENV-*2019-233.*

Yours sincerely
Michael D'Souza BSc (Hons)
Senior Environmental Officer.

You old cow, Joyce, thought Fiona as she read the emailed letter again. She might have guessed what she was up to when the mayor showed up at fish and chips night. The old school tie wins again.

'Do you want me to call the contractors and let them know there is a delay?' asked Melissa.

'Yes please. And it will only be a delay, not a cancellation.' Don't think you'll be having the last word on this one, Joyce, she thought. Fiona forwarded the email to Paul, marking it FYI, and went to the kitchen to fix herself a cup of tea.

It had, by any benchmark, been something of a day. Almost five thousand litres of water had emptied into the basement by the time Martin switched off the mains. Gerry, bless him, had secured the basement and prevented any residents from entering, and advised Tredwell Trades that their services would be needed in the next twenty-four hours for the clean-up. Melissa went down there in wellies to take photos and had already completed and sent the preliminary forms for the insurance claim. Of course, Fiona received a stream of residents through her office all day complaining about the inconvenience of the water being turned off, not being able to access their vehicles and generally anxious about the state of their belongings in the storage units. And then there was the shouted and expletive-filled phone call from her boss before she'd even got out of her car. She guessed he'd been given the heads-up by Tredwell Trades. Thanks for that, boys, she thought. Vincent had demanded that Tredwells be given access to the basement immediately. When she had explained that it was unsafe until the water receded, he gave her a mouthful. She was incompetent, had taken her eye off the ball and might think she was all cosy with the residents, but a *man* would have at least maintained the plumbing system. He'd like to know what more nasty surprises were lurking at his village that he didn't know about. Fiona had refrained from bringing up the unexplained transactions to and from the

Reserve Fund. She picked up the selection of photos Melissa had passed to her and studied the photo on the top, frowning, then slid them into an envelope and tucked it in her handbag. They could wait for another day.

HARLEY

Meira wasn't responding to his polite requests to be let in, so Harley went around to Martin's balcony, where he was rewarded with a bowl of chicken mince and a cushion on the floor. Martin forgot to put him outside when he went to bed. Before the flood the previous evening, Harley had slept in the sun on Meira's balcony. When she arrived home in the afternoon, he'd kept his own counsel until Paul finished his tea and left. He mewed at the door and she let him in.

'Yes, I am back,' she told him as he twined around her legs. 'Released.'

She turned to go back inside. 'I hear Mr Havelock has been feeding you. Did he buy you some chicken?' Harley followed her to the freezer. 'You will need to wait until it defrosts. But we can read while we wait.' Meira put the container of raw mince in the kitchen sink and then filled the sink with hot water. Wiping her hands dry with a tea towel, she went to the couch and picked up the book on top of the stack. She read to him from the dust jacket.

'*In a world not quite like this one, two lovers will be tested beyond their understanding.*' Meira looked over the book at him. 'Apparently, this book is *audacious*. What do you think? Shall we read an audacious book?' She rifled through the pages. 'I think we should.' Meira settled into the couch, curling her legs up under her, and Harley found his place on the carpet in the sun and went back to sleep.

He had startled some time later when there was a knock on the door. He looked up, astonished, when Martin came in carrying a basket of hot food and proceeded to set it out on the kitchen table. Harley jumped onto the back of the couch to get a better look. Behind him, Meira gathered plates and cutlery and took a bottle of wine from the fridge. Martin poured and Harley watched as they sat opposite each other and held their glasses in the air.

'To the emergency call system.'

'Indeed.'

Harley watched them eat from the back of the couch. Meira appeared to have forgotten about his own dinner defrosting in the sink. Feeling somewhat put out, he let himself out through the balcony and went to see what Joyce was doing.

16 · 3ᴿᴰ TUESDAY

JOSH

Josh looked at the empty space on the shelf he had made in the storage unit. The mice were gone. Drowned? But where was the cage? It couldn't have been carried off by floodwaters (Josh had envisaged the flood as torrents of fast-flowing water that washed violently back and forth between the basement walls, hurling boxes above Japanese tsunami-style waves) because the bars of the storage units were too small. Unless it had been smashed to pieces. Josh imagined the fate of his charges, tossed about on a sea of muddy water, terrified and unable to escape until the cage dashed itself against an antique sideboard and they were thrown into the waves and sank to the bottom of the turbulent basement sea. He choked down a sob and sorrowfully laid a hand on the shelf.

'Rest in peace, my little friends.'

He turned to make his sad departure and was startled to find the president of the Residents' Committee standing at the entrance to the storage unit. He blushed furiously and tried to think of something to excuse his presence. Paul was smiling.

'It's alright, son. They're safe in my villa. You can come and get them when you've finished your shift.'

HARLEY

Harley had been asleep in the lee of the wind in Pat's garden. It was one of his favourite spots when the northerly blew, and Pat would sometimes bring Bobby inside and put out a plate of leftover chicken if she noticed him there. This afternoon, Bobby was also sleeping; dozing in front of the windows, leash already attached ahead of his afternoon walk. Harley, who had been keeping an eye on the dog, watched him open his eyes and contemplate the empty chicken plate through the glass. Harley lifted himself off the soil. He'd need to move fast if Bobby came outside. He'd seen him shoot through the round opening in the glass door before.

Bobby's eyes drifted shut again. Harley settled and licked his flank where specks of dirt still rested on his coat. He was working his way up to his shoulder when movement from the window caught his eye. Bobby was on his feet, stretching. On stiff legs, he walked to the door and nosed his way through, heading for the plate. Harley lifted his haunches and watched as the dog snuffled at the dried flecks of chicken meat and, unable to coax anything off the plate, trotted to the agapanthus to pee instead. Raising his head as well as his leg, he spotted Harley, barked and staggered. Harley made for the fence. The dog, needing to recover from his three-legged stumble, was well behind him when he cleared the fence. Harley made up for the insult by sitting on the path outside the gate to wash while the dog whined. He knew that Bobby could, if he wanted, squeeze under the gate and get to him, but there were now noises coming from inside the house and he figured the dog would return to his owner. He was wrong, and Bobby eventually succumbed, pushed himself under the gate, and gave chase.

FIONA

Fiona opened Microsoft Outlook and began an email to Vincent.

> To: vincent@tredwellexclusiveretirement.com.au
> From: fiona@tredwellforresthall.com.au
> Dear Vincent
> I need to raise an important matter regarding the management of the Harewood Hall Reserve Fund. Last week, with the kind assistance of Jessica in the finance team, I checked the recent

fund transactions in Dynamics and found several that I cannot account for in my own income and expenditure records. These transactions are substantial amounts and in one instance were for almost the entire balance of the fund. (I have attached a printout from Dynamics with the transactions highlighted.) I'm afraid that none of these transactions have appeared on the monthly Reserve Fund statements that head office sends to the residents.

I know you will appreciate the seriousness of this matter. Please be reassured that I have not disclosed my concerns to the Residents' Committee as I am sure there is a reasonable explanation and no need to worry them. Please call me if you wish to discuss it further.

Kind regards, Fiona

She opened Dynamics and at the login page, entered her email address and password. The computer pinged. *Incorrect login or password. Please enter a valid login and password.* She re-entered her details. The computer pinged again, this time with the helpful advice to remember that passwords were case sensitive. Fiona entered her details in a third time, typing slowly and checking the keys. The computer pinged for a third time. *You have exceeded the number of attempts to login and your access to Dynamics has been locked. Contact your system administrator for further assistance.*

Fiona groaned in frustration. She should have known that access to the accounting system was too good to be true and she'd eventually be kicked off. She wondered how they found out. She rang Lidia.

'Did you ask Jessica for access to Dynamics?'

'No, but Toni did. Why?'

'Did she get in?'

'No, Jessica wasn't at her desk and she was put through to the CFO.' Lidia cackled down the phone. 'Apparently he gave her a mouthful. *Village managers have no right*, that sort of thing. Let me guess. You've been kicked off.'

'Afraid so.'

'Good while it lasted?'

'Yeah. I bet Jessica got a talking to.'

'Toni didn't tell him it was Jessica, but the access logs will show it was her. Poor kid, she didn't know.'

'She does now.'

Fiona ended the call and contemplated her screen, still blinking its instruction to contact her system administrator. Not much point in doing that, she thought, and the email she'd just sent wasn't likely to get any attention either. There was a light tap at the door. Paul and Martin walked through and closed the door behind them.

'Time for a chat?' Paul asked, his face at odds with the lightness of his words. As they sat, his hand reached into his pocket and Martin opened his notebook to the back page.

JOYCE

Joyce was on her balcony, watching the storm come in from the north. The wind had picked up, but she could not yet hear the thunder. That would come later, well after she had closed the window shutters and begun their dinner. Tonight, she would cook John Dory with shiitake mushrooms and ginger. It was from the Gourmet Traveller Fast Recipes collection and would only take her fifteen minutes. She had bought the fish from the market this morning and planned to pair it with the last of the Spy Valley Pinot Gris that she and Peter had discovered when they were on holiday in Marlborough for their wedding anniversary last year. Perhaps she would pour herself a glass while she cooked.

The cat she had seen on the balcony last week darted around the western corner of the building and Joyce leaned over the railing to watch its progress as it aimed for the cover of the grevilleas that were planted against the wall. The wind gusted and she gripped the handrail to steady herself. Bobby came racing behind the cat, unsure if he was barking at the cat or the wind. As usual, his red leash trailed after him. Joyce leaned over further to see what the cat would do, now on her very tiptoes.

She saw the cat bolt towards the staff entrance, where its escape was blocked by the new door to the basement. Bobby danced at the cornered cat, which arched its back and hissed a warning. As the dog paused, confused at the cat's reaction, the cat slipped past him and headed for the gum trees. Good luck with climbing those, thought Joyce. The wind gusted again, and she heard a loud crack overhead. Startled, she looked up, and overbalanced.

JOSH

Josh walked up from the western-side villas to his car in the staff carpark. He had finished his shift and now the wind had picked up and was catching the mouse cage that he carried in his right hand. He thought Paul had been pretty good about the mice. He said they hadn't been hurt in the flood, but the basement wasn't a healthy place for them to live. They had talked for a while about whether it was right to take them back to the research centre. Josh told Paul about his fears for their safety. He said he hadn't intended to be an animal-rights warrior, but the more he thought about it, the more he felt bad about sending them back there. He didn't have a better plan though, and now he was stuck. Every solution he thought of put the mice at risk. There was no alternative that would guarantee a happy outcome. Paul had said he didn't know the answer himself and had Josh talked to his parents about the problem? Josh hadn't and Paul suggested that he take the mice home, confess and talk it through with them. As Josh struggled to keep the cage upright in the wind, he thought he might call Emily and they could go talk to his parents together.

Turning to round the western corner of the Harewood Hall heritage building, head down into the wind, Josh didn't see the dog and cat drama unfolding under Joyce's balcony. He gripped the cage with both hands and continued towards his car, which was parked in its usual place under the bottlebrush. Suddenly, Martin's new cat raced across his path. Josh startled, and then was knocked below his right knee. He heard a yelp and, his hands already occupied trying to right the cage, stumbled as Bobby's leash tangled around his feet. He pitched forwards, losing his hold on the mice and knocking his shin on the curbing. The cage tumbled out of his hands, bounced once and came to a stop on its side underneath the gum trees. Winded, he tried to suck in air while Bobby raced around the garden, barking and searching for the missing cat.

HARLEY

Harley sat on top of the fence on the northern side of the lemon-scented gums. Below him, Bobby ran in circles. Josh was on his hands and knees under the trees and the plastic and wire cage from the basement was on the ground out of reach in front of him. Harley could see two white mice cowering in the corner of the upturned cage. Safely beyond Bobby's field of vision, he lifted his front left paw and gave it a quick clean.

Harley also heard the crack and crouched, ready to run. Above him, the leaves on the opposite side of a gum tree drooped a little lower than before. Harley looked up as the leaves lifted high in a gust of wind, as though the tree were breathing out, and then tumbled downwards. There was another crack as the branch tore from the trunk and thudded onto the ground, falling on top of the mouse cage, crushing the frame and popping the door. The two mice raced across the access road towards the holes in the building's limestone footings. Above them, Joyce righted herself and stumbled inside. Harley jumped off the fence and circled Josh, who was crawling on his hands and knees to retrieve the destroyed mouse cage. The cat paused to consider the boy and the empty cage, then loped after the mice toward the basement, crossing the road in front of a silver car, which had braked sharply in front of the fallen branch.

17 · ONE WEEK LATER

FIONA

Sitting at her desk, Fiona read through the contract specifications one more time then attached the document to the email and pressed send. She was inviting tenders for maintenance and refurbishment work in the village. After the flood, Vincent had announced that Tredwell Trades would be wound up and no longer available for work. Each village manager was to appoint their own maintenance and refurbishment contractors. According to Vincent, work had dried up in the industry downturn and, coupled with unspecified losses following the Harewood Hall flood, that meant the business was no longer viable.

She collected her bag and went out to reception.

'Melissa, I'm off. I should be back by noon.'

'Say goodbye to Jessica for me.'

'I will. Don't forget to pass that phone number on to Paul for me.'

'Already done it.'

'Of course you have.'

Fiona waved to the morning-tea ladies. Joyce, cradling a brace on her wrist, and Pat were in deep conversation over a travel brochure and didn't notice her. Bobby was under Pat's feet with the leash tangled on the floor and gave two thumps of his tail as she walked past. Outside in the sun, a long scar glinted on the closest lemon-scented gum. The tree-pruning contractor said that it was not a concern and the tree would heal itself. He had even attended a Residents' Committee meeting to reassure them. The garden bed under the tree where the pipe had burst was now levelled and mulched. Further up the road in the staff carpark, Josh's car was parked in its customary spot under the bottlebrush, its roof littered with flowers. Fiona had saved him from the perplexed professor by claiming the ruined mouse cage as village property. It wouldn't have done either of them any good for the village to be outed as the location of the missing mice. She'd had to have words with Josh, of course, and given him a formal warning so he understood the severity of what he'd done. She'd also called in the pest control contractor.

As Fiona walked to her own car, Josh and Martin came up from the basement carrying gardening tools. Visitors had parked on the verge outside the west-end villas and broken two more sprinklers. Martin was using it as an opportunity to teach Josh how to repair the reticulation. With Fiona's permission, Martin had appropriated the Tredwell Trades storage unit to rehome the tools he had donated to the village. He also convened a working group to design a men's shed on the southern side of Harewood Hall. Fiona understood that Roy was a member of the working group. Which might, she thought, explain why she had heard so little of him in the past week.

Fiona got in her car and headed back down the hill. She was going to a farewell morning tea for Jessica. Lidia had organised it at her village and all the local village managers were attending. At the end of last week, head office had announced that Jessica would be leaving the business to spend more time with her family, effective immediately. Fiona noted that head office had not given Jessica a send-off. Usually head office staff were treated to a fancy morning tea in the boardroom, but not this time. It didn't matter: Lidia and her residents were always looking for an excuse to bake, and their clubhouse had a pretty view across the river. Fiona was looking forward to spending a couple of hours eating cake and chatting with her colleagues.

The following day, Melissa was at reception talking to Paul and Roy. Fiona could hear from her voice that she was working hard to keep her emotions in check as they made small talk, waiting for her to come out of her office. Through her window, she saw Gerry, and then Molly, Elaine, Pat and Bobby making their way through the gardens and to the entrance doors. It had only needed one phone call from Melissa to gather the faithful. Fiona felt a lump rising in her own throat and pushed it down. She would not give Vincent the satisfaction.

The company secretary sat in one of the tub chairs in Fiona's office, tapping on his mobile phone. His back was curled, his shoulders hunched, and his legs stretched out in front of him. He looked uncomfortable, she thought. Never mind. He looked up, impatient to get the job done and return to head office.

'Finished?'

She smiled ruefully and turned off her computer. 'All done.'

'Is it always this noisy?' He frowned at the crowd gathering in reception.

'No.' She didn't feel the need to elaborate. They had stopped paying for her advice exactly twenty-nine minutes ago when the company secretary and his dark-blue Mercedes circled into the Harewood Hall driveway, parked in the universal parking bay and handed Fiona her notice. I bet he knows the mayor too, she thought.

Fiona picked up her packing box, placed her handbag and redundancy notice on top and walked out of her office. She didn't believe for a minute the company secretary's well-rehearsed words about company cashflow issues. As she entered the reception lobby, the crowd of residents filled the space and gave a deep sigh when she appeared. Paul was the first to embrace her.

'Take care of yourself,' he said. 'We'll be in touch when the dust settles.'

They hugged her one by one.

'This is such a shock.'

'Did you have any idea?'

'What will we do without you?'

'Surely they can't do this without any notice.'

'Who is going to run the village?'

'I'm calling the Fair Work Commission.'

'Where's Vincent? He needs to explain himself.'

Someone said *photo* and they all went outside to stand in the portico while Gerry shuffled them inwards to get them in the frame.

18 · TWO WEEKS LATER

PAUL

Paul locked the door of his villa and walked down the path to the heritage building. On his left, the uncurtained windows of villa twenty-six looked out at the pruned rosebushes, the front doorstep still unencumbered by pot plants or outdoor shoes. There had been no interest in the property since Dr Godden decided to go to The Residence instead. Between them, Paul and Martin had cleared the junk mail and pulled any summer grass that appeared in the paving. Bobby stretched out in the sun across the path. Pat waved to Paul through the window and he let himself in through the gate.

'Are you coming to morning tea?' he asked her at the door.

'Not just yet, Paul,' she replied. 'Don't wait for me.'

At the café, Paul waved to Melissa in reception and sat down at his favourite table. He was the only person in the café, and he gave a quick thanks for the moment's solitude. Over the past week he had received a stream of confused and angry residents through his villa, demanding to know why Fiona had been dismissed and who would run the village now that she was gone. Paul didn't have the answers. It didn't help that Vincent had kept radio silence. Paul had made call after call to head office, only to receive messages that Vincent was travelling interstate, or in a board meeting, or had visitors in his office and would return his call as soon as he was free. He never did. With no-one else to blame, residents had turned on Paul, accusing him of hiding information and criticising the committee for failing to let Vincent know how much they needed Fiona.

Paul had confided his frustrations in Martin who, in an uncharacteristic move, had brought everyone to attention at the last fish and chips night by tapping on a glass with a spoon and then telling them all to leave Paul alone. It wasn't Paul's fault that they no longer had a village manager and if they wanted to do something useful, they should camp outside Vincent's Peppermint Grove home – Martin had found the address on Google – until he gave them an answer.

And then Mary Johnson had suffered a stroke and the village manager's mobile phone had rung unanswered in the office. Richard had travelled with his wife to the hospital and it fell to Paul to attend with the ambulance and lock up the heritage building after they had left. Poor Mary was due home tomorrow, and no-one had made arrangements to support her and Richard now that Mary was unable to feed and dress herself.

Paul opened the local newspaper. Above the fold on page three he read 'Clear Your Desk! Residents Farewell Beloved Retirement Village Manager'. The iconic front façade of Harewood Hall dominated the page, its sandstone walls solid and immovable. The residents were gathered under the portico, glaring at the camera. Fiona stood in the middle, holding her packing box. Bobby's leash lay puddled at her feet. Bobby himself had his broad back to the camera.

> *Residents of the exclusive Harewood Hall Retirement Village were given a rude shock last week when their manager, Mrs Fiona Boston, was handed her notice and told to vacate the premises immediately.*
>
> *'It is such a shock,' said 97-year-old Molly, who has lived at Harewood Hall for 16 years. 'Who will look after us now?'*
>
> *Mrs Boston, a local resident, said she had been advised that her position had been made redundant effective immediately. This newspaper understands that many retirement village operators are experiencing large decreases in profit margins.*
>
> *The owner of Harewood Hall, Sydney businessman and philanthropist Vincent Tredwell, who recently made a significant donation to Professor Malcolm Graves' world-breaking medical research on deadly parasitic infections, said that Mrs Boston was a respected member of the retirement-living community and he wished her well in her future*

career. He declined to comment on yesterday's police raid on the eastern suburbs office of Tredwell Trades. Eyewitnesses reported that drug squad officers were in attendance. The Police Commissioner said the raid followed a tip-off from an unnamed whistle-blower but refused to say whether it was part of a wider operation to address the methamphetamine crisis.

19 · THREE WEEKS LATER

HARLEY

Harley lifted his head and sniffed the air in Martin's apartment. His new bed in the corner of the living room was empty. Harley preferred to sleep on the couch, but tactfully started the night in the bed before moving.

Tonight, there was something different in the apartment. Something he had felt before. He didn't need to investigate to know what it was. He waited a moment, savouring the warmth of the circle he had made on Martin's end of the couch. It had been good, but it was time to move on. He jumped off the couch, eased himself through the partly closed balcony door and headed down to the basement.

20 · FOUR WEEKS LATER

JOSH

Josh and Emily walked to the funeral from Josh's house. At the end of the street, they opened the iron gate in the cemetery fence and walked along the radial path to the centre and then out again to the muster point at the northern entrance. The day was warm, and Josh was uncomfortable in his suit jacket.

'So, I saw Sarah yesterday ...'

Emily laughed. 'Did you see her, or did she see you first?'

'OK,' he capitulated, 'she saw me first. Anyway, you know her brother Simon lives in one of those townhouses next to Harewood Hall. We went to a party there once, remember? With all of the med students.'

'That was when Sarah met Simon's friend. Zac. The one she's moved in with. So fast. We sat on the balcony and ate pizza.'

'Yeah, that's the one. His flatmate, Lisa, has moved out and that bedroom on the first floor is available.'

'Nice. Great place to live.'

'Well,' he hesitated. 'I thought maybe we could take it. Me and you.'

'What, move in together?' She looked at him with an expression he couldn't read.

'Yeah. Me and you. And Simon. Obviously.' He looked at his feet.

'I'd love to, babe.'

He smiled at the ground. 'Cool. That's great. I'll let him know.'

They continued walking in silence. Josh stole a look at her face. Seeing she was smiling, he reached for her hand.

They arrived just before the cortege. Josh was surprised by the size of the gathering, which included a large group of children wearing the uniform of the high school at the foot of Harewood Hall. The hearse rolled in through the gates and the crowd followed it up the boulevard to the chapel, Josh and Emily slipping in behind the students. Inside, they hung back while the relatives and residents found seats, then sat in the plastic chairs that had been provided at the back of the chapel for the extra-large crowd. Martin's son, who Josh only knew by name and had flown over from Melbourne, was the first to speak. He talked about a golden childhood of roast dinners and cycling through suburban streets. His dad, he said, had taught him to repair a puncture, build a model aeroplane and make his bed every morning. He owed him his own attention to detail that had taken both him and his sister far in their chosen careers. He owed his father less in terms of interpersonal relationships; these skills he learned from his mother, which was why he was able to stand in front of them all and speak more than a word or two. The audience laughed good-naturedly.

The state manager of Engineers Australia spoke about Martin's contribution to the profession and the principal of the high school talked at length about his many years of service, coaching struggling students in maths and physics, as well as his daily attention to the school grounds. When they reached the first of the two songs in the order of service, all the students rose in their seats on the second chord and stood during the opening bars.

'Excellent,' murmured Emily, and stood as well. To his right, Josh saw Paul flip his order of service to the back page and then rise. He looked at his own program. The song was in Italian. He turned his open palms upward at Emily. 'We learned it in school,' she stage-whispered, then turned to the front to sing along with the choir.

Afterwards in the anteroom, Josh and Emily stood to one side, eating sandwiches and drinking tea. Josh could see Paul speaking with Jean and Geoff Hockey. Paul pantomimed a swinging punch to an invisible stomach followed by a two-handed shove to the chest and a backwards stagger. Jean held her hand over her mouth. Geoff had both hands shoved in his pockets and shook his head in disbelief. Pat and Molly sat in two of the chairs provided for the elderly mourners and looked up gratefully as Peter Wise brought them both cups of tea. Molly gestured for Emily to come over to her. Josh watched as Emily bent down for Molly to whisper in her ear and saw her blush as she giggled. Peter Wise joined his wife and Elaine, one a thin column of black, white and grey, and the other a broad splash of pink and green. Elaine listened intently, leaning in as Joyce spoke and patting her arm from time to time. Further across the room, Fiona, Anwesha and Meira juggled teacups and shortbread as they talked, Fiona bending to the shorter women to make herself heard. Melissa and her boyfriend, a lean, muscled man in a slender suit, talked with the Johnsons, who appeared to be getting ready to leave.

'Excuse me.'

Josh turned to see a tall woman beside him wearing a navy-blue skirt suit with a plain white blouse. She had a long, familiar face and held her large hands clasped in front of her.

'Are you Josh? I'm Elise Havelock. We've spoken on the phone.'

Later in the afternoon, when Elise and William had left in the funeral director's limousine and the residents walked back along the boulevard to their cars, Josh and Emily took the long way home to Josh's house on the opposite side of the cemetery. Here, the trees were tall and dense, and, despite the season, the air was cool and quiet and smelled of soil and stone. Emily threaded her arm through his and they strolled, savouring the silence. Here and there, fresh flowers were placed on old gravestones. It was comforting, Josh thought, to know that people who had long since died were honoured in this way. He wondered if the people who placed the flowers had known them personally. It didn't seem possible, in this old section of the cemetery, where the graves dated back one hundred years and more. Josh liked to think of the people lying here, at the end of his street. Not cast away on the edge of town, but in the centre of his suburb, where he worked and ran every day.

'Josh, look,' Emily whispered and grabbed his arm, pulling him to a stop. She pointed to a gravestone two rows over that was higher than the rest. On top of the stone sat a small grey cat with black markings and a faded muzzle. It was watching them and stood up as they approached.

'Hey, fella,' said Josh, threading his way through the old graves. 'You're an old boy, aren't you?'

He crouched and the cat jumped down and trotted to him, mewing and head bumping the back of his hand. His coat was soft, and he had a firm layer of fat under his skin. Josh gathered him into his arms. Emily crouched next to him and inspected the cat's ears.

'He doesn't have a collar, but he's been spayed,' she said. 'He's friendly. Maybe he's been microchipped.'

Josh rubbed the top of the cat's head with his fingertips. It was warm. 'If he hasn't, can we keep him?'

She smiled back at him. 'Yes. Yes, we can.'

A NOTE ABOUT RETIREMENT LIVING AND AGED CARE

Before I started writing, I had the good fortune to work in the retirement living and aged care industry. Some 180,000 people live in retirement villages in Australia and over one million people receive aged care services. In the main, our older people are safe, comfortable and happy, but from time to time, we hear terrible stories about neglect, abuse and unfair contracts. The last few years have been especially difficult as we try to keep people safe from COVID-19 and still connected with their loved ones. Mistreatment of our elderly (whether they are in care or living independently) is never acceptable and must always be investigated and put right. For my part, I found villages and aged-care services to be run by dedicated staff who are mortified when things go wrong, and, in an environment where money is tight, never stop trying to find ways to make the last years of our lives good ones. I love them. Also, they don't import drugs to prop up their businesses. I made up that bit.

I have also worked alongside some wonderful residents' committees. They organise social events, donate to charity, volunteer in the gardens, tutor at local schools, run men's sheds, sweep driveways, endorse budgets, open the doors for emergency services, walk each other's dogs, take each other to medical appointments, visit their neighbours in hospital, mediate disputes, the list could go on and on. They taught me what positive aging looks like beyond the catchphrase and that every person has a backstory. They also showed me the honour and decency in living in community with good humour, common sense and neighbourly compassion. I love them too. None of the characters in *The Cast Aways of Harewood Hall* are real people, and Harewood Hall is not a real place, although Perth residents may recognise the building that is now known as Montgomery House and run by the Aegis Aged Care Group as a residential aged care facility. It is true that the building was once a psychiatric hospital, but in my novel I have turned it into a retirement village and built freestanding villas on what is now a lovely local park. As far as I know, Montgomery House does not have a carpark basement, a resident cat, or Pudding or Coco: these were all products of my imagination.

ACKNOWLEDGEMENTS

Thank you for reading *The Cast Aways of Harewood Hall*. It was my first manuscript to be accepted for publication and I am grateful to Fremantle Press for choosing a story by a total unknown. I'm afraid my response when you called me was a bit gormless, but I hope since then I have demonstrated that I can be relied on to do what is needed when you ask. Thank you, Georgia Richter, for making editing such a pleasure, and to the rest of the team – Jane, Claire, Chloe, Kirstie and Cathy – for guiding Harley and his friends through to the bookshelves.

Thank you to my family, friends, former colleagues and residents who shared their stories about aging, aged care, and retirement living and let me adapt them for this book. Special thanks to Jack, who was my working model for Josh, and Lidia and Paul, who kindly gave me permission use their names.

Thank you to my family and friends who read early drafts.

Finally, thank you and every bit of love to my husband, Ross, who continues to go to work and come home each day to a wife who wants to talk about made-up people.

Karen Herbert

Fifteen-year-old Darren Davies is found facedown in the Weymouth River with a gunshot wound to his chest. The killer is never found. Ten years later, his mother receives a visit from the local police. Sandra's best friend has been found dead on a remote Pilbara road. And Barbara's DNA matches the DNA found under Darren's fingernails. When the investigation into her son's murder is reopened, Sandra begins to question what she knew about her best friend. As she digs, she discovers that there are many secrets in her small town, and that her murdered son had secrets too.

'… tautly plotted, brilliantly characterised, and laced with venomous moments that lay bare the town's racial and criminal histories. *The River Mouth* marks the debut of a brilliant new voice in Australian crime fiction.' *David Whish-Wilson*

FREMANTLEPRESS.COM.AU

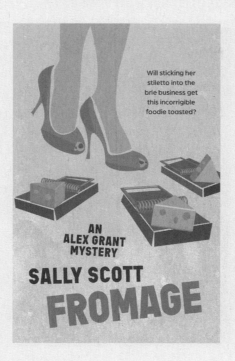

Will sticking her stiletto into the brie business get this incorrigible foodie toasted?

AN ALEX GRANT MYSTERY

SALLY SCOTT

FROMAGE

Journalist Alex Grant is enjoying the last days of her summer holiday in Croatia when she is accosted by an old school friend, Marie Puharich, and her odious brother, Brian, both there to attend the funeral of their fearsome grandfather's two loyal retainers. The only upside of the whole sorry business is meeting Marco, the family's resident adonis. An incorrigible foodie, Alex is unable to resist Brian's invitation to visit the family creamery in Australia's south-west to snoop around for stories and eat her body weight in brie. But trouble has a way of finding Alex, not least because her curiosity is the size of a giant goudawheel. What begins as a country jaunt in search of a juicy story will end in death, disaster and the destruction of multiple pairs of shoes.

'A rollicking, delicious and chaotically disastrous mystery.' *Readings*

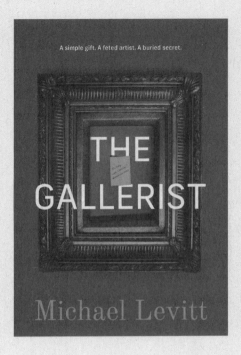

Mark Lewis, a former surgeon, has found solace in running a small art gallery. When Jan, a local woman, brings him a painting for valuing, it looks uncannily like a painting by the enigmatic artist James Devlin. Yet Jan claims it was done by a seventeen-year-old boy called Charlie.

As Mark searches for the painting's true provenance, he is joined by the attractive and clever Linda de Vries. But the pair will learn that James Devlin is a man whose past is as blank as an empty canvas, and he is determined to keep it that way.

'… a clever novel with an ingenious plot set in the Australian art world.' *Good Reading Magazine*

FROM FREMANTLEPRESS.COM.AU

When Australian expat Simone moves to London to start a career, getting pregnant is not on her agenda. But she's excited to start a new life with her baby and determined to be a good mother. Even though her boyfriend Paul's cold and grey apartment in the Barbican Estate seems completely ill-suited for a baby. Even though Simone and Paul have only known each other for a year. Even though she feels utterly unprepared for motherhood. The arrival of Paul's cousin Rachel in the flat should be a godsend. But there is something about Rachel that Simone doesn't trust. Fighting sleep deprivation and a rising sense of unease, she begins to question Rachel's motives, and to wonder what secrets the cousins share.

'… a quietly unsettling portrait of new motherhood and how we should always trust our innermost instincts.' *Reading Matters*

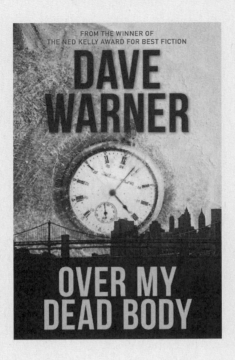

Cryogenicist Dr Georgette Watson has mastered the art of bringing frozen hamsters back to life. Now what she really needs is a body to confirm her technique can save human lives. Meanwhile, in New York City, winter is closing in and there's a killer on the loose, slaying strangers who seem to have nothing in common. Is it simple good fortune that Georgette, who freelances for the NYPD, suddenly finds herself in the company of the greatest detective of all time? And will Sherlock Holmes be able to save Dr Watson in a world that has changed drastically in 200 years, even if human nature has not?

'… *Over My Dead Body* is a witty, enjoyable tale that provides a new take on the Sherlock Holmes canon.' *Murder, Mayhem and Long Dogs*

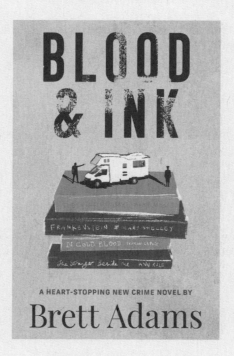

Literature professor Jack Griffen has recently suffered a nervous breakdown. His wife has divorced him and she and their adult daughter have decamped to the USA.

Into the void steps exchange student Hieronymus Beck, claiming to be the professor's greatest fan. The pair spend hours talking about the anatomy of crime fiction, the roles of heroes and villains, and Beck's favourite book of all time, *In Cold Blood*.

But everything changes when Jack finds Hiero's list. Five sheets of paper. Five ways to commit a murder. His student has told him he's writing a crime novel, but what else is he doing? Caught up in his protégé's dangerous game, the mild-mannered professor finds himself asking how far will he go to save a life. As far as murder?

First published 2022 by
FREMANTLE PRESS

Fremantle Press Inc. trading as Fremantle Press
25 Quarry Street, Fremantle WA 6160
(PO Box 158, North Fremantle WA 6159)
fremantlepress.com.au

Cover illustration and design by Nada Backovic, nadabackovic.com
Printed by McPherson's Printing, Victoria, Australia

 A catalogue record for this
book is available from the
National Library of Australia

ISBN 9781925816990 (paperback)
ISBN 9781760990008 (ebook)

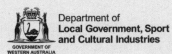

Fremantle Press is supported by the State Government through the Department of Local
Government, Sport and Cultural Industries.

Fremantle Press respectfully acknowledges the Whadjuk people of the
Noongar nation as the traditional owners and custodians of the land
where we work in Walyalup.